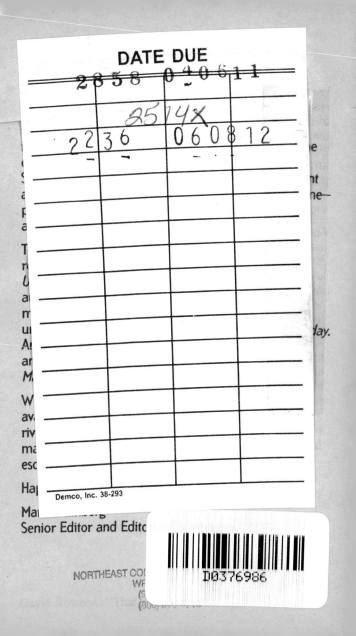

DATE DUE

2858	040611
2514X	
2236	060812

Demco, Inc. 38-293

D0376986

When **Tess Gerritsen** was a third-year medical resident, one of her patients presented her with a bag of romance novels. By the second chapter of the first book, she was hooked. She has been reading and writing romances ever since—and using her medical knowledge to add to her intricate and dramatic stories. A *New York Times* bestselling author, she is also writing mainstream medical thrillers with much success.

Annette Broadrick believes in romance and the magic of life. Since 1984, when her first book was published, Annette has shared her view of life and love with readers all over the world. Among her many awards is the *Romantic Times Magazine* Lifetime Achievement Award for both series romance and series romantic fantasy.

A native Texan, **Mary Lynn Baxter** knew instinctively that books would occupy an important part of her life. Always an avid reader, she became a school librarian, then a bookstore owner before writing her first novel. Now Mary Lynn is an award-winning author who has written more than thirty novels, and many of her titles have appeared on the *USA Today* bestseller list.

TAKE5

Quick Reads. Great Escapes.

NEW YORK TIMES
BESTSELLING AUTHOR

Tess Gerritsen

Annette Broadrick

Mary Lynn Baxter

HARLEQUIN®

TORONTO • NEW YORK • LONDON
AMSTERDAM • PARIS • SYDNEY • HAMBURG
STOCKHOLM • ATHENS • TOKYO • MILAN • MADRID
PRAGUE • WARSAW • BUDAPEST • AUCKLAND

ISBN 0-373-83495-0

TAKE 5, VOLUME 4

Copyright © 2001 by Harlequin Books S.A.

The publisher acknowledges the copyright holders
of the individual titles as follows:

UNDER THE KNIFE
Copyright © 1990 by Terry Gerritsen

ADAM'S STORY
Copyright © 1987 by Annette Broadrick

RETURN TO YESTERDAY
Copyright © 1987 by Annette Broadrick

EVERYTHING BUT TIME
Copyright © 1984 by Mary Lynn Baxter

MARRIAGE, DIAMOND STYLE
Copyright © 1991 by Mary Lynn Baxter

This edition published by arrangement with Harlequin Books S.A.

® and TM are trademarks of the publisher. Trademarks indicated with ® are registered in the United States Patent and Trademark Office, the Canadian Trade Marks Office and in other countries.

Visit us at www.eHarlequin.com

Printed in U.S.A.

CONTENTS

CONTENTS

UNDER THE KNIFE

Tess Gerritsen

With a steady hand, Dr. Kate Chesne injected two hundred milligrams of Pentothal sodium into her patient's intravenous line. "It will take a minute or so." She squeezed Ellen's shoulder in a silent gesture of reassurance. "Let yourself float," Kate whispered. "Think of the sky…clouds…."

Ellen gave her a calm and drowsy smile as the O.R. door swung open and the surgeon walked in. Dr. Guy Santini moved to the table and squeezed the patient's hand. "Still with us, Ellen?"

She smiled. "On the whole, I'd rather be in Philadelphia."

Guy laughed. "You'll get there. But minus your gallbladder."

Kate watched as her patient's jaw fell slack. She called softly, "Ellen?" brushing her finger across Ellen's eyelashes. There was no response. Kate nodded at Guy. "She's under."

"Well, let's get this show on the road," he said, heading out to scrub. "All her labs look okay?"

"Blood work's perfect."

"EKG?"

"I ran it last night. Normal." Ellen O'Brien was only forty-one. Except for a gallstone, she was in perfect health.

As the team took its place around the operating table, Kate's gaze traveled the circle of masked faces. Except for the intern, they were all comfortably familiar. There was the circulating nurse, Ann Richter. Next there was Guy, homely and affable, his brown eyes distorted by thick bottle-lens glasses. Opposite Guy stood the intern and last there was Cindy, the scrub nurse, a dark-eyed nymph with an easy laugh.

Guy made the first incision. As a line of scarlet oozed to the surface of the abdominal wall, the intern automatically dabbed away the blood with a sponge. Then Guy made a deeper incision, exposing the layer of fat. "Muscles seem a little tight, Kate,'' he observed. ''We're going to have trouble retracting.''

''I'll see what I can do.'' Turning to her medication cart, she reached for the tiny drawer labeled Succinylcholine. Given intravenously, the drug would relax the muscles. She frowned. ''Ann? I'm down to one vial. Hunt me down some more, will you?''

''That's funny,'' said Cindy. ''I'm sure I stocked that cart yesterday afternoon.''

Kate drew up 5 cc's of the crystal-clear solution and injected it into Ellen's IV line. She sat back and waited.

Guy's scalpel began to expose the abdominal muscle sheath. ''Still pretty tight, Kate,'' he remarked.

''It's been three minutes. You should notice some effect by now.''

''Not a thing.''

''Okay. I'll push a little more.'' Kate injected another 3 cc's into the line. ''I'll need another vial soon, Ann,'' she warned.

A buzzer went off on the cardiac monitor. What Kate saw on the screen made her jump to her feet in horror.

Ellen O'Brien's heart had stopped.

In the next instant the room was in a frenzy. The intern clambered onto a footstool and thrust his weight again and again on Ellen's chest.

As panic swirled around her, Kate fought to stay in control. She injected vial after vial of adrenaline. I'm losing her, she thought. Dear God, I'm losing her. Then she saw one brief fluttering across the oscilloscope.

''Let's cardiovert!'' she called out. ''Two hundred watt.''

Cindy darted around to the defibrillator and hit the charge button. The needle shot up to two hundred. Guy grabbed the paddles, slapped them on Ellen's chest and released the electrical charge.

Ellen's body jerked like a puppet, then the fluttering slowed to a ripple. It was the pattern of a dying heart. It was over. She wasn't responding to their efforts.

Fighting tears, Kate gazed around at the bloodied gauze and empty vials littering the floor. Soon it would be swept up and incinerated; the only clue to the tragedy would be a body in the morgue.

THE NEXT day, Kate was back at the hospital. Still shaken, she was trying to piece together the mystery of Ellen's death.

Guy Santini entered the physicians' lounge, sat next to Kate and tugged off his surgical cap. Silently he handed her Ellen O'Brien's chart.

"The EKG," he said. "You told me it was normal."

"It was."

"You'd better take another look."

Puzzled, she opened the chart. The first detail she noted was her own initials at the top. Next she scanned the tracing. For a solid minute she stared at the series of twelve black squiggles. The pattern was unmistakable. A third-year medical student could have made the diagnosis. "That's why she died, Kate," Guy said.

"I couldn't have made a mistake like this!"

"It's right there in black and white. For God's sake, your initials are on the damn thing!"

They stared at each other, both shocked by the harshness of his voice.

"I'm sorry," he apologized. "She'd had a heart attack. And we took her to surgery." He gave Kate a look of utter misery. "I guess that means we killed her."

Kate flinched and closed the chart.

"There's more, Kate. A letter arrived this morning. Hand delivered by personal messenger to hospital administration." He pushed a sheet of paper across the table.

She took one look at the letterhead and felt her stomach drop away: Uehara and Ransom, Attorneys at Law.

"One of the best firms in town," explained Guy. "You and the hospital are being sued for malpractice. And David Ransom is personally taking on the case."

Her throat had gone dry. "But I've explained what happened!"

"That isn't the issue. It reflects badly on the whole hospital. If the case goes to trial, there'll be publicity and you know how the Chief of Staff feels about that.'' He paused. ''They are suspending you, Kate, and word is, they want your resignation.''

So there it was. The blow.

''When is the next Quality Assurance meeting?'' Kate asked.

''It's next Tuesday. I'll make sure the O'Brien case is on the agenda and you can present your record to the committee. A judgment by your peers might help.''

''Thank you, Guy.'' Kate stood up. ''This is all so overwhelming. I need some air.''

As she rode the elevator down, something inside her seemed to snap. By the time the doors slid open, she was shaking violently.

Dear God, I'm being sued. She'd always thought that lawsuits happened to other people.

Suddenly feeling sick, she swayed against the lobby telephones and her gaze fell on the local directory. If only they knew the facts, she thought. If I could explain to them...

It only took seconds to find the listing: Uehara and Ransom, Attorneys at Law.

''MR. RANSOM is unavailable.''

The gray-haired receptionist had eyes of pure cast iron.

''But I have to see him!'' Kate insisted.

''Doctor, you're wasting your time! Mr. Ransom never meets with defendants.'' The telephone rang and the receptionist's attention was directed to the call.

The sounds of voices suddenly drew Kate's attention. She turned and saw, just down the hall, a small army of young men and women emerging from a conference room. Which one was Ransom? None of the men looked old enough.

It took Kate a split second to make her decision. Swiftly, she moved toward the conference room.

Blinding sunshine poured in through the southerly windows, spilling across the head and shoulders of a lone man seated at the far end of a long table, streaking his fair hair with gold.

His attention was focused on a sheaf of papers lying in front of him.

Kate swallowed hard. "Mr. Ransom?"

The man looked up. "Yes? Who are you?"

"I'm so sorry, Mr. Ransom!" cut in the receptionist's outraged voice.

"I only want to talk to him!" Kate wrenched her arm free.

"Just who are you? " The roar of Ransom's voice echoed in the vast room.

"Kate—" She paused. "Doctor Kate Chesne."

A pause. "I see. Show her out, Mrs. Pierce."

"I just want to tell you the facts!" Kate persisted. "Or would you rather not hear what really happened to Ellen O'Brien!"

That made him look up sharply. "Hold on, Mrs. Pierce. I've changed my mind. Let Dr. Chesne stay."

Mrs. Pierce muttered something unintelligible as she walked out. The door closed behind her.

"Well, Dr. Chesne," David said. "Have a seat. Unless you'd rather scream at me from across the room."

His cold flippancy made him seem all the more unapproachable but she forced herself to move toward him. He was younger than she'd expected, not yet in his forties. Establishment was stamped on his clothes, from his gray pinstripe suit to his Yale tie clip. But a tan that deep and hair that sunstreaked didn't go along with an Ivy League type. He's just a grown-up surfer boy, she thought. He certainly had a surfer's build, with those long, ropy limbs and broad shoulders. A slab of a nose and a blunt chin saved him from being pretty. But it was his eyes she found herself focusing on. They were a frigid, penetrating blue. "I'm here to tell you the facts, Mr. Ransom," she said.

"Don't bother." Reaching into his briefcase, he pulled out Ellen O'Brien's file. "I have everything I need right here."

"Not everything."

"And now you're going to supply the missing details."

"What I'm going to supply you with is the truth."

"Oh, naturally." He slouched back in his chair. "Tell me

something," he asked. "Does your attorney know you're here?"

"I haven't talked to an attorney—"

"Then you'd better get one. Fast. Because you're damn well going to need one."

"This is nothing but a big misunderstanding." She hesitated. Then, "I'm a very…careful person, Mr. Ransom. And I don't make stupid mistakes. The night Ellen O'Brien came into the hospital, Guy Santini admitted her. But I wrote the anesthesia orders and checked the lab results. And I read her EKG. It was a Sunday night and the technician was busy so I even ran the strip myself. I wasn't rushed. I took all the time needed and more, because Ellen was a member of our staff. I went over her lab tests with her."

"And you told her everything was normal."

"Yes. Including the EKG."

"Then you obviously made a mistake. I have the tracing right here, and it plainly shows a heart attack."

"That's not the EKG I saw! The one I saw was normal."

"Then how did this abnormal one pop into the chart?"

"Someone put it there, of course."

"Who?"

"I don't know."

"You must have a theory."

"I don't. I've gone crazy trying to figure it out! We do dozens of EKGs every day at Mid Pac. It could have been a clerical error. A mislabeled tracing. Somehow, that page was filed in the wrong chart."

"But you've written your initials on this page."

"Those are my initials. But I didn't write them."

"What are you saying? That this is a forgery?"

"It has to be. I mean, yes, I guess it is…." Suddenly confused, she shoved a strand of hair off her face. His utterly calm expression rattled her.

"All right," he relented. "Let's assume for the moment you're telling the truth. I can think of only two explanations for why the EKG would be switched. Either someone's trying to destroy your career—"

''That's absurd. I don't have any enemies.''

''Or someone's trying to cover up a murder.''

At her stunned expression, he gave her a superior smile. ''Since the second explanation obviously strikes both of us as absurd, I have no choice but to conclude you're lying.'' He leaned forward. ''Come on, Doctor, level with me. Was there a slip of the knife? A mistake in anesthesia?''

''I told you, there were no mistakes!''

''Then why is Ellen O'Brien dead?''

She stared at him, stunned by the violence in his voice. And the blueness of his eyes. A spark seemed to fly between them, and with a shock, she realized how attractive he was. Too attractive. And that her response to him was dangerous.

''No answer?'' he challenged smoothly. ''Maybe you'd better review your textbook on EKGs.''

''I don't need a textbook. I know what's normal!''

He looked bored. ''Really—'' he sighed ''—wouldn't it be easier just to admit you made a mistake.''

Wearily she slumped back in her chair. ''I wish I could admit I made a mistake,'' she said quietly. ''Ellen trusted me and I let her die. It makes me wish I'd never become a doctor. But I love my work. And now it looks as if I'll lose my job....'' Her head drooped in defeat. ''And I wonder if I'll ever be able to work again....''

David regarded her bowed head in silence and fought to ignore the emotions stirring inside him. He could usually tell if someone was lying. All during Kate Chesne's little speech, he'd been watching her eyes. They had been absolutely steady and forthright and as beautiful as a pair of emeralds.

The last thought startled him, popping out as it did, almost against his will. She was a beautiful woman, though she had a prizefighter's square jaw. Her shoulder-length mahogany hair was a riot of waves. Curly bangs softened a prominent forehead. It wasn't a classically beautiful face, but then he'd never been attracted to such faces.

Suddenly he was annoyed not only at himself but at her, at her effect on him. He looked down at his watch, then stood up. "I have a deposition to take and I'm already late. So if you'll excuse me…"

He was halfway across the room when she called out, "Mr. Ransom? I know my story sounds crazy. But I swear to you, it's the truth."

"Whether I believe you or not is irrelevant," he said. "So don't waste your time on me, Doctor. Save it for the jury."

*

TEN-KNOT WINDS were blowing in from the northeast as the launch bearing Ellen O'Brien's last remains headed out to sea. The minister tossed a lei of yellow flowers off the old pier. The blossoms drifted away on the current, a slow and symbolic parting that brought Ellen's family to tears.

The sound floated over the crowded dock to the distant spot where Kate was standing alone and ignored.

There were others present from the hospital, a group of nurses and a pair of obstetricians.

The far-off glint of sunlight on fair hair made Kate focus on the end of the pier where David Ransom stood, towering above the others.

Wind gusted in from the sea, drowning out the minister's final words. When at last it was over, Kate found she didn't have the strength to move. She watched the other mourners pass by and soon, the pier was empty. When she finally reached her car, she felt utterly weary. As she fumbled for her keys, her purse slipped out of her grasp, scattering its contents and she could only stand there, paralyzed by defeat. She had the absurd image of herself standing frozen to this spot. She wondered if anyone would notice.

David noticed. Even as he waved goodbye and watched his clients drive away, he was intensely aware that Kate Chesne was on the pier behind him. He'd been startled to see her here. Then halfway across the parking lot, he heard something clatter against the pavement and he saw that Kate had dropped her purse.

Almost against his will, he was drawn toward her. She

didn't notice his approach. He crouched beside her, scooped a few errant pennies from the ground, and held them out.

"Looks like you need some help," he said.

"Thank you."

For a moment they stared at each other. "I didn't expect to see you here," he remarked.

"It was—" she shrugged "—a mistake, I think."

"Did your lawyer suggest it?"

She looked puzzled. "Why would he?"

"To show the O'Briens you care."

Her cheeks suddenly flushed with anger. "Is that what you think? That this is some sort of strategy?"

"It's not unheard of."

"Why are you here? To prove to your clients you care?"

"I do care."

"And you think I don't?"

"I didn't say that. Don't take everything I say personally."

"I take everything you say personally."

"You shouldn't. It's just a job to me."

Angrily, she shoved back a tangled lock of hair. "And what is your job? Hatchet man?"

"I don't attack people. I attack their mistakes. And even the best doctors make mistakes. But it's incompetents like you that make my job so easy."

Rage flared in her eyes, as sudden and brilliant as two coals igniting, and he thought she was going to slap him. Instead she whirled around, slid into her car and slammed the door. The Audi screeched out of the stall.

As he watched her car roar away, he couldn't help regretting those brutal words he'd said in self-defense. That perverse attraction he'd felt to her had grown too compelling.

He turned to leave, but something caught his eye. Glittering on the pavement was a silver pen. He picked it up and studied the engraved name: Katharine Chesne, M.D. For a moment he stood there, thinking about its owner. Wondering if she, too, had no one to go home to. And it suddenly struck him, as he stood alone on the windy pier, just how empty he felt.

THE WHINE of the door swinging closed made Guy Santini glance up. Ann Richter stood across the lab table. They looked at each other in silence.

"I see you didn't go to Ellen's services, either," he said.

"I wanted to. But I was afraid." Silently, she held out a letter. "It's from Charlie Decker's lawyer. They're asking questions about Jenny Brook."

"What?" Guy snatched the paper from her hand. "You're not going to tell them, are you? Ann, you can't—"

"It's a subpoena, Guy."

"Lie to them, for God's sake!"

"Decker's out, Guy. He was released from the state hospital a month ago. I even think he's following me...."

"He can't hurt you."

"Can't he?" She nodded at the paper he was holding. "Henry got one, just like it. So did Ellen. Just before she..." Ann stopped, and only now did Guy notice how haggard she was. "It has to end, Guy," she said softly. "I can't spend the rest of my life looking over my shoulder for Charlie Decker."

He crumpled the paper in his fist. "You could leave the islands, you could go away for a while. Look, I'll give you the money—" He fumbled for his wallet and took out fifty dollars, all the cash he had. "Here. I'll send you more."

"I'm not asking for your money."

"Go on, take it. Please, Ann," he urged quietly.

Slowly, she reached out and took it. Then she announced, "I'm leaving tomorrow. For San Francisco. I have a brother—"

"Call me when you get there. I'll send you all the money you need." She didn't seem to hear him.

He watched as she walked slowly to the door, and he said, "Thank you, Ann."

She didn't turn around. She simply paused in the doorway, gave a little shrug, and vanished out the door.

KATE WAS exhausted. She had stayed out late, avoiding the inevitable return to her empty house. Since it was Friday night, she decided to treat herself to an evening out. She had supper alone at a trendy little seaside grill where everyone but her seemed to be having a grand old time.

Next she tried a movie. She found herself wedged between a fidgety eight-year-old boy on one side and a young couple passionately making out on the other. She walked out halfway through the film. She never did remember the title, only that it was a comedy, and she hadn't laughed once.

By the time she got home, it was ten o'clock. She was half undressed and sitting listlessly on her bed when she noticed that the telephone light was blinking. She let the messages play back as she wandered over to the closet.

"Hello, Dr. Chesne, this is Four East calling to tell you Mr. Berg's blood sugar is ninety-eight.... Hello, this is June from Dr. Avery's office. Don't forget the Quality Assurance meeting on Tuesday at four...."

She was hanging up her skirt when the last message played back.

"This is Ann Richter. Please, I have to talk to you right away. I'm leaving for San Francisco tomorrow. It's about Ellen. I know why she died...."

There was the click of the phone hanging up, and then a soft whir as the tape automatically rewound.

Kate grabbed the phone book from her nightstand. Ann's address and phone number were listed; her line was busy. Again and again Kate dialed but she heard only the drone of the busy signal. She slammed down the receiver and knew what she had to do next.

THE TRAFFIC heading into Waikiki was bumper-to-bumper.

As usual, the streets were crowded with a bizarre mix of people. Tonight, Kate found the view through her car window frightening, all those faces, drained of color under the glow of streetlamps, and a wild-eyed evangelist on one corner, waving a Bible as he shouted, "The end of the world is near!"

She was still jittery ten minutes later when she climbed the steps to Ann's apartment building. As she reached the door, a young couple exited, allowing Kate to slip into the lobby.

The elevator whined upward: three, four, five. Except for a faint hydraulic hum, the ride was silent.

On the seventh floor, the doors slid open.

The corridor was deserted. A dull green carpet stretched out before her. As she walked toward number 710, she saw that the door was slightly ajar. "Ann?" she called out.

There was no answer.

She gave the door a little shove. Slowly it swung open and Kate froze, taking in a toppled chair, scattered magazines, and bright red splatters on the wall. Then her gaze followed the trail of crimson as it zigzagged across the beige carpet, leading to Ann's body, lying facedown in a puddle of blood.

Beeps issued faintly from a telephone receiver dangling off an end table. The cold, electronic tone was like an alarm, screaming at Kate to move. But she remained paralyzed.

The first wave of dizziness swept over her. All her medical training, all those years of working around blood couldn't prevent this response. Through the drumbeat of her own heart she became aware of another sound, harsh and irregular. Breathing.

Someone else was in the room.

A flicker of movement drew her gaze to the living room mirror. Only then did she see the man's reflection. He was cowering behind a cabinet, and they spotted each other in the mirror at the same instant. As the reflection of his eyes met hers, she imagined she saw, in those hollows, the darkness beckoning to her.

He opened his mouth but no words came out, only an unearthly hiss, like a viper's warning just before it strikes.

She turned to flee and heard her own scream echo off the walls, the sound as unreal as the image of the hallway flying past.

The stairwell door lay at the other end and she hit it at a run. One flight into her descent, she heard the door above spring open again and slam against the wall. Again she heard the hiss, as she stumbled to the sixth-floor landing and grappled at the door. It was locked tight.

Footsteps thudded relentlessly down the stairs. She couldn't wait; she had to keep running.

She dashed down the next flight but the fifth-floor door was locked, too. He was right behind her.

She flew down the next flight and the next. Her purse flew off her shoulder but she couldn't stop to retrieve it. Sheer panic made her wrench at the next door. To her disbelief, it was unlocked. She found herself in the parking garage and tore off blindly into the shadows.

She heard the stairwell door fly open as she plunged toward the exit ramp. Her legs, stiff from running, refused to move fast enough. She could hear the man right behind her. The ramp seemed endless, but in a last, desperate burst of speed, she tore around the final curve. Too late, she saw the headlights of a car coming up the ramp toward her.

She caught a glimpse of two faces behind the windshield, a man and a woman, their mouths open wide. As she slammed into the hood, there was a brilliant flash of light, then nothing.

*

ONLY NOW, as the sun spilled in across her bed and a profound exhaustion settled over her, did Kate finally drift toward sleep. She didn't hear the knock, and was only vaguely aware that someone was approaching her bed.

Through a blur of sleep, she saw David's face.

"No fair, Mr. Ransom," she whispered. "Kicking a girl when she's down..." Turning away, she gazed down dully.

"Stop it, Kate. Please."

She fell instantly still. He'd called her by her first name.

"I'm not here to...kick you while you're down." Sighing, he added, "I guess I shouldn't be here at all."

"Why did you come?"

He gave a sheepish laugh. "To return this. You dropped it."

He placed the pen in her hand. "Thank you," she whispered.

"How are you feeling?" he asked, for want of anything else to say.

She gave a feeble shrug. "Tired. Sore." She paused and added, "Lucky to be alive."

His gaze shifted to the bruise on her cheek and she automatically reached up to hide it.

"The bruise will fade. What matters is that you're safe."

"Am I?" She looked at the door. "There's been a guard out there all night. How did you get past him?"

"I know Lt. Ah Ching. He told me what happened. We worked together years ago. When I was with the prosecutor's office."

"You?"

He smiled. "Yeah. I've done my civic duty."

"Then you've talked to him about what happened?"

"He said your testimony's vital to his case."

"Did he tell you Ann Richter left a message on my recorder just before she was killed?"

"About what?"

"Ellen O'Brien. 'I know why she died.' Those were her exact words."

David stared at her, finding himself drawn deeper into the spell of those green eyes. "Maybe she just figured out what went wrong in surgery—"

"The word she used was why. That implies a purpose for Ellen's death."

"Murder on the operating table? Come on."

She turned away. "I should have known you'd be skeptical. It would ruin your precious lawsuit, wouldn't it? To find out the patient was murdered."

"What do the police think?"

"How would I know?" she shot back in frustration.

There was a knock on the door. A nurse came in with the discharge papers. David watched as Kate sat up and obediently signed each one. The pen trembled in her hand.

"Do you have somewhere to go?" he asked. "After you leave here?"

"Guy Santini, a doctor friend of mine, and his wife Susan

have this beach cottage they hardly ever use. They occasionally take their young son William there to play in the ocean."

"You'll be staying there alone? Is that safe?"

She didn't answer. It made him uneasy, thinking of her in that cottage, alone, unprotected. He had to remind himself that she wasn't his concern.

He stood up to leave and as he walked out of the room, he heard her say softly, "I don't think I'll ever feel safe again."

"YOU HAVEN'T told me the whole story," said David.

Police Lt. Pokie Ah Ching took a mammoth bite of his Big Mac, chewed fiercely, then grunted, "What makes you think I left something out?"

"You've thrown some heavy-duty manpower into this case. You're fishing for something big."

"Yeah. A murderer," Pokie said.

"Kate happens to be a friend of mine—"

"Hogwash! I'm a detective, Davy. And I happen to know she's the defendant in one of your lawsuits." He snorted. "Since when're you getting chummy with the opposition?"

"Since I started believing her story. Two days ago, she came to me and I laughed her out of my office. Then this nurse, Ann Richter, gets her throat slashed. Now I'm beginning to wonder. Was Ellen O'Brien's death malpractice? Or murder?"

"Murder, huh?" Pokie shrugged and took another bite. "That'd make it my business, not yours."

"Look, I've filed a lawsuit that claims it was malpractice. It's going to be pretty damned embarrassing, not to mention a waste of time, if this turns out to be murder. Level with me, Pokie. For old times' sake."

"Don't pile on the sentimental garbage, Davy."

"We were talking about the case."

Pokie sat back and studied him for a moment. "Okay." He sighed. "What do you want to know?"

"What's so important about Ann Richter's murder?"

Pokie answered by grabbing a folder from the chaotic pile

of papers on his desk. He tossed it to David. "M.J.'s preliminary autopsy report. Take a look."

"I see M.J. hasn't lost her touch for turning stomachs," David said. "Now, this finding doesn't make sense. Is M.J. sure about the time of death?"

"M.J.'s always sure. She's backed up by mottling and core body temp."

"Why the hell would the killer cut the woman's throat and then hang around for three hours?"

"To clean up. To case the apartment."

"Was anything missing?"

Pokie sighed. "No. That's the problem. And no sign of sexual assault."

"So you've got a brutal murder and no motive."

"Take another look at that autopsy report. Read me what M.J. wrote about the wound."

"'Severed left carotid artery. Razor-sharp instrument.'"

"Those are the same words she used in another autopsy report two weeks ago. That victim was an obstetrician named Henry Tanaka."

"Ann Richter was a nurse."

"Right. And before she joined the O.R. staff, she used to moonlight in obstetrics. Chances are, she knew Henry Tanaka."

David suddenly went very still. He thought of another nurse who'd worked in obstetrics. And was now dead. "Tell me more about that obstetrician," he said.

"Henry Tanaka's office was over on Liliha. Two weeks ago, he stayed behind to catch up on some paperwork. His wife says he always got home late. But she implied it wasn't because of paperwork."

"Girlfriend?"

"What else?"

"Wife know any names?"

"No. She figured it was one of the nurses. Anyway, about seven o'clock that night, a couple of janitors found the body. At the time we thought it was some junkie after a fix. There were drugs missing from the cabinet."

"Narcotics?"

"Naw, the good stuff was locked up in a back room. The killer went after worthless stuff, but he was smart enough not to leave prints. The only lead we had was that as one of the janitors was entering the building, he spotted a woman running across the parking lot. It was drizzling and almost dark, but he says she was definitely a blonde."

"So what came of your lead?"

"Nothing much. Then Ann Richter got killed." He paused. "She was blond. Kate Chesne's our first big break. Now at least we know what our man looks like."

"What kind of protection are you giving Kate?"

"She's tucked away on the North Shore. I got a patrol car passing by every few hours."

"That's all?"

"No one'll find her up there."

THE SUN slanted down on Kate's back, its warmth lulling her into an uneasy sleep. She lay with her face nestled in her arms as the waves lapped at her feet and the wind ruffled the pages of her paperback book. On this lonely stretch of beach, she had found the perfect place to hide away.

Little by little, she was tugged awake by the wind in her hair, by a vague hunger for food. She hadn't eaten since breakfast and already the afternoon had slipped toward evening.

Then another sensation wrenched her fully awake. It was the feeling that she was being watched. When she rolled over and looked up, David was standing there.

He was wearing jeans and an old cotton shirt, the sleeves rolled up in the heat. Though her swimsuit wasn't particularly revealing, something about his eyes seemed to strip her. Sudden warmth flooded her skin.

"You're a hard lady to track down," he said.

"That's the whole idea of going into hiding." Grabbing her towel and book, she rose to her feet.

"I have to talk to you, Kate."

"I have a lawyer. Why don't you talk to him?"

"It's about the O'Brien case—"

"Save it for the courtroom," she said over her shoulder as she walked away.

"I may not be seeing you in the courtroom," he yelled, catching up to her as she reached the cottage. She let the screen door swing shut in his face.

In the middle of the kitchen she halted, suddenly struck by the implication of his words. Slowly she turned and stared at him through the screen. "What does that mean?" she asked.

"I'm thinking of dropping out."

Still staring at him, she pushed the screen door open. "Come inside, Mr. Ransom. I think it's time we talked."

Silently he followed her into the kitchen and stood by the breakfast table, watching her. The fact that she was barefoot only emphasized the difference in their heights.

She swallowed nervously. "I have to dress. Excuse me." She fled into the bedroom and grabbed the first clean dress within reach, a flimsy white import from India. When she finally ventured back into the kitchen, she waved vaguely toward a chair. "Sit down, Mr. Ransom. I'll make some coffee."

"By the way," he asked, "can we cut out the 'Mr. Ransom' bit? My name's David."

He settled into a chair across from her and their eyes met levelly over the kitchen table.

"What made you change your mind?" she asked.

In answer, he pulled a piece of paper out of his shirt pocket. It was a photocopy of a local news article. "Did you know the victim, Henry Tanaka?"

"He was on our O.B. staff, but I never worked with him."

"Look at the newspaper's description of his wounds."

Kate tried to swallow. "That's how Ann—"

He nodded. "Same method. Identical results."

"How do you know all this?"

"Lt. Ah Ching saw the parallels almost immediately. That's why he slapped a guard on your hospital room. If these murders are connected, there's something systematic about all this. And those people knew each other. They even worked together."

"But Ann was a surgical nurse—"

"Who used to work in obstetrics."

"What?"

"Eight years ago, Ann Richter went through a very messy divorce. She needed extra cash, fast. So she did some moonlighting as an O.B. nurse. The night shift. The same one Ellen O'Brien worked. They knew each other, all right. Tanaka, Richter, O'Brien. And now they're all dead."

The scream of the boiling kettle tore through the silence but she was too numb to move. David rose and fixed the coffee.

"How did Ann react to Ellen's death?"

Kate was silent for a moment, remembering. "She seemed...paralyzed. But we were all upset. Afterward she went home sick. That was the last time I saw her. Alive, I mean...."

"She must have known something. Maybe they all did."

Softly Kate ventured, "Then you think Ellen was murdered."

"That's why I'm here. I want you to tell me. Convince me it was murder and that I should drop out of this case."

"I can't think of anything. It was a routine operation!"

"What about the surgery itself?"

"Faultless. Guy's the best surgeon on the staff. Anyway, he was barely through the muscle layer when—" She stopped.

"When what?"

"He was having trouble retracting the abdominal muscles. So I injected a dose of succinylcholine."

"That's pretty routine, isn't it?"

She nodded. "But in Ellen, it didn't seem to work. I remember asking Ann to fetch me another vial because there was only one in the drawer."

"What happened after the second dose?"

"A few seconds went by. And then her heart stopped."

They stared at each other. Then he leaned forward, his eyes hard on hers. "If you could prove it—"

"But I can't! That empty vial went straight to the incinerator. And there's not a body left to autopsy." She looked away, miserable.

"Who has access to the anesthesia carts?"

"They're left in the operating rooms. I suppose anyone on the hospital staff could get to them. Doctors. Nurses. Maybe even the janitors. But it's not someone on the staff. I saw the killer, David! That man in Ann's apartment was a stranger."

"Who could have an associate in the hospital. Maybe even someone you know. Look at the systematic way these murders are being carried out. As if our killer has some sort of list. My question is: Who's next?"

The clatter of her cup dropping against the saucer made Kate jump. I saw his face, she thought. If he has a list, then my name's on it.

"He's out there," she whispered. "Looking for me. And I don't even know his name." The touch of David's hand on her shoulder made her tremble.

"He can't hurt you, Kate. Not here." David's breath seared her neck. Then suddenly it was his lips. His face burrowed through the thick strands of her hair to press hungrily against her neck.

He swung her around to face him. The instant she turned, his mouth was on hers.

She felt herself falling under the force of his kiss, until her back suddenly found the kitchen wall. With the whole hard length of his body he pinned her there, belly against belly, thigh against thigh. Her lips parted and his tongue raged in, claiming her mouth. There was no doubt in her mind he intended to claim the rest of her, as well.

She scarcely heard the telephone ringing. It took all her willpower to swim against the flood of desire. "The telephone—"

"Let it ring." His mouth slid down to her throat.

But the sound continued.

"David. Please…"

Groaning, he wrenched away and she saw the astonishment in his eyes. The phone rang again. Jarred to her senses at last, she grabbed the receiver and managed a hoarse "Hello?"

"Dr. Chesne?" a voice whispered, barley audible.

"Yes?"

"Are you alone?"

"No. Who is this?" Her voice suddenly froze.

"Be careful, Kate Chesne. For death is all around us."

*

THE RECEIVER slipped from her grasp as she reeled back in terror. "It's him," she whispered. "It's him!"

David scrabbled for the receiver. "Who is this? Hello? Hello?" Cursing, he slammed it down. "What did he say? Kate!"

"He said to be careful, that death was all around...."

"Get your things together. You can't stay here," he snapped.

She didn't ask where they were going. Driven by the need to get away, she began to pack. As David thrust the key in the ignition minutes later, she was seized by a wild terror that the car wouldn't start. But it did. The ironwood trees lunged at them as David sent the BMW wheeling around.

"How did he find me?" she sobbed.

"That's what I'm wondering." David hit the gas pedal as the car swung onto paved road.

"No one knew I was here. Only the police."

"Who took you to the cottage?" he asked.

"Susan Santini, Guy's wife, drove me."

"Did you stop at your house?"

"No. My landlady brought my suitcase to the hospital."

"He might have been watching the lobby entrance."

"But we didn't see anyone follow us."

"People almost never do. As for your phone number, he could've looked it up in the book. The Santinis have their name on the mailbox."

High on the hillside, the lights of houses flashed by, each one an unreachable haven of safety. In all that darkness, was there a haven for her? She huddled against the car seat, wishing she never had to leave this small cocoon of safety.

"...and there's plenty of room. So you can stay as long as you need to."

"What?" Bewildered, she turned and looked at him. "I don't understand. Where are we going?"

He glanced at her, his tone strangely unemotional. "My house."

THE NEXT day Kate was still unnerved. Ellen's death, Ann's murder, the phone call the night before. All of it left her severely on edge. As did spending the night in David's house. He'd been a total gentleman, but part of Kate wished he hadn't.

He'd awakened her early in order to look at mug shots to identify Ann's killer. They'd rode in silence to the police station. Kate was scared, but felt comforted by David's presence.

Lt. Pokie Ah Ching slid the book of mug shots toward Kate. "See anyone you know, Dr. Chesne?"

Kate scanned the photographs and immediately focused on one face. The man gazed straight ahead with wide eyes. It was the look of a lost soul. Softly she said, "That's him."

"You positive?"

"I remember his eyes." Both men were watching her intently.

"That's our man," Pokie said with grim satisfaction.

"Who is he?" she asked.

"A nutcase," replied Pokie. "The name's Charles Decker. That photo was taken five years ago, right after his arrest."

"On what charge?"

"Assault and battery. He kicked down the door of a medical office. Tried to strangle the doctor."

"A doctor?" David's head came up. "Which one?"

"Henry Tanaka. And this morning I got word from the lab. Decker's fingerprints were on the Richter woman's doorknob."

"What was his motive?" Kate asked.

Pokie shrugged. "All I got is a theory." Sighing, he fished out a spiral notebook. "Here's what I got so far. Decker, Charles Louis, white male born in Cleveland thirty-nine years ago. Parents divorced. Joined the navy at twenty-two. Got shipped here to Pearl six years ago. Served as corpsman aboard the USS Cimarron.''

"Corpsman?'' Kate questioned.

"Assistant to the ship's surgeon. Had a decent service record, couple of commendations. Seemed to be moving up the ranks okay. And then, five years ago, something snapped.

"He'd put in for permission to marry a woman named Jennifer Brook. It was granted. But then he and his ship sailed for six months of classified maneuvers off Subic Bay. When he returned to Pearl, Jennifer wasn't waiting on the pier and Decker jumped ship.''

"She found another guy?'' David guessed.

"No. Miss Brook was dead. Complications of childbirth,'' explained Pokie. "She had some kind of stroke in the delivery room. The baby girl died, too. Decker never even knew she was pregnant.

"That's when the man lost it,'' continued Pokie. "Found out Tanaka was his girlfriend's doctor, showed up at the clinic and just about strangled him. The police were called, but a day later Decker got out on bail. Bought himself a Saturday-night special, put the barrel in his own mouth, pulled the trigger.'' Pokie closed the notebook.

The ultimate act, thought Kate. Buy a gun and blow your own head off. How he must have loved that woman. But he was alive. And he was killing people.

Pokie saw her questioning look. "It was a very cheap gun. It misfired. Turned his mouth into bloody pulp. But he survived. After rehab, he was transferred to the state hospital. The nuthouse. He regained function of just about everything but his speech.''

"He's mute?'' asked David.

"No. He can mouth words, but his voice is more like a hiss.''

A hiss, thought Kate. The memory of that unearthly sound, echoing in Ann's stairwell. The sound of a viper about to strike.

Pokie continued. "About a month ago, Decker was discharged from the state hospital. He was supposed to be seeing a shrink called Nemechek. But Decker never showed up.''

"Have you talked to Nemechek?" asked Kate.

"Only on the phone. He's at a conference in L.A. Should be back on Tuesday. Swears his patient was harmless, but he's covering his butt."

"So that's the motive," said David. "Revenge. Why was Ann Richter killed?"

"It seems she and Tanaka were, how do I put it, very well acquainted. He was seen at her apartment more than once. Remember that blond woman the janitor saw running through the parking lot? The night he was killed, I think she went to pay him a social call. Instead she found something that scared the hell out of her. Maybe she saw Decker. And he saw her."

"Then why didn't she go to the police?" asked Kate.

"Maybe she didn't want the world to know she was having an affair with a married man. Who knows?"

"So she was just a witness," said Kate. "Like me."

Pokie looked at her. "There's one big difference. Decker can't get to you. Right now no one outside this office knows where you're staying. Let's keep it that way." He sighed. "It might take a while to find him. But hang in there, Doc. The man can't hide forever."

As they rose to leave, Kate asked. "What about Ellen O'Brien? Does she have some connection to all this?"

Pokie looked down at Charlie Decker's photo. Then he shut the folder. "No," he answered. "No connection at all."

"But there has to be a connection!" Kate blurted as they walked out of the station. "Some piece of evidence he hasn't found—"

David shrugged. "Right now I have to agree with him. I don't see how Ellen O'Brien fits into this case."

"But you heard what he said! Decker assisted the ship's surgeon—"

"Decker's profile doesn't fit the pattern, Kate. A psycho who works like Jack the Ripper doesn't bother with drug vials and EKGs. That takes a different kind of mind."

She stared down the street. "The trouble is, I can't see any way to prove Ellen was murdered. I'm not even sure it's possible."

David paused on the sidewalk. "Okay." He sighed. "So we can't prove anything with what we know now. Maybe we should start with the person who connects Tanaka and Decker—Jennifer Brook."

"What do you mean? Obviously she's dead."

"But the hospital should have her records, right?"

"Of course! And since I'm still technically on staff, I can request them." A renewed vitality came over Kate. "David, take me to the hospital. Now."

"JENNIFER BROOK," said the hospital records clerk. "And this patient is deceased?"

"Yes," said Kate.

The woman rose reluctantly from her chair. "You'll have to wait."

"Why do I get the feeling we'll never see her again?" muttered David.

Kate sagged weakly against the counter. "Just be glad she didn't ask for your credentials. I could get in big trouble for showing hospital records to the enemy."

"Who, me?"

"You're a lawyer, aren't you?"

"I'm just poor old Dr. Jones from Arizona. Remember?"

They both turned at the sound of footsteps. The clerk reappeared, empty-handed.

"The chart's not there," she announced.

"Was it released from the hospital?" David snapped.

"We don't release originals, Dr. Jones." The clerk sank down in front of her computer and typed in a command. "See? There's the listing. It's supposed to be in the file room." She was about to clear the screen when David stopped her.

"Wait. What's that notation there?" he asked.

"That's a chart copy request." She punched another button and a name and address appeared: "Joseph Kahanu, Attorney at Law, Alakea Street. Date of request: March 2."

David frowned. "That's only a month ago."

Kate looked at David and grabbed his hand. They stepped away from the clerk. "How do you feel about meeting a colleague?"

David nodded. "Let's go."

THE PAINT in the hall to Kahanu's office was chipping, the carpet threadbare.

"Great address," whispered David, knocking on the door.

It was answered by a huge Hawaiian. "You're David Ransom?" he asked gruffly.

David nodded. "And this is Dr. Chesne."

The office was suffocating and Kate recognized all the signs of a struggling law practice: the ancient typewriter, the cardboard boxes stuffed with client files, the secondhand furniture.

"I haven't called the police yet," said Kahanu.

"You're aware Decker's wanted for murder?"

Kahanu shook his head. "It's a mistake."

"Did Decker tell you that?"

"I haven't been able to reach him."

"You know two people have been murdered."

"They've got no proof he did it."

"The police say they do. They say Charlie Decker's a dangerous man. A sick man. He needs help."

"That what they call a jail cell these days? Help?" He mopped his brow, as though buying time to think. "Guess I got no choice now," he muttered. "One way or the other, the police'll be banging on my door." He pulled out a folder and tossed it on the battered desk. "There's the copy you asked for. Seems you're not the only one who wants it."

David frowned. "Has someone else asked for it?"

"No. But someone broke into my office last week. Tore apart all my files. Didn't steal anything, and I even had fifty bucks in the cash box. I couldn't figure it out. But this morning, after you called, I got to thinking. Wondering if that file's what he was after."

"But he didn't get it."

"The night he broke in, I had the papers at home."

"Is this your only copy?"

"No. I ran off a few just now. Just to be safe."

David handed Kate the chart. "You're the doctor."

The first few pages recorded a routine obstetrical admission. The patient, a healthy twenty-eight-year-old woman at thirty-six weeks of pregnancy, had entered Mid Pac Hospital in the early stages of labor. Kate turned to the delivery-room record.

Here things began to go terribly wrong. The nurse's neat handwriting broadened into a frantic scrawl. The entries became terse, erratic, with some blotted-out sentences totally unreadable.

On the next page was the last entry: Resuscitation stopped. Patient pronounced dead at 01:30.

"She died of a cerebral hemorrhage," Kahanu said.

"And the baby?" Kate asked.

"A girl. She died an hour after the mother."

"Kate," David murmured. "Look at the names of the personnel in attendance."

Kate's gaze dropped to the three names. As she took them in, her hands went icy. Henry Tanaka, M.D. Ann Richter, RN. Ellen O'Brien, RN.

Kahanu turned to the window. "Four weeks ago Charlie Decker came to my office for a legal opinion about a possible malpractice suit."

"On this case?" said David. "But Jenny Brook died five years ago. And Decker wasn't even a relative."

"He paid for my services, Mr. Ransom. In cash. So I subpoenaed the chart for him. I contacted the doctor and the two nurses who'd cared for Jenny Brook. But they never answered my letters."

"They didn't live long enough," explained David. "Decker got to them first."

"My client didn't kill anyone."

"Your client had the motive, Kahanu. And you provided him with their names and addresses."

"You've never met Decker. He's not a violent man. I know a killer when I see one. There's something about their eyes. Something missing. A soul, maybe. I tell you, he wasn't like that."

Kate leaned forward. "What was he like, Mr. Kahanu?" The Hawaiian paused. "He was real...ordinary. Mostly skin and bones, like he wasn't eating right. I felt sorry for him. He looked like a man who's had his insides kicked out. He didn't say much. But he wrote things down for me. I think it hurt him to use his voice." Kahanu shook his head. "I still don't see why he even bothered, you know? The woman's dead. The baby's dead. All this digging around in the past, it won't bring 'em back."

*

OUTSIDE THE police station David muttered an oath as he slid into the driver's seat and slammed the car door. "We just got the brush-off."

Kate stared at him. "But they've seen Brook's file. They've talked to Kahanu—"

"Pokie says there's not enough evidence to open a murder investigation. As far as they're concerned, Ellen O'Brien died of malpractice. End of subject."

"Then we're on our own."

"Wrong. We're pulling out." Suddenly agitated, he drove out from the curb. "Things are getting too dangerous."

"They've been dangerous from the start."

"Okay, I admit it. Up till now I wasn't sure I believed you—"

"You thought I was lying?"

"There was always this nagging doubt. But now we're hearing about stolen hospital charts. People breaking into lawyer's offices. There's something weird going on here, Kate. This isn't the work of a raging psychopath. It's too methodical." He frowned at the road ahead. "And it all has to do with Jenny Brook. There's something about her hospital chart that our killer wants to keep hidden."

"But we've gone over that thing a dozen times, David!"

"Then we're overlooking something. And I'm counting on

Charlie Decker to tell us what it is. I say we sit tight and wait for the police to find him.''

She turned away. "I can't really expect you to understand. It's not your fight.''

But he did understand. And it worried him, that note of stubbornness in her voice. "You're wrong,'' he told her.

"You don't have anything at stake.''

"Don't forget I pulled out of the case.''

"Oh. Well, I'm sorry I cost you your fee.''

"You think I care about the money? It's my reputation I put on the line. And all because I believe that crazy story of yours. Murder on the operating table! I'm going to look like a fool if it can't be proved!''

"I've put you in a compromising position, haven't I?''

His answer was a curt nod.

"I'm sorry.''

"Look, forget about it, okay?'' He got out and opened her door. "Are you coming inside?''

"Only to pack.''

"You're leaving?''

"I appreciate what you've done for me,'' she answered tightly. "You went out on a limb and you didn't have to.''

"And just where do you plan to go?''

"I'll stay with friends.''

"Suit yourself,'' he said and stalked off to the house.

While she was packing, he paced back and forth in the kitchen, trying to ignore his growing sense of uneasiness. Finally he stormed toward her bedroom.

She noticed him in the doorway. "I'm almost finished,'' she said, tossing her nightgown on top of the other clothes. "Have you called a cab yet?''

"No, I haven't.''

"Well, could you call one now?''

"I'm not going to.''

"Fine,'' she said calmly. "Then I'll call one myself.'' She started for the door, but he caught her by the arm.

"Kate, don't. I think you should stay. It's not safe out there.''

They were standing so close he could almost feel the heat mounting in waves between them as their gazes locked. Her eyes suddenly went wide with surprise. And need. Despite her bravado, he could see it brimming there in those deep, green pools.

"What the hell," he growled, "I think both our reputations are already shot."

And then he hauled her into his arms and kissed her. It was a long and savagely hungry kiss. Almost immediately he felt her respond, her body molding itself against his. It was a perfect fit. Her arms twined around his neck and as he urged her lips apart with his, the kiss became desperately urgent. Her moan sent a sweet agony of desire knifing through him.

The same sweet fire was now engulfing Kate. She felt him fumbling for the buttons of her dress, then with a groan of frustration, he tugged it off. The lace bra magically melted away and his hand closed around her breast. Under his pleasuring stroke, her nipple hardened instantly and they both knew that this time there would be no retreat.

Already she was groping at his shirt, until together they stripped it off his shoulders. She immediately sought his chest, burying her fingers in the bristling gold hairs.

By the time they'd found the evening glow of his bedroom, his shoes and socks were tossed to the four corners, his pants were unzipped and his arousal was evident.

The bed creaked in protest as he fell on top of her, his hands trapping her face beneath his. They couldn't wait. With his mouth covering hers and his hands buried in her hair, he thrust into her, so deeply that she cried out against his lips.

He froze. "Did I hurt you?" he whispered.

"No...oh, no...."

It took only one look at her face to tell him it wasn't pain that had made her cry out, but pleasure in him, in what he was doing to her.

He let her take him to the very brink and surrendered himself to the fall. In a frenzy he took control and plunged them both over the cliff. The drop was dizzying.

The landing left them weak and exhausted. Outside, the waves roared against the seawall.

"Now I know what it's like to be devoured," she whispered as the glow of sunset faded.

"Is that what I did?"

She sighed. "Completely," she whispered as she closed her eyes and drifted off to blissful sleep.

THE NEXT evening Kate let David talk her into dinner. A full stomach and a few glasses of wine left her flushed and giddy as they walked to the parking garage. She clung to his arm. She was going home with David.

Today had been difficult and she was grateful for the company. The hospital's Quality Assurance meeting had felt more like a firing squad. They had upheld the administration's decision to suspend her. After the meeting, the hospital's attorney approached her, asking for her signature on resignation papers. She'd ripped them into shreds. Finally, thanks to David, the day's anxieties had dissipated.

She slid onto the leather seat of the BMW and the familiar feeling of security wrapped around her like a blanket. In spite of David's occasional emotional retreat, she was in a capsule where no one, nothing, could hurt her.

The feeling shattered when David glanced in the rearview mirror and swore softly. "David, is something wrong?"

He frowned at the mirror. "I think we're being followed." Kate whipped her head around. "Are you sure?"

"I only noticed because it has a dead left parking light. It pulled out behind us when we left the garage. It's been on our tail ever since." He took his foot off the gas pedal.

She went rigid in alarm. "Why are you slowing down?"

"To see what he does."

The headlights seemed to hang in the distance.

"Smart guy," said David. "He's just far enough behind so I can't read his license number."

"There's a turnoff! Oh, please, let's take it!"

He veered off the highway and shot onto a two-lane road

that cut through dense jungle. The same pair of headlights twinkled behind them, refusing to vanish.

"I'm going to lose him. Hold on."

She was thrown sideways by the violent lurch of the car. Houses leaped past as the BMW rounded corners at a speed that made her claw the dashboard in terror.

Without warning, David swerved into a driveway and instantly cut off the engine. Then he was pulling her down into his arms and she lay, wedged between the gearshift and his chest, listening.

With mounting terror, she watched a flicker of light slowly grow brighter in the rearview mirror. From the road came the faint growl of an engine and then it faded away. Only when there was total silence did they creep up and peer through the rear window.

The road was dark. The car had vanished.

"What now?" she whispered.

"We get the hell out of here. While we still can."

Only when they reached the highway did Kate allow herself a breath of relief. She knew by the direction they were headed that David was taking her to his house.

A few minutes later David slipped the key into the lock of his front door. They could hear the telephone ringing.

David shot to answer it. "Hello," he barked into the receiver.

Pokie's voice boomed across the wires. "Have I got news for you! We got him."

"Decker?"

"I'll need Dr. Chesne down here to identify him. Half an hour, okay?"

"Where you holding him? Downtown station?"

There was a pause. "No, not the station. The morgue."

UNDER THE harsh morgue lights, the corpse's face looked waxen.

"Some yachtie found him this evening, floating facedown in the harbor," explained Pokie.

Nodding, Kate whispered. "That's him."

Pokie grinned. "Bingo," he grunted.

M.J., the medical examiner, ran her gloved hand over the dead man's scalp. "Feels like we got a depressed skull fracture here...looks like he's been in the water quite a while."

Suddenly nauseated, Kate turned and buried her face against David's shoulder.

He guided Kate away from the body drawers. "Come on. Let's get the hell out of here."

The medical examiner's office was a purposefully cheering room, complete with hanging plants and old movie posters. Pokie poured coffee from the automatic brewer and handed two cups to David and Kate. He settled into a chair across from them. "So that's how it wraps up," he said. "No trial. No hassles."

"How did he die, Lieutenant?" Kate whispered.

Pokie shrugged. "Happens now and then. Some guy who's had a little too much to drink falls off a pier, bashes his head." He glanced at M.J. "What do you think?"

"Can't rule out anything yet," mumbled M.J.

"Just how long was he in the water?" asked David.

"A day. More or less."

"A day? Then who the hell was following us tonight?"

Pokie grinned. "You just got yourself an active imagination."

"I'm telling you, there was a car!"

"Well, it sure wasn't my guy in the drawer," said M.J.

"When are you going to know the cause of death?" David snapped.

"Still need skull X rays. I'll open him up tonight, check the lungs for water. That'll tell us if he drowned."

Pokie nodded. "Well, it's over, Doc. Our man's dead. Looks like you can go home."

"Yes," she said in a weary voice. "Now I can go home."

WHO WERE you, Charlie Decker?

That refrain played over and over in her head as she sat in the darkness of David's car and watched the streetlights flash by. Who were you?

"It's too easy, David," she said softly.

He glanced at her. "What is?"

"The way it's all turned out. Too simple, too neat..." She stared off into the darkness, remembering Charlie Decker's face in the mirror. "My God. I saw it in his eyes," she whispered. "It was right there, staring at me." "What?"

"The fear. He was terrified. He must have known something. And it killed him. Just like it killed the others...."

"You're saying he was a victim? Then why did he threaten you? Why did he make that call to the cottage?"

"Maybe it wasn't a threat...." She looked up. "Maybe he was warning me. About someone else."

"But the evidence—"

"What evidence? A few fingerprints on a doorknob? A corpse with a psychiatric record?"

"And a witness. You saw him in Ann's apartment."

"What if he was the real witness? Four people, David. And the only thing that linked them was a dead woman. If I only knew why Jenny Brook was so important."

"Kate, the man's dead. The answers died with him. Don't turn this into an obsession!" Gripping the steering wheel, he forced out an agitated breath. When he spoke again, his voice was quiet. "Look, I know how much it means to you, clearing your name. But in the long run, it may not be worth the fight. That's why I think you should settle out of court. Before your name gets dragged through the mud."

"Is that how they do it in the prosecutor's office? 'Plead guilty and we'll make you a deal'?"

"There's nothing wrong with a settlement."

"Would you settle? If you were me?"

There was a long pause. "Yes. I would."

"Then we must be very different." Stubbornly she gazed ahead.

They drove the rest of the way in silence. A cloud of gloom filled the car. They both seemed to sense that things were coming to an end; he guessed it had been inevitable. Already he could feel her pulling away.

When they reached her house, David walked her to the front door.

"Would you like to come in for a cup of coffee?" she asked.

"Not right now. But I'll call you."

Automatically she thrust the key in the lock and gave the door a shove. It swung open. As the room came into view, she halted, unable to believe what she was seeing.

Dear God, she thought. Why is this happening?

She felt David's steadying hand as the room swam, and then her eyes refocused on the opposite wall.

On the flowered wallpaper the letters "MYOB" had been spray painted in bloodred. And below them was the hollow-eyed figure of a skull and crossbones.

*

"NO DICE, Davy. The case is closed."

Pokie Ah Ching splashed coffee from his foam cup as he weaved through the crammed police station.

"Don't you see, it was a warning!"

"Probably left by Charlie Decker."

"Kate's neighbor checked the house yesterday. That message was left when Decker was already dead."

"So it's a kid's prank."

"Yeah? Why would some kid write MYOB? Mind your own business?"

"You understand kids? I don't. Like I said, Davy, I'm busy."

David leaned across the desk. "Last night I told you we were followed. You said it was all in my head."

"I still say so."

"Then Decker turns up in the morgue. Four deaths. Tanaka. Richter. Decker. And Ellen O'Brien—"

"Death on the operating table isn't in my jurisdiction."

"But murder is. There's a hidden player in this game, Pokie.

Someone smart and quiet and medically sophisticated. And very, very scared.''

''Of what?''

''Kate Chesne. Maybe she's been asking too many questions. Maybe she knows something and doesn't realize it. But she'd made our killer nervous enough to scrawl warnings all over that wall.''

Pokie flipped open a report on his desk, a rude gesture that said the meeting was definitely over.

David rose to leave. He was almost to the door when Pokie snapped: ''Hold it, Davy. Where's Kate right now?''

''She's at my house.''

''Then she is in a safe place.'' Pokie waved the report. ''This just came in from M.J.'s office. It's the autopsy on Decker. He didn't drown.''

''What?'' David snatched up the report. Skull X rays show compression fracture, probably caused by lethal blow to the head. Cause of death: epidural hematoma.

Pokie spat out an epithet. ''The man was dead hours before he hit the water.''

David threw the report at Pokie. ''Obviously there's a killer out there. And with or without your help, I'm going to protect Kate.''

ONE THING Kate could not do was sit and wait. The police had closed their case with Decker's death, but she knew there was a killer at large. And it was only a matter of time before he found her.

Earlier in the day, when David had left to meet with Pokie, she had made an appointment with Decker's psychiatrist, Dr. Nemechek. She glanced at her watch as she pulled into a parking spot on the grounds of the mental health facility. 2:00. She was right on time.

As arranged, Dr. Nemechek met her in the lobby. He was a thin, slouching man with tired eyes. They walked together on the hospital grounds. All around them, white-gowned patients wandered aimlessly like dandelion fluffs.

Dr. Nemechek paused and gazed around sadly at his kingdom of shattered minds. "Charlie Decker never belonged here," he remarked. "I told them that he wasn't criminally insane. But the court had their so-called expert from the mainland. So he was committed." He shook his head. "That's the trouble with courts. They look at their evidence. I look at the man."

"And what did you see when you looked at Charlie?"

"He was withdrawn. Very depressed. Maybe delusional."

"Then he was insane."

"But not criminally so. Insanity can be dangerous. Or it can be a merciful shield against pain. That's what it was for Charlie—a shield. His delusion kept him alive. That's why I never tried to tamper with it."

"The police say he was a murderer."

"Ridiculous. He was a perfectly benign creature with no reason to kill anyone."

"What about Jenny Brook? Wasn't she his reason?"

"Charlie's delusion wasn't about Jenny. It was about her child. One of the doctors told him the baby was born alive. Only Charlie got it twisted around in his head. That was his obsession. Every August, he'd hold a little birthday celebration. He'd tell us, 'My girl's five years old today.' He wanted to find her. But I knew he'd never really try. He was terrified of learning the truth."

A sprinkling of rain made them both glance up at the sky. "Is there any possibility he was right?" she asked.

"Not a chance." A curtain of drizzle had drifted between them. "The baby's dead, Dr. Chesne. For the last five years, that child only existed in Charlie Decker's mind."

THE BABY'S DEAD.

As Kate drove the mist-shrouded highway back to David's house, Dr. Nemechek's words kept repeating in her head.

If the girl had lived, what would she be like now? Kate wondered. Would she have her father's dark hair and eyes?

A face took shape in her mind and at that instant, fog puffed across the road. With that, the image wavered, dissolved; in its place was another child's face. There was a break in the clouds; as the sunlight broke through, so did the revelation.

Why the hell didn't I see it before?

Jenny Brook's child was still alive.

And he was five years old.

IT WAS five-thirty and the lone clerk who remained in Medical Records grudgingly took Kate's request slip and went to the computer terminal.

"This patient's deceased," she noted.

"I know," said Kate. "Could you please get me the chart?"

"It may take a while to track it down. Why don't you come back tomorrow?"

"I need the chart now." Kate felt like adding: It's a matter of life and death.

The clerk looked at her watch, then vanished into the file room, returning fifteen minutes later with the record. Kate retreated to a corner table and stared down at the name on the cover:

Brook, Baby Girl.

The child had never even had a name.

The chart contained only the hospital fact sheet, death certificate, and a scrawled summary of the infant's short existence. Death had been pronounced August 17 at 2:00 a.m., an hour after birth. The cause was cerebral anoxia: the tiny brain had been starved of oxygen. The death certificate was signed by Dr. Henry Tanaka.

Kate turned to the copy of Jenny Brook's chart, which she'd brought with her.

"...28-year-old female, G1P0, 36 weeks' gestation, admitted via E.R. in early labor..."

A routine report, she thought. There were no surprises, no warnings of the disaster to come. Kate closed the chart. Suddenly feverish, she returned to the file clerk. "I need another record," she said.

"Not another deceased patient, I hope."

"No, this one's still alive. William Santini."

It took only a minute for the clerk to find it. Kate was almost afraid to open it, to see what she knew lay inside.

A copy of the birth certificate stared up at her. Name: William Santini. Date of Birth: August 17. Time: 03:00.

August 17, the same day. But not quite the same time. Exactly one hour after Baby Girl Brook had left the world, William Santini had entered it.

Two infants; one living, one dead. Had there ever been a better motive for murder?

"Don't tell me you still have charts to finish," remarked a familiar voice.

Kate's head whipped around. Guy Santini had just walked in the door. She slapped the chart closed but the name was scrawled in bold black ink across the cover. In a panic, she hugged the chart to her chest, smiling automatically.

"I'm just…cleaning up some paperwork." She managed to add, "You're here late."

"Car's in the shop so Susan's picking me up." He glanced across the counter. "Where's the help around here, anyway?"

"She was, uh, here just a minute ago," said Kate inching toward the exit.

He frowned. "Is something wrong?"

"No. I've really got to go." She turned and was about to flee when the file clerk yelled: "Dr. Chesne!"

"What?" Kate spun around.

"The chart. You can't take it out of the department."

Kate looked down at the folder. She didn't dare return it while Guy was standing here; he'd see the name.

They were both frowning at her.

"Look, if you're not finished with it, I can hold it right here," the clerk offered.

"No. I mean…"

Guy laughed. "What's in that thing, anyway?"

Kate placed the chart facedown on the counter. "I'm not finished with it."

"Then I'll hold it for you." The clerk reached over, apparently poised to expose the patient's name. Instead she scooped up Guy's request list. "Why don't you sit down, Dr. Santini?"

she suggested. "I'll bring your records over." Then she vanished into the file room.

Time to get the hell out of here, thought Kate. She felt Guy's eyes on her back as she moved slowly and deliberately toward the exit. Only when she'd made it into the hall and heard the door thud shut behind her did the impact of what she'd discovered hit her. Guy Santini was her colleague. Her friend.

He was also a murderer. And she was the only one who knew.

Kate fled the hospital and headed out into the downpour.

She'd parked at the far end of the lot. The storm had become fierce, and by the time she got to the car, her clothes were soaked. It took a few seconds to fumble through the unfamiliar set of keys, another few to unlock the door. Just as she slid onto the driver's seat, a hand seized her arm.

She stared up to see Guy Santini.

"Move over," he said.

Escape was impossible. Guy was blocking the driver's exit and she'd never get out the passenger door in time.

Before she could even plan her next move, Guy shoved her aside and slid in. The door slammed.

"Your keys, Kate," he demanded.

The keys had dropped beside her on the seat.

"Give me the damn keys!" He suddenly spotted them and shoved the key into the ignition. The second he did, she lashed out, but he seized her wrist and wrenched her sideways so hard she was thrown back against the seat.

"If I have to," he said, "I swear I'll break your arm." He threw the gear in reverse and the car jerked backward. Then, hitting the gas, he spun the car out into the street.

"Where are you taking me?" she asked.

"Anywhere. I'm going to talk and you're going to listen."

"About what?"

"You know what the hell about!"

Her chin snapped up as they approached an intersection and turned onto the freeway. She watched in despair as the speedometer climbed to sixty.

"It was none of your business, Kate," he said. "You had no right to pry."

"Ellen was my patient, our patient—"

"That doesn't mean you can tear my life apart!"

"What about her life? And Ann's? They're dead, Guy!"

"And the past died with them! I have to protect my son. And Susan. You think I'd stand back and let them be destroyed?"

"They'd never take him away from you! Not after five years!"

"You think all I'm worried about is custody? Oh, we'd keep William all right. It's Susan I'm thinking of." The highway was slick with rain, the road treacherous.

"I don't understand," she persisted, scanning the road ahead for a stalled car, a traffic jam, anything. "What do you mean about Susan?"

"She doesn't know. She thinks William is hers."

"How can she not know?"

"For five years, it's been my little secret. She was under anesthesia when our baby was born. It was a nightmare, all that panic to do an emergency C-section. That was our third baby, Kate. Our last chance. And she was born dead...." He paused. "I didn't know what to do. What to tell Susan."

"You took Jenny Brook's baby as your own."

"It was an act of God. Can't you see that? The woman had just died. And there was her baby boy, this absolutely perfect baby boy, crying in the next room. And Susan, already starting to wake up. Can't you understand? It would have killed her to find out. God gave us that boy! We all felt it. Ann. Ellen. Only Tanaka—"

"He didn't agree?"

"Not at first. I argued with him. I practically begged him. It was only when Susan opened her eyes and asked for her baby that he finally gave in. So Ellen put the boy in Susan's arms. And my Susan, she just looked at him and then she, she started to cry...." Guy wiped his sleeve across his face. "That's when we knew we'd done the right thing."

Yes, Kate could see the perfection of that moment. But that

same decision had led to the murder of four people. Soon it would be five.

The car suddenly slowed; she looked up. Traffic was growing heavier. Far ahead lay the Pali tunnel, curtained off by rain. She knew there was an emergency telephone near the entrance. If he would just slow down a little more...

The chance never came. Guy veered off onto a thickly wooded side road and roared past a sign labeled: Pali Lookout. The last stop, she thought. Set on a cliff high above the valley, this was the overhang where ancient warriors once were flung to their deaths. It was the perfect spot for murder.

A last flood of desperation made her claw for the door. He yanked her back and she flew at him with both fists. Guy struggled and lost control of the wheel. The car swerved off the road.

It was Guy's strength that decided the battle. He threw all his weight into shoving her back. Then, cursing, he grabbed the wheel and spun it wildly to the left. The right fender scraped trees as the car veered back onto the road.

Guy stopped the car and killed the engine. For a long time he sat in silence. The rain had slowed to a drizzle and beyond the cliff's edge, mist swirled past.

"That was a damned crazy stunt you pulled," he said quietly. "Why the hell did you do it?"

Slowly she bowed her head. "Because you're going to kill me," she whispered. "The way you killed the others."

"I'm going to what?"

She looked up, searching his eyes for some trace of remorse. "Was it easy?" she asked softly. "Cutting Ann's throat?"

"You mean you really think I—" Suddenly he began to laugh. It was soft at first, then it grew louder and wilder until his whole body was racked by what sounded more like sobs than laughter. He didn't notice the new set of headlights, flickering through the mist. Another car had wandered up the road. This was Kate's chance to throw open the door, to run for help. But she didn't. In that instant she knew that Guy was incapable of murder.

Without warning, he shoved his door open and stumbled out. At the edge of the lookout, he halted, his head bowed.

Kate got out of the car and followed him. She didn't say a thing, just reached out and touched his arm. She could almost feel the pain, the confusion, coursing through his body.

"Then you didn't kill them," she said.

*

FROM SOMEWHERE in the mist came the hard click of metal. Kate and Guy froze as footsteps rapped slowly across the pavement. Out of the gathering darkness, a figure emerged, and even in the dusk, Susan Santini's red hair seemed to sparkle with fire. But it was the dull gray of the gun that held Kate's gaze.

"Move out of the way, Guy," Susan ordered softly.

Guy could only stare mutely at his wife.

"It was you," Kate murmured. "Not Decker."

Slowly, Susan turned her unfocused gaze on Kate. "You don't understand, do you? But you've never had a baby, Kate. You've never been afraid of someone hurting it or taking it away. That's all a mother ever worries about."

A low groan escaped Guy's throat. "My God, Susan. Do you understand what you've done?"

"You wouldn't do it. So I had to. All those years, I never knew about William. Then I had to hear it from Tanaka."

"You killed four people, Susan!"

"Not four. Only three. I didn't kill Ellen." Susan looked at Kate. "She did."

Kate stared at her. "What do you mean?"

"That wasn't succinylcholine in the vial. It was potassium chloride. You gave Ellen a lethal dose." Her gaze shifted back to Guy. "I didn't want you to be blamed, darling. So I changed the EKG. I put her initials on it."

"And I got the blame," finished Kate.

Nodding, Susan raised the gun. "Yes, Kate. I'm sorry. Now please, Guy. Move away."

"No, Susan."

She frowned at him. "They'll take William away from me. Don't you see?"

"I won't let them. I promise."

Susan shook her head. "It's too late, Guy. I've killed the others. She's the only one who knows."

"But I know!" Guy blurted out.

"You won't tell. You're my husband."

"Susan, give me the gun." Guy moved slowly, his hand held out to her. "Please, darling. Nothing will happen. I'll take care of everything. Just give it to me."

She retreated a step and almost lost her balance. Guy froze as the barrel of the gun swayed in his direction.

"You're not going to hurt me, Susan."

"I love you," she moaned.

"Then give me the gun. Yes, darling. Give it to me...."

The distance between them slowly evaporated and Guy, at last sensing he had won, quickly closed the gap. Seizing the gun by the barrel, he tried to tug it from her hands.

But she didn't surrender it. "Let go!" she screamed.

The gun's blast seemed to trap them in freeze-frame. They stared at each other in astonishment, then Guy stumbled backward, clutching his leg.

"No!" Susan's wail rose up and drifted through the mist. Slowly she turned toward Kate, desperation in her eyes.

That's when Kate ran. Blindly, into the mist. She heard a pistol shot. A bullet whistled past and thudded into the dirt near her feet. There was no time to get her bearings, to circle back toward the road. She just kept running.

The ground suddenly rose upward. Through fingers of mist, she saw the sheer face of the ridge, sparsely stubbled with brush. Her only escape route lay to the left, down the crumbling remains of the old Pali road. She had no idea how far it would take her.

The old road was full of cracks and potholes. In places it had crumbled away entirely and young trees poked through, their roots rippling the asphalt. Darkness was falling fast; it would cut off the last of her visibility. But it would also be a cloak in which to hide.

But where could she hide? On her right, the ridge loomed steeply upward; on her left, the pavement broke off sharply at the cliff's edge. She had to keep running.

A gust of wind swept the road. For an instant, the mist cleared. She saw looming to her right the face of the ridge, covered by dense brush. Halfway up was the mouth of a cave. If she could reach it before Susan passed this way, she could hide until help arrived. If it arrived.

She threaded her way into the shrubbery and began clambering up the mountainside, clawing for roots and branches to pull herself up. The sound of footsteps made her freeze. Desperately, Kate hugged the mountain, willing herself to blend into the bushes.

By the time she reached the cave's mouth, her hands had cramped into claws. It took her last ounce of strength to drag herself up into the muddy hollow. There she collapsed, fighting to catch her breath.

Closing her eyes, she focused on a mental image of David. If only he could hear her silent plea for help.

It was the footsteps that told her darkness would come too late to save her. Through the tangle of branches fringing the cave mouth, she saw against the sky's fading light the velvety green of a distant ridge. The mist had vanished; so had her invisibility.

"You're up there, aren't you?" Susan's voice floated up. "I almost missed it. But there's one unfortunate thing about caves. They're dead ends."

Rocks rattled down the slope and slammed onto the road. She's climbing the ridge, Kate thought frantically. She's coming for me....

Her only escape route was right into Susan's line of fire.

A twig snapped and more rocks slithered down the mountain. Susan was closing in.

Swiftly Kate groped around and came up with a fist-size

rock. It wasn't much against a gun, but it was all she had. And Susan was already halfway up the slope.

Their eyes met. One was fighting for her life, the other for her child. There could be no compromise.

Susan took aim; Kate hurled the rock.

It skimmed the bushes and thudded against Susan's shoulder. Crying out, Susan slid a few feet, then grabbed hold of a branch. There she clung for a moment, stunned.

Kate scrambled out of the cave and began clawing her way up the ridge. Even as she pulled herself up, some rational part of her brain was screaming that the ascent was impossible, that the cliff face was too steep.

A bullet ricocheted off a boulder. Kate cringed but Susan's aim was wide.

Kate looked up to find herself staring at an overhanging rock, laced with vines. Could she drag herself over the top? Would the vines hold her weight?

When at last she cleared the overhang, she was too exhausted to feel any sense of triumph. She hauled herself over the top and rolled onto a narrow ledge. Susan was right behind her.

A final gunshot rang out. What Kate felt wasn't pain, but surprise. There was the dull punch of the bullet slamming into her shoulder. Then she was rolling, over and over, tumbling toward oblivion.

It was a halekoa bush that saved her life. It snagged her by the legs, breaking her fall, and as she lay there, she became aware of a strange shrieking in the distance; to her confused brain, it sounded like an infant's wail, and it grew louder.

The hallucination dragged her into consciousness, turning into the wail of police sirens. The sound of help.

Then, across her field of vision, a shadow moved. Susan said nothing as she slowly pointed her gun at Kate's head.

"Don't do this, Susan. You need help. I'll see you get it."

The barrel still hovered at her head. Then, through the wind's scream, she heard a voice calling her name. Another hallucination, she thought.

But there it was again; David's voice, shouting her name, over and over.

"Please, Susan," she whispered. "Can't you see? If you kill me, you'll destroy your only chance of keeping your son!"

Her words seemed to drain all the strength from Susan's arms. Slowly, she let the gun drop. For a moment she stood motionless, her head bent. Then she turned and gazed over the ledge, at the road far below. "It's too late now," she said. "I've already lost him."

A chorus of shouts from below told them they'd been spotted.

Susan stared down at the gathering of men. "It's better this way," she insisted. "He'll have only good memories of me. That's the way childhood should be, you know..."

Perhaps it was a sudden gust that threw Susan off balance; Kate could never be certain. All she knew was that one instant she was poised on the edge of the rock and then she was gone.

She fell soundlessly, without uttering a cry.

It was Kate who sobbed. As the world spun around her she cried, silently, for the woman who had just died, and for the others who had lost their lives. And all in the name of love.

DAVID HAD to wait four hours to see her. Four hours of pacing the fourth-floor waiting room.

At midnight, a nurse at last poked her head into the room. "Are you Mr. Ransom?"

He spun around. "Yes!"

"Dr. Chesne's out of surgery."

"Then... She's all right?"

"Everything went just fine. If you'd like to go home, we'll call you when she—"

"I have to see her."

"I'm sorry, but we only allow immediate family into..." Her voice trailed off as she saw the look in his eyes. "Five minutes, Mr. Ransom. That's all. You understand?"

He ran to her room, then stilled at the sight of her.

"You're all right," he whispered, pressing his lips to her palm. "Thank God you're all right...."

"I don't remember...."

"You've been in surgery. Three hours. It seemed like for-ever. But the bullet's out."

She remembered, then. The wind. The ridge. And Susan. "She's dead?"

He nodded. "There was nothing anyone could do."

"And Guy?"

"He won't be able to walk for a while. I don't know how he made it to that phone. But he did."

For a moment she lay in silence, thinking of Guy, whose life was now as shattered as his leg. "He saved my life. And now he's lost everything...."

"Not everything. He still has his son."

Yes, she thought. William will always be Guy's son. Not by blood, but by love. Out of all this tragedy, at least one thing would remain intact and good.

IT WAS raining hard when David came to see her late the next afternoon. She was sitting alone in the solarium, gazing at the courtyard below.

"Out of bed, I see. You must be feeling better," he said.

She managed a wan smile. "I guess I never was one for lying around all day."

"Oh. I brought you these." He handed her a small foil-wrapped box of chocolates.

"Thank you," she murmured. "And thank you for the roses." Then she turned and stared out at the rain.

There was a long silence.

"I hear you're getting your old job back," he finally said.

"Yes. I guess that's something else I have to thank you for. I'm told you made a lot of phone calls."

"Just a few. Nothing, really." He took a deep breath. "So, you should be back at work in the O.R. in no time. With a big raise in pay, I hope."

"I'm not sure I'm taking the job."

"What? Why on earth wouldn't you?"

She shrugged. "I've been thinking about other places."

"You mean besides Mid Pac?"

"I mean...besides Hawaii. There's really nothing keeping me here."

There was another long silence. Then he said, "Isn't there?"

She didn't answer. He watched her, sitting so still.

"Dr. Chesne?" A nurse appeared. "Are you ready to go back to your room?"

"Yes," Kate answered. "I think I'd like to sleep."

"You do look tired." The nurse glanced at David. "Maybe it's time you left, sir."

"No," said David. "Not until I've finished making a fool of myself. So could you leave us alone?"

The nurse hesitated. Then, sensing that something momentous was looming, she retreated.

Kate was watching him, her green eyes filled with uncertainty. He reached down and gently touched her face.

"Now tell me the real reason you want to leave."

She was silent. But he saw the answer in her eyes. "My God," he muttered. "You're a bigger coward than I am."

"A coward?"

"That's right. So am I." He turned away and began to wander restlessly around the room. "I didn't plan to say this. Not yet, anyway. But here you're talking about leaving. And it seems I don't have much of a choice." He went to her and tilted her face up. "All right, then. I love you. I love your stubbornness and your pride. And your independence. I didn't want to. But now I can't imagine ever not loving you." He pulled away, offering her a chance to retreat.

She remained perfectly still.

"It won't be easy, you know," he said.

"What won't?"

"Living with me. There'll be days you'll want to wring my neck or scream at me, anything to make me say 'I love you.' But just because I don't say it doesn't mean I don't feel it. Because I do."

Kate was silent. David took her hand in his and touched her fingers to his lips. "Kate, have you been listening?"

"Yes, I've been listening," she replied softly.

"And?" he asked. "Do I hear the verdict? Or is the jury still out?"

"The jury," she whispered, "is in a state of shock. And badly in need of mouth-to-mouth—" If resuscitation was what he'd intended, his kiss did quite the opposite.

"Now, fellow coward," he murmured. "Your turn."

"I love you," she said happily.

"That's the verdict I was hoping for." He kissed her again, with all the joy he felt in his heart. "Will you marry me, Kate, my love?"

"A life sentence, huh?" She smiled. "Yes, darling, I can't think of a better way to spend my life, than with you."

ADAM'S STORY

Annette Broadrick

~~~~~~~⚜~~~~~~~

Adam St. Clair paused outside his hotel to look up and down
the Monterrey, Mexico thoroughfare. The February wind off
the mountains made him raise the collar of his sheepskin-lined
denim jacket and settle his Stetson more firmly on his head.
Hunching his shoulders, Adam started toward his car.

Tonight was the night. He wasn't sure how he knew exactly.
He'd followed countless leads since joining the agency that
was trying to stop the flood of drugs crossing the border into
the United States. Most of those leads had led nowhere. Some
had gotten him into the circle of men who made their living
bringing drugs in from South America.

He'd had no trouble with his cover. Playing the part of a
Texas rancher came naturally—that's what he'd always been.
But two years ago, he'd also become a man determined to do
what he could for his country.

If all went well tonight, he'd have the information necessary
to nail one of the leaders, unless the informant changed his
mind.

Adam had removed his hat and now he ran his hand through
his tawny hair, causing the waves to fall into curls across his
forehead. His sister, Felicia, had always teased him about his
curls. His mouth lifted into a slight smile at the memory.

He forced his thoughts back to the job at hand. Adam knew
that what he was doing was dangerous, and felt a twinge of
guilt that he'd never told Felicia about this part of his life. But
there was no reason for her to be involved. Since she'd been
living in Los Angeles for several years, he'd had no need to
explain his periodic trips to Mexico.

He glanced at his watch. It was time to go.

HER EYES flew open, and Caitlin Moran sat up in bed. She
looked around her one-room cabin, trying to decide what had

awakened her. The darkness outside showed no sign of impending dawn.

Caitlin continued to sit there, listening intently. Something was wrong. She slid out of bed, absently pulled on her heavy robe to offset the chill of the mountains and padded to the window.

She could see nothing in the clearing except the heavy frost that tinted the blades of grass silver. Nothing moved. She could hear no sound of an intruder.

Disturbed, but unsure why, Caitlin turned away from the window.

What could be wrong?

Reluctantly, she crawled back into bed, pulling up the blankets.

Caitlin wasn't alarmed because she was alone. She had lived in her small cabin, high in the mountains near Monterrey, for more than five years. Being alone was a way of life she had chosen.

Staring up at the roof over her head, she tried to calm her mind, willing herself to fall asleep again.

Instead, scenes of violence began to race across the screen of her mind. She saw two cars traveling fast over twisting and narrow mountain roads, their headlights blinding.

A shadowed face appeared, indistinct at first, but with concentration Caitlin began to see more details. Gray-green eyes with a look of determination and agitation stared back at her, a frown making the brows draw together over a well-formed nose. A strong jaw was clenched, the lines around the tight-lipped mouth making deep grooves in the face.

Caitlin had never seen the man before, but she would never forget him.

Who was he? Tawny curls fell across his forehead, giving a deceptively boyish look to an otherwise stern face. She tried to get more, but nothing came. She sighed, frustrated by her ability to see so much that she didn't want to see, and her inability to pick up more when she tried.

She had lived with her frustration long enough to know

there was little she could do to rid her mind of the pictures and messages she received.

She forced herself to turn over, trying to clear her mind. Instead she began to remember how she had slowly made a place for herself in these mountains.

About once a month she began to take the vegetables she had grown and her handwoven rugs and fabrics down to the small settlement a few miles from her cabin. There she would trade for supplies.

The people of the village at first stared at her reddish-gold hair and blue eyes with distrust. Why was she living there? What did she want?

How could she explain to them that she was searching for some answers? She was looking for her sanity, her belief in herself. By the time she'd finally been released from the hospital, she'd known her life would never be the same again. Her loving parents were gone. Friendships had evaporated, and the man she loved had withdrawn from her.

The stoic natives would probably not be impressed to know that she had run from the world and chosen their small corner of the universe to find peace.

Caitlin had been grateful for the many summers she had spent with her aunt in San Antonio. She had enjoyed learning Spanish and by the time she returned to Seattle each fall, she had continued to increase her grasp of the language. Now she couldn't remember the last time she'd spoken English. Probably not since her aunt had passed away.

Caitlin had grown used to the villagers. She understood and identified with their need for privacy. They didn't bother her, and she didn't bother them.

She remembered the day she had been on her way out of the village, leading her burro, when she heard a baby crying. There was no baby near her, yet she heard the choked whimpering very clearly in her head.

Since she had moved to the mountains, the pictures and impressions she kept seeing had slowly disappeared. Now they were back, and she wasn't sure what to do.

The choked crying of the baby seemed to fill her mind once

more, and Caitlin made her decision. She began to thread her way through the streets in an effort to locate the infant.

When she paused in front of a small house, there was no actual sound coming from within. Yet she felt certain the baby was inside. She could see in her mind's eye the baby being held in its mother's arms.

Caitlin tapped on the door. After a long moment, a young woman with tired, reddened eyes peered out at her. In Spanish, Caitlin said, "Your baby is ill?"

"Oh, yes! I fear he is dying!" was the reply.

"May I help?" Caitlin reached into her cloth bag and pulled out a smaller one. "I have had some experience in healing with these herbs."

When Caitlin stepped into the dimly lit room, she saw the other women, sitting in a circle around the infant, weeping.

The poor child struggled for every breath. He seemed incapable of crying at this point. Caitlin asked for boiling water, and as soon as it was brought to her, she crushed some leaves into it and quickly made a tent with a blanket lying nearby. She held the baby, sitting under the blanket and breathing with him, absorbing the aromatic fumes.

Then she began to croon to him, rubbing her hands over his body and talking to him in a low voice, explaining that breathing was easy, part of life, that there was nothing to fear from life, that he would enjoy it.

Time meant nothing to her as she worked with the baby. Slowly his breathing eased, and his temperature lowered. His color improved, and after several hours he dropped off into a deep, healing sleep.

When Caitlin stood up to place him in his bed, she turned and looked at the mother with a smile. "What is your baby's name?"

"Miguel."

Caitlin gently stroked the infant's back.

"I believe Miguel will be all right now. When he awakens, make him a liquid from soaking these leaves in boiling water for five minutes. Give him this much—" she showed the woman "—every two hours. By tomorrow he will be ready to eat again."

A clamoring of voices broke out from all the women, but Caitlin was too tired to decipher what they were saying. Clearly, they were elated with her success.

She began to back out of the room, saying over and over, *"De nada, de nada."*

The next day Antonio, Miguel's father, appeared at her door, together with his father and two brothers, asking what they could do to pay her for saving the young child's life. She tried to explain they owed her nothing, but they insisted. When they saw how simply she was living, they told her they would bring her new furniture.

And they had. Over the months each one had shown up at her doorstep with a new offering—a beautifully carved bed, a small round table with four matching chairs, a rocker.

Eventually the surrounding mountainside heard the story of the fair-haired healer who knew mysterious ways to use the plants of the fields and forests to bring strength and peace to a troubled body and soul. Caitlin felt truly blessed to have found what she could do with her life. And she was content...

She was almost asleep, when suddenly, an image of the same face leaped into her mind, a look of dread and horror in its taut expression.

Caitlin involuntarily screamed, "No!"

She shook with the intensity of the feeling that gripped her. The man was in danger. But where was he?

Throwing back the covers, she leapt up and pulled on jeans and a shirt, then socks and her hiking boots.

Grabbing her heavy hooded coat and the bag she always carried, Caitlin stepped outside.

The crude shelter that protected Arturo, her burro, lay several yards from her front door, and she hastened toward his stall. She found his bridle and blanket, then grabbed his halter and led him away from the warmth of his home, much to his loudly voiced irritation.

"Oh, hush, Arturo," she scolded. "It won't be long until dawn, anyway."

Caitlin hurried down the path, leading the burro and trying to get her bearings.

A desperate sense of urgency pushed her on, but she couldn't pinpoint where it was leading her. She was moving away from the village.

The path narrowed to no more than a trail where deer and other animals followed the mountain ridge over into the next valley.

Caitlin had never been here before. As far as she knew, no one lived in these parts. But coming over a ridge, she saw a light moving in the distance. She paused, watching the headlights of two cars.

One vehicle seemed to be chasing the other through the mountain stillness, following twisting, turning roads. She remembered seeing them earlier in her mind. She tied Arturo to a young sapling and hurried toward the lights.

She watched with mounting horror while one car began to ram the back of the other, making the driver lose control. The lead car careened back and forth, grazed a tree, then rolled as though in slow motion, coming to rest at the edge of the steep precipice.

From her position, Caitlin watched as the scene continued to unfold. She broke into a run, then abruptly halted when two men leapt out of the second vehicle and ran to the other car. Their voices carried in the night.

"Where is he? Is he dead?" one asked in Spanish.

"If not, he will be soon enough. Let's get that car over the side. If anyone finds him, they'll think he was just driving too fast and lost control."

Caitlin could hardly believe what she was hearing. She continued down the mountainside, a sense of helplessness overwhelming her. Not only was she outnumbered, she had a hunch those two wouldn't hesitate to kill her if they knew she'd been a witness. She watched as the men pushed on the car until it toppled over the side and exploded on impact.

The noise shook the ground, and Caitlin grabbed the limb of a nearby tree to keep her balance.

She heard one of them say, "Let's roll him over the side,"

just as Arturo protested the noise, the night, and being left alone. Caitlin froze.

One of them glanced up in her direction.

"What was that?"

"Who knows? There's all kinds of animals out here."

The other man headed back to the car. "Let's go. Nobody's going to find him here, anyway."

The car turned around and left, returning the way it had come. Caitlin felt paralyzed with shock. In all her experience, she had never witnessed anything so deliberately cruel and callous.

She went on down the hillside, now having no trouble distinguishing where she was going. Unnoticed, the sky had begun to lighten, signaling a new day.

As soon as she reached the injured man's side, she fell to her knees.

His skin was icy, and her heart sank. She felt for a pulse, but her hand was shaking so much she couldn't find any sign of life. His clothes were covered with dirt, his features all but obscured by blood.

She couldn't leave him lying there while she went for help. It would take her hours. He needed help now, unless it was already too late.

Making up her mind, Caitlin began to climb the mountain once again. She would bring Arturo down and attempt to take the man to the village.

Perhaps it was too late to save him, but he deserved a decent burial.

Decent. The word seemed to ring in her head. He had been a decent man. A kind man. A man who had not deserved to die this way.

By the time Caitlin reached Arturo, tears cascaded down her cheeks. There were many times when she found life particularly puzzling. Now was one of those times. Why had she seen him so clearly if she wasn't going to be given the opportunity to save him?

She dried her eyes with the sleeve of her shirt. Whatever the reason, she was there, and she was going to see that he wasn't abandoned. Turning, she guided the burro back down the side of the mountain.

With infinite care and tenderness, she straightened the unknown man's legs and turned him so that he was lying on his back. She knelt and began to wipe the blood away from his face. It had come from a gash across his forehead, just beneath his hairline.

There was no expression on his face. He looked as though he were asleep. He had a beautiful face—clean, clearly defined, with high cheekbones and a strong jawline. His lips, in repose, looked as though they were made for smiling.

She sat and stared at him for a few moments until she realized she was wasting time. Then she placed her arms around him, her head resting on his chest where his coat had fallen open, in an attempt to get him upright.

She froze, her eyes closing in a spasm of excitement. An almost indiscernible rhythm had reached her ear.

It was a heartbeat.

*

NEVER HAD a place looked so good to her as her own clearing once they arrived. Caitlin wasn't sure where she had found the strength to get the man onto Arturo's back, so now she led the burro inside and slid the unconscious man onto the bed.

He hadn't moved. His skin felt clammy to the touch, and his gray color evinced his state of shock.

"But you're alive," she whispered. "You're going to make it."

Searching in her bag for her penlight, Caitlin carefully lifted each of the man's eyelids, shining the light into his pupils and watching them retract slightly. The movement was sluggish, but at least there was some response, thank God. There was no doubt that he suffered from a concussion, but his brain was still functioning.

The gash on his head no longer bled, and Caitlin knew she

would have to stitch it, but not until she could clean and disinfect it.

First things first. She had to get him out of his coat and boots, and try to make him more comfortable. From her quick check before she'd loaded him onto Arturo, he had no broken bones, for which she was thankful. His head injury was serious enough.

When she slipped his arm out of his coat sleeve, Caitlin flinched at the sight of a shoulder holster under his arm. She wondered how many law-abiding people wore them. *Or get run off the road, for that matter.* She unfastened the holster and pulled it away from him, staring at the pistol in it. She didn't know what to do with it.

Was he dangerous? When he came to, would he try to kill her?

No. He was a decent man. Somehow she knew that. But whatever he was mixed up in was highly dangerous. She was a witness to that.

With sudden decision she wrapped the gun in a towel and hid it in her suitcase. Then she returned to the man lying unconscious on her bed.

ADAM THOUGHT he was dreaming when he finally managed to focus his eyes. And he felt as though an oversize sledgehammer was continually tapping on his skull. It was difficult to concentrate.

The rustic cabin he seemed to occupy was immaculate, the furnishings sparse. Except for the statue of a small deer in front of the fireplace, there was no ornamentation, unless he counted the woman.

The glow from the fire tinted her skin apricot. She stood with her back to him, wearing a pair of panties that covered a deliciously curved derriere. Her long reddish-blond hair fell to her waist in waves and curls.

He watched her as she dressed, unaware of him. Who was she? And what was he doing here?

His last memory was sitting in his car in front of his hotel in Monterrey. He'd had something important to do. What was it?

The throbbing pain increased when he frowned. He touched his forehead and felt a large welt that was extremely tender. On his jaw, he felt the roughness of a beard.

She turned toward him, reaching for her blouse. She had very delicate features. Her eyes were framed with dark lashes, and very blue.

"Who are you?" he said, his voice husky.

She grabbed her blouse to her breast in surprise, and turning her back to him, tugged it on, then a pair of jeans. Walking over to the bed, she sat down beside him and took his hand.

"I'm Caitlin," she said, smiling. "Who are you?"

The room kept receding from him and he blinked. "Adam," he finally muttered, his throat dry.

"Adam," she repeated slowly. At last she had a name for him. She liked it. "You're going to be fine, Adam. You got a nasty blow to your head, though." She reached up and brushed his hair from his forehead, careful not to touch his wound.

He couldn't think. Her touch felt so soothing; it went with the sound of her voice, which was so familiar, the tone as gentle as her touch...Adam drifted off to sleep, his expression serene.

Time didn't seem to have any meaning to him, and he kept fading in and out of consciousness. He would open his eyes to daylight, close them, then reopen them to deep shadows. But he was always aware of her presence. What had she said her name was? Caitlin, that was it. Caitlin with the soft voice and soothing hands.

Vaguely he was aware of her instructions to eat. From some distant place she urged him to turn so that she could stroke him with a warm, wet cloth, offering a balm to his aching body. He tried to tell her he could bathe himself, but somehow he couldn't find the words.

Once he woke up to find her sleeping curled up by his side. He smiled. Shifting slightly, he moved so that his hand could touch her arm. He found the closeness comforting.

Sometime during those many hours, Caitlin became a part of his thoughts, whether he was conscious or unconscious. Her presence kept the fear and confusion he was experiencing at bay.

Caitlin.

At last the day came when Adam could focus without the hazy double vision that had plagued him. He lay there quietly looking around the now familiar room.

At first he didn't see Caitlin, then she moved into his line of vision. Her reddish-blond hair hung in a single braid across her shoulder, and he smiled at the tranquil picture she made placing wood on the fire.

When she moved away from the fireplace, he tried to keep her in sight by turning his head—a mistake as he discovered when the pain in his head magnified.

But Caitlin glanced up, and when she saw him watching her, she smiled, making her eyes sparkle.

"How do you feel?" she asked, taking his hand in hers.

"Like my head's been used for batting practice," he managed to say. "Where are we?" he asked, his curiosity finally piqued.

"The mountains. In Mexico."

"What am I doing here?"

"You were badly injured not too far from here. Since there's no town nearby, I brought you to my home to help you recover."

He thought about that for a moment. He knew he was hurt. He'd never felt so much pain before.

"How long have I been here?"

"I'm not sure, exactly. I'm afraid I lost track of time…you've been so ill."

Not that it mattered. He was content to lie there looking at her very lovely, expressive face.

Caitlin was touched by his tender expression. And slightly alarmed. He mustn't grow attached to her. She felt the inner warning that she was too late—her loving care of him had created a bond between them.

"Where do you live, Adam?" she asked then, gently releasing his hand and folding her own together.

Adam had to think about her question for a moment. His home. Where was it? "On a ranch...in Texas. Near Mason." His eyes sought hers. "Do you know where that is?"

He watched her as she shook her head. That was all right. He'd show her someday, when he felt better.

"What are you doing here in Mexico, Adam?"

Good question. He frowned once again.

Car lights shining in the rearview mirror. He'd been going somewhere, meeting someone.... Danger.

With a sudden start Adam felt along his side.

"Where's my pistol?"

"I put it in my suitcase, where it would be safe," she said.

The pistol didn't need to be safe. *They* needed to be safe. They would be safer if he had the gun nearby.

"How long have I known you?"

Unconsciously Caitlin reached for his hand once more. "Just since the accident."

"You don't know why I'm here?"

"Not very clearly, I'm afraid. I've picked up that you were on your way to meet someone important to you, and you never made it."

"What do you mean, 'picked up'?"

Her grip on his hand tightened, and he watched several expressions move across her face.

"I see pictures in my head," she said in a hesitant voice. "That's how I knew about you, that you were nearby, that you would be hurt."

She wasn't making much sense. But then, nothing made much sense to him at the moment.

"You mean my accident."

"Yes, except that it wasn't an accident. You were forced off the road and almost killed."

Bright lights reflected in a rearview mirror, almost blinding him... Yes. He remembered now. He didn't know where they came from. Suddenly they were behind him, coming up fast.... She had been there. She... "You saved my life," he said.

Caitlin felt as though she were drowning in the gray-green eyes that gazed up at her.

"I'm glad I was able to," she managed to say.

They studied each other in silence for a while, then Adam's thoughts seemed to drift. He stirred restlessly. "Somehow I have to tell them—"

"I know. There are people who need to know that you're alive," Caitlin responded. "But they will wait, Adam. First, you need to mend."

His eyes drooped shut. "So tired."

Without considering her actions, she leaned down and kissed his cheek. "I know. Go to sleep now. You have plenty of time. The worst is behind you."

Adam smiled at her touch. He loved her soft scent, her warm touch, her tranquil presence. He loved...

The next time he opened his eyes the room was in shadows. Caitlin sat in a small rocker before the fire, doing handwork.

"Do you live here alone?" he asked.

She glanced around, then came over to his side, automatically touching his hand, then his cheek. "Not totally. Chula keeps me company from time to time." She nodded to the deer statue in front of the fireplace.

Adam frowned, as she went to the kitchen area where she picked up a small bag. Returning to the fireplace, Caitlin took some oats from the bag, placing them in a small bowl.

His eyes widened when the statue unfolded its legs and got up, stepping daintily across the rug to eat.

He began to understand how Alice must have felt when she stepped through the looking glass.

Caitlin brought him a bowl of stew and sat down beside him. When he finished the last spoonful of food, she said, "Why don't you rest now?"

Adam frowned. "All I do is sleep."

"I know, but it's the best thing for you. You're making excellent progress, you know."

His mind returned to the cause of his injuries.

"Did you see what happened to me?"

Caitlin nodded, her expression somber.

"Tell me everything you can remember."

Once again she took his hand, unobtrusively keeping watch over his pulse. He didn't need to get upset. As briefly as possible, she explained what she had witnessed.

When she fell silent, Adam lay there, staring into space. Two men tried to kill him. Why? How had they known about the meeting with the possible informer?

And how was he going to find them?

"Did you get a look at the men?"

"Not a clear look, but I would know them again."

He wished he understood how Caitlin had known what was going to happen. And how could she identify two men she'd only seen in the dark? He couldn't deny that there was something different about her... Adam drifted off to sleep once more.

Caitlin watched him for a long time, grateful to see that he was resting easier. A tea that she had given him should help to combat his pain.

With any luck at all, he would sleep through the night. She smiled to herself, wondering what she would do if he woke up sometime and found her by his side? Once he was awake more, she would get the sleeping bag out and sleep near the fire. He must not think she wanted anything more from him.

Caitlin had been aware of his thoughts earlier. He was attracted to her, just as she was attracted to him. But it would be better left unacknowledged. His life existed outside of the mountains. She had no desire ever to leave them.

She already knew that Adam would hold a very special place in her heart. And why not? A person didn't save another's life every day.

Caitlin lay awake for several hours that night, thinking of Adam. There was a reason he'd come into her life, a lesson she would learn from the experience. She only hoped it didn't involve more pain than she could handle.

*

As THE DAYS slowly passed, Adam's returning strength became apparent. He stayed up longer now than he spent in bed. Adam found a quiet pleasure in following Caitlin around as she worked outside, feeding the burro, milking the goat, gathering eggs, as well as feeding half the wildlife in the mountains.

He was surprised to discover the number of people who called on her, either to bring her items in payment for her assistance or to ask for herbal remedies.

On one rather warm day Adam sat outside in the sunshine and watched Caitlin prepare her garden for spring planting.

Spring. It certainly felt that way today. How long had he been there?

He knew that several weeks had gone by. The weather had warmed considerably since he first came to Mexico. No doubt everyone knew he was missing by now. Why had no one come looking for him?

Maybe they had. How could anyone have found him up here? He would have to find a way back to Monterrey. Soon. But not today.

Adam glanced up at the sound of Caitlin's laughter. Chula was nudging her with her nose. He smiled at the picture she made, playing with the deer. She seemed so content with her life, so innocent in many ways.

She was different from anyone he had ever known. A very special person. What was it she had told him about seeing pictures in her mind? Knowing when something was going to happen? There was a word for it. Psychic. She was psychic.

"Caitlin?"

The sound of his voice seemed to startle her. "Yes?" She walked over to where he sat. He had shaved that morning for the first time, and Caitlin couldn't control her reaction to his good looks. She tried to cover her feelings by saying, "All you need is a sombrero, and you'd be part of the land of *maana.*" He smiled.

"That's what I wanted to talk to you about. I need to get some exercise. Could we take a short walk?"

"Where would you like to go?" she asked.

"How about showing me where you found me?"

She shook her head. "I really think that's too far for you to walk. But we can start out in that direction."

Adam soon discovered what she meant. He was more than ready to rest when she suggested they sit down. "Don't you ever get lonely living up here?" he asked.

"Loneliness is a state of mind. The loneliest time of my life occurred when I lived in the city of Seattle."

"Ah—so you didn't suddenly appear here on the planet and choose this place to reside."

She laughed at his whimsy.

"I'm afraid not. Is that what you thought?"

"I'm not sure what to think about you."

She grinned. "I take it you're not used to people who know what you're thinking."

He shook his head. "Sorry, I can't buy that one. I'm still trying to get used to the idea you saw what happened to me before it occurred."

Caitlin gazed out over the vista of mountains and trees. "You've been trying to figure a way to ask me to go home with you."

Her quiet words caught him unprepared, but before he could comment, she continued. "The feelings you've been having about me are very natural, Adam, but don't mistake gratitude for something else."

"How do you know what I'm thinking and feeling?" he demanded.

"Partly because I was once very ill myself. It's easy to become dependent on those who are caring for you."

"You think that's why I'm attracted to you?" he asked.

"I know there's a sexual awareness between us. It's very strong."

"But you don't intend to do anything about it, do you? You see me only as your patient, is that it?"

"I believe that's the wisest course to follow, yes. We come from different worlds. It's better not to get too involved."

"What's wrong with my world?"

"Nothing," she replied. "But the world you live in is too painful for me."

"In what way?"

"People don't want their thoughts and emotions revealed. They need their masks to face life."

"What do you hide, Caitlin?" he asked softly.

"Fear," she said. "Fear of rejection. Fear of being hurt."

"So you stay up here where you're safe."

"Yes."

He stood up and held out his hand. "Let's go home."

ADAM STAYED outside most of the next day. He was definitely on the mend. His body could attest to that. Just thinking about Caitlin created certain body changes that were uncomfortable as well as embarrassing. He had never wanted another woman the way he wanted Caitlin, and yet he had never even kissed her.

Since he'd moved out of her bed—he smiled when he recalled how that had happened—they had carefully avoided physical contact.

He sat down at the table, thinking about the night he'd seen her dragging out a sleeping bag.

"What are you doing?" he'd asked, frowning.

She seemed surprised. "Going to bed. Why?"

"You don't have to sleep on the floor."

Caitlin registered no expression. "Yes, I do."

"Since when? You've seemed quite comfortable curled up by my side."

He watched a lovely flow of color in her face. "I didn't realize you knew I was there," she murmured, and knelt on the sleeping bag.

Adam spoke again. "If anyone's going to bed down on the floor, it will be me."

She looked up at him with dismay. "You won't be able to sleep down here. And you need your rest, Adam."

He'd continued to look at her until she'd gotten up and reluctantly walked over to the bed....

Adam lay in front of the fireplace late that night, unable to sleep. He heard the quiet rustling of covers and knew Caitlin was no more asleep than he was.

"Caitlin? Can't you sleep?"

There was a short silence, then a sigh. "Not really. Would you like me to make us something to drink?"

"Sounds good to me."

He could hear her pour water into a pan, stoke up the stove, hear the clatter of cups. After a while she appeared beside him, holding out a cup.

He sat up to take it, and she sat down in her rocking chair. Caitlin wore her hooded velour robe, its navy blue color emphasizing the red of her hair and the fairness of her complexion. She gazed at the fire.

"Have you ever been in love, Caitlin?"

Her gaze moved from the flames until her eyes met his. "I thought I was...once."

"Tell me about it."

"Rick and I became engaged our sophomore year of college." Her gaze returned to the fire. "We were both only children and spoiled—although unaware of that, of course. We'd had happy childhoods—things had always happened the way we wanted them to. We were going to marry after graduation, wait three years to have children—"

She stopped speaking and made a slight dismissing gesture with her hand.

"It didn't work out that way." She watched the dancing flames. "The accident ended everything."

"What sort of accident?"

"Mom, Dad and I were on our way home from a football game when we were hit head-on by a speeding car. I happened to be in the back seat. That's what saved me. They say Mom was killed instantly and Dad died at the hospital."

"My God!"

"I was in a coma for several weeks. When I began to come out of it I 'saw' the accident happen, as though I was a witness. Then I 'watched' Rick when he heard of the accident. I saw him visit me in the intensive care unit while I was unconscious.''

"Is that when you developed your psychic abilities?"

"No. They were just there after the accident. When I regained consciousness, I knew what the doctors were going to say before they said it. More importantly, I knew what they weren't saying.''

"How did Rick take the change in you?" Adam asked.

"He was appalled when he discovered that I could tell what he was thinking and feeling, particularly when it was contrary to what he was saying. That's when I knew our relationship was over, and that at best, it had been a very shallow one.''

"What happened then?"

"Eventually I was well enough to go home. Only there was no home for me. And I didn't understand what had happened to me. I was not only trying to come to terms with my grief, but I was also convinced I was losing my mind.''

They sat in silence, and Caitlin realized that she was experiencing a sense of security she hadn't felt since her parents' deaths.

Adam propped himself up on one elbow. "I don't believe you were losing your mind. In my line of work our intuitive powers are often the only thing that saves us. Obviously your abilities were enhanced in some way. But that doesn't make them any less real.''

"What *is* your line of work, Adam?"

He smiled. "I assumed you already knew that.''

"I know you're not what you appear to be. You have a secret life that few people know about. You're a decent, honest man, but you don't let many people get close to you.''

Adam's eyes narrowed slightly. "I can see why your friends would be uneasy. A person can't have any secrets from you.''

"I don't know why you carry a gun," she said.

He studied her in silence for a few moments.

"Before I can explain that," he finally said, "I need to give you a little background." He paused. "The St. Clair ranch has been in my family for several generations," he began. "I was just a kid when my dad died, leaving my mom, sister and me to run it. Thank God we had a dependable foreman, or we'd never have made it. Mom died when I was a teenager, and I had to look after my sister, Felicia.''

''Is she tall, blond, with green eyes?'' Caitlin asked.

Adam grinned. ''That's her.''

''And she's in love with the man who runs the ranch with you?''

Adam abruptly sat up. ''Dane Rineholt?''

''Is he part owner of the ranch?''

Slowly Adam relaxed. Caitlin's abilities were definitely unsettling. ''Yes,'' he said, ''as a matter of fact he is.'' In a musing tone he added, ''So Felicia's in love with Dane. That explains a lot.''

''Didn't you know?'' She was surprised that he hadn't been aware of something that came to her so clearly. In her mind, she saw them together. ''Is Felicia at the ranch now?''

Adam shook his head. ''Not that I know of.''

Caitlin could see Felicia at the ranch and feel her tremendous grief. She thought Adam was dead. She must have come home when she heard he was missing.

''She loves you very much,'' she murmured.

''No more than I love her.'' He stretched out on the sleeping bag. ''Dane had been at the ranch a few years before I found out he was working with the authorities to help stop the drug smuggling across the border. It sounded exciting to me, and I insisted on getting in on it.''

''Is that what you're doing down here now?''

''Yes. However, I've learned there's more drudgery than excitement, and more danger than I anticipated.''

''Did those men who tried to kill you know who you were?''

''I wish I knew. I've been working undercover, getting involved with a group of smugglers. In the process other dealers have been pushed out.'' His gaze met hers. ''Several factions could have wanted to get rid of me without even knowing I'm an agent.''

Caitlin shivered. ''You're lucky to be alive.''

"Yes. But I wouldn't have made it without you." He studied her profile. "You never told me how you got from Seattle to the mountains of Mexico. What made you move?"

"I had an aunt who lived in San Antonio. When I was younger, I spent part of my summer vacation with her. She loved the mountains, and we always went to Monterrey whenever I visited.

"During the months after the accident, I would remember the peace and serenity I'd always felt here."

"Caitlin, no one can escape life indefinitely."

"I'm not escaping from life. I have my own life here, and I'm content with it."

"You feel safer being alone, you mean." Adam slowly got to his feet. He took her hand, gently pulling her up to stand in front of him.

Cupping his hands around her face, he tilted her head so that she was looking up at him from only a few inches away. "You've allowed no room in your life for love," Adam said, pulling her closer while he did what he'd been wanting to do for days...weeks...a lifetime.

Adam kissed her. He took his time, lazily exploring her with his mouth, his hands, his entire body. She felt so good in his arms, better, if possible, than his dreams and imaginings had led him to believe. He knew in that moment that he never wanted to spend another day without her.

Caitlin felt as though she were in shock. She had forgotten how it felt to have someone's arms around her, hugging her. She hadn't known how it would feel to be pressed so closely to this man.

His kiss seemed to paralyze her, as though by his touch Adam had taken possession of her soul. No one had ever kissed her in the lazy yet very thorough way he was doing.

Was he aware of the growing feelings for him that had become a part of her? Did he know what his touch was doing to her?

Sometime during that kiss Caitlin tentatively began to respond. Her tongue met his in a shy greeting, and she slid her arms timidly around his neck in an effort to get closer to him.

When her knees gave way, Adam lifted her in his arms and placed her on his sleeping bag. While one arm held her close to him, he slipped the robe from her shoulders.

Her voluminous flannel gown demurely buttoned from the waist to the ruffled neckline. Adam fumbled with the buttonholes for a moment, then slipped his hand inside her gown and felt the heat of her body against his palm.

Adam wanted her so badly he ached with it. When his hand slid to her breast and encircled it, he felt her body move convulsively.

"It's all right, love," he said in a low, gentle voice. "I want to love you, that's all." He leaned down and placed his mouth over the tip of her breast, his tongue playfully nudging the sensitive peak.

Deep-rooted alarms began to jangle within Caitlin. She had always been shy, even with Rick. She knew that once she gave herself to Adam she would never be the same again.

She lowered her trembling hands from around his neck so that she could move away from him. Instead, her hands slid to his hair, the soft curls wrapping around her fingers as he had managed to wrap himself around her heart.

Adam felt her stiffen, her hands restlessly clutching his head to her breast. Her rapid breathing resulted in a soft panting that he found extremely erotic. Reluctantly he raised his head and looked down at her flushed face and kiss-swollen lips. The expression in her eyes was so vulnerable that it almost brought tears to his.

She saw his eyes burning with desire and a deeper emotion that almost frightened her with its intensity.

"I love you, Caitlin."

The words scarcely made a ripple in the silence around them, but their impact was so profound they could have been shouted.

"You can't," she finally managed to say. "You mustn't."

"Why not?"

"It won't work."

"On the contrary, my love. I think you...me...us...work very well together." He glanced down at his hand where it rested lovingly cupped around her breast. "There's nothing to be afraid of, you know," he continued. "Loving someone is very natural. I think you'll find it quite enjoyable, once you get used to the idea."

Caitlin closed her eyes. "I can't, Adam. Don't ask that of me."

"Why not?" he finally asked, shifting away from her.

"Surely that's obvious. Our lifestyles are not exactly compatible." She turned to watch the fire. "Somehow I can't see you spending the rest of your life here."

"And is this where you intend to spend the rest of your life, Caitlin?"

"Yes."

"I see," Adam finally said in a low voice.

Did he? Could he possibly see and understand the pain she had escaped from?

Caitlin knew that Adam wanted to make love to her. She didn't need her psychic abilities for that. She even knew that he was sincere. For now. Once he returned to his real life, he'd realize how out of place she would be.

"Your head hurts," Caitlin said, feeling his physical and emotional pain as though it were her own.

"Among other things," he acknowledged wryly.

"I'll bring in more wood. You'd better try to get some sleep." He got up and closed the door quietly behind him.

She hadn't wanted to hurt him. But wasn't it better to face reality now?

*

CAITLIN WOKE UP the next morning to the scent of freshly brewed coffee, and realized she had overslept. Adam had drawn the curtain that shielded the bed from the rest of the room, leaving that corner in shadows.

As soon as she was dressed, Caitlin slid the curtain back, unsurprised to discover herself alone in the cabin. Opening the door, she looked around the clearing, then wandered over into the lean-to. Adam was milking the goat.

"You have talents I never suspected," she said, trying to lighten the atmosphere.

He had filled the pail and was setting it aside when she spoke. He glanced up at her, then looked away, but not before she saw the expression of love and hurt in his eyes.

"I thought you could use some help this morning," he responded, his tone even. Without looking at her, he said, "I'm leaving today."

She'd known that as soon as she opened her eyes, but hadn't wanted to face it.

Caitlin returned his pistol and holster to him, and after breakfast, they set out.

She set an easy pace, but by the time they reached the village, Adam knew he'd pushed himself. He was running on nerves and sheer willpower. There was no point in delaying his return to Texas. And there was a definite danger in staying. He loved Caitlin, but to share that cabin without making love to her was a torture he could not continue.

They walked along the main street, with Caitlin pointing out the shops, and ended up at a small tavern where Adam talked to the owner. He needed transportation north. Without money or identification, that might prove difficult.

"What's wrong?" Caitlin asked when he returned to their table.

"I hadn't realized how remote we are. There's very little traffic here. I'm going to have to stick around and take my chances on getting out."

Caitlin could see the lines of strain around his eyes. She felt the dull throb of pain in his head. This was too soon for him to be so active, but she knew he had to go.

They left the tavern, and Caitlin went to buy a few supplies. She had nothing more to do in the village.

"I really need to start back. It will be dark soon," she told Adam, and placed her hand on the sleeve of his coat. "Take care of yourself. God bless."

She turned and walked away, forcing herself not to glance back.

"Wait!" She turned to find him striding toward her. "I'll be damned if I'm going to tell you goodbye in the middle of some godforsaken Mexican settlement." He took her by the elbow and began to walk beside her. "I'll go partway with you."

Caitlin could feel her heart pounding. This was much harder than she could handle.

"Are you going to be okay?" he asked.

She nodded without looking at him.

"Aren't you even going to talk to me?"

"What do you want me to say?"

"How about 'I'm going to miss you, Adam'?"

She stopped. They were above the settlement now, out of sight of civilization. The western sun bathed him in a golden glow. She would never forget the way he looked at that moment. She forced herself to meet his gaze, her eyes filling with tears.

"I'm going to miss you, Adam," she managed to say.

With slow, deliberate movements, he slipped his arms around her, pulling her close to him. "I'm going to miss you, too, darlin'."

Caitlin rested her head against his chest. "Oh, Adam," was all she could say.

Adam tilted her head so that his mouth found hers. He didn't know how he was going to walk away from her. She had become as necessary to him as the air that filled his lungs and gave him life. He loved her.

Caitlin felt as though she no longer had a will of her own. Her response to his kiss left no doubt in either one's mind that she shared his feelings.

The whine of a bullet and the cracking sound of the discharge came simultaneously, and Adam reacted automatically. He pushed Caitlin toward the ground, shoving her behind a boulder. Another shot was fired, and pieces of the rock ricocheted around them.

"Are you all right?" he whispered. She nodded.

The sudden attack left them both stunned. Violence had no business here, and yet it had found them.

"I've got to see who this is. Stay here, okay?"

Adam's gun was already in his hand, and he crept farther away from the trail, circling the area where the gunshots had been fired. It hadn't occurred to him that someone was still out to kill him. How had they traced him to the village? Now he'd walked right into their hands without suspecting anything, making no attempt to cover his tracks.

Because of his carelessness he'd managed to involve Caitlin. Damn. A cold fury swept over him. He would find out who this was.

The woods were silent. The gunman had stopped firing. Adam paused, torn between going after him and getting Caitlin away from there. He couldn't take any chances with her life. He turned back to where he'd left her.

She sat huddled, head resting on her drawn-up knees. He knelt down beside her. "I've lost him for the moment," he whispered. "There's no telling who he is. He could have been sitting there in the tavern for all I know."

Caitlin raised her head, her face totally without color. Slowly she shook her head. "No, he wasn't. I would have noticed him." She paused. "He's the man who drove the car that forced you off the road."

Adam studied her intently, not liking the look of her eyes. She was going into shock. "Are you sure?"

"Reasonably."

"Damn! I wish I could see him…know who I'm looking for."

He stood, pulling her up, too. She winced and moved away from him. "Look, Adam. I'll go on back to the cabin. If you return to the village, maybe someone will be able to point him out. Everyone would know if there's a stranger in town. I should have thought to ask."

"I wasn't thinking very clearly myself today." All of his thoughts had been on the pain of leaving.

She tried to move away from him, but he still held her arm. "I don't want you continuing on that path." He guided her behind the rocks for some distance until he spotted a trail he had seen earlier. "Follow that until you get over the ridge. I'll be along shortly."

"There's no reason for you to come back to the cabin. You need to stay at the village. I'll be okay."

He saw no point in standing there debating the issue. He would see what he could find, then return to the cabin.

Without commenting on her statement, he leaned over and gently kissed her, then watched as she turned away and began to follow the path.

After thoroughly searching the area, Adam found nothing but some shell casings. Whoever it was must have decided to wait for another time.

Adam silently thanked him for the warning. He would be better prepared next time.

He started back up the trail. He had to know that Caitlin was all right.

Glancing down, he caught sight of color, and bent closer to examine what looked to be blood. He touched one of the small drops and confirmed his suspicion.

She'd been hit. And she hadn't even told him.

Damn her! Why hadn't she said something? He should have known that her shocked condition was more than just being scared. And now he remembered that she'd kept her arms across her chest, her hands tightly gripping her shoulders.

Her shoulder! Of course. He hadn't seen it because his mind had been on the gunman.

SHE HAD MADE considerable progress along the trail, but had stopped to rest.

She sat next to a large tree, her body braced against it, her head back and her eyes closed. Her hand still clutched her shoulder, but now the blood had soaked through her heavy handwoven shirt, and was dripping down her arm.

When Adam reached out to touch her, he absently noted that his hand was shaking. "Let me see," he said, his voice gruff.

Her eyes flew open. "What are you doing here?"

He knelt beside her. "Why didn't you tell me you were hurt, dammit?" he said. "How bad is it?"

"I'm all right, Adam. It's just a flesh wound," she said. "There was no reason for you to come back."

He lifted her shirt away, exposing her shoulder. The bullet had grazed her upper shoulder, leaving a jagged tear. He picked her up and started toward the cabin.

"Adam, don't carry me. You're in no condition—"

"If you know what's good for you, you won't say another word," he said through clenched jaws. "Not one... more...word."

By the time Adam reached the clearing, Caitlin was either asleep or unconscious. It was now dark. He shoved the cabin door open with his foot and felt his way over to the bed.

Adam lit the lamp, covered Caitlin with a blanket and built a fire.

He pumped some water into a bowl and made preparations to clean her wound. Quickly undressing her, he left only her panties, then covered her with a blanket, leaving the wounded area exposed.

"How are you feeling?" he asked in a neutral tone, while he bathed and cleaned it.

"All right," she whispered.

The weakness in her voice filled him with pain, but there was no sense letting her know how upset he was. He tried to smile, but his lips barely moved.

"We've reversed our roles, I guess," she said in response to his smile.

"Looks that way."

"Adam, please don't feel you have to stay here with me. I know you need to get back to Monterrey."

"Dammit, Caitlin, don't you understand that things have changed now? Whoever is after me knows approximately where they can find me and that I'm with you. I can't go off and leave you unprotected."

"They don't want me. Even if they managed to find this cabin—which is doubtful—once they discovered you were gone, they'd have no further interest in me."

"A nice thought to hold." He got up and added wood to the fire. "Do you want something to eat?"

"Not particularly."

Caitlin was asleep by the time the food was ready, and he decided that rest was the best thing for her.

Adam ate, then paced the floor. Periodically he checked the bandage he'd placed on her shoulder. He knew her arm and shoulder would be stiff and sore by morning, but there should be no infection.

Remembering how effective it was for relieving pain, Adam made up some of the tea she had given to him. He almost laughed at the sleepy face she made as she drank it. Served her right. However, the brew worked, and that was the important thing. She would be able to rest more comfortably now.

When Caitlin woke up, bright sunlight flooded the room. She was alone in the cabin and was reminded of the morning before. Adam must be outside.

Her shoulder felt much better. She knew it was healing. She'd slept so well the night before, no doubt partly due to that potent tea.

It took her a while to pull on her clothes. Adam still hadn't returned, so she went looking for him. She discovered that the animals had all been fed but Adam was nowhere around. Puzzled, she returned to the cabin. Only then did she notice that he hadn't made coffee, but a note was propped against the coffeepot.

Please forgive me for not waking you to say goodbye. We said that yesterday, and I wasn't sure I could leave you today if I didn't get away now. I have no choice at the moment but to go, but I'll be back. You and I have some unfinished business.

Don't forget me

Adam

Caitlin stared at the note for a long time. Of course there was no reason for him to linger. He knew she was going to be all right.

She kept reading the last line over and over. *Don't forget me.*

How could she possibly forget him? He'd said he would come back, and she believed him.

A part of her life was finished now, but she felt richer because of what she had experienced.

She had learned about love, its pain as well as its beauty. Perhaps one couldn't exist without the other.

ADAM'S ENTRY into the village was different today. After making sure no one was in sight, he slipped into the tavern by the rear entrance. When the owner was alone, he signaled to him.

"Have any strangers come into town recently? Besides me," Adam added.

The man thought for a moment. "No."

"Are you sure? Think about it."

"Well-l-l-l." The man scratched his head. "Alfredo Cortez, he's lived here a few weeks—"

"You mean, since February?"

"Oh, yes. I'd say since then…possibly. He comes in here every afternoon—sits around and visits."

"Does he ever say why he's here, like maybe because he's looking for someone?"

"Maybe… He doesn't bother anybody, you know."

Adam felt the frustration of being the outsider. Obviously this Cortez had managed to mingle with the locals.

"Thanks for your help," Adam said to the owner. He wished he had some money on him. He might have learned more.

Adam slipped out of the tavern without seeing anyone. He would find Antonio's home and explain about Caitlin's injury. He knew how much the villagers cared for her. She would be safer with them than if he stayed to look after her.

An hour later Adam was several miles from the village, headed north. With no I.D., he decided to stay as invisible as possible and get to the border. He'd worry about getting across once he got there.

For the next several days Adam walked, hitched rides, slept in lean-tos when he could and continued north. By the time he made it to the border, he was almost too weak to stand. The next hurdle was to cross into the States.

Getting across the Rio Grande took three days. He spent most of that time in the border patrol office trying to convince them he was who he said he was. Eventually he was allowed to call his superiors in San Antonio who confirmed that he'd been reported missing, presumed dead.

His next call was to Dane. He was more than a little surprised when Felicia answered.

"What are you doing at the ranch?" he asked.

"Adam? Is that really you? Where are you?"

He told her, then spoke to Dane, explaining that he needed a ride home.

A couple of Agency men showed up, and he gave them as full a report as possible. He discovered that the man he had been gathering evidence on had been arrested and that a successful conclusion to the case seemed certain.

No one was sure who was behind the attempts on Adam's life. At this point it was anybody's guess.

By the time Dane and Felicia arrived, Adam's store of energy was gone. He slept all the way back to the ranch and did little more than sleep and eat for the next week.

Adam's disappearance had caused one good thing to happen: Dane and Felicia had gotten married during the time they had spent looking for him. They were expecting a baby in late fall.

So Caitlin had been right about them.

Caitlin. She was never out of his thoughts. He wouldn't be whole again until he returned to her.

In the meantime…he bought a car and drove to San Antonio. Robert McFarlane, head of the regional office, had called a private meeting with him.

Adam filled Rob in on everything that had happened. Then he had some questions of his own.

"Was that informant ever contacted?" Adam asked.

"Yes. By Zeke Taylor—not long after you disappeared."

"That makes sense. Zeke's the only other agent who knew about the contact. How did it go?"

"The man gave Zeke all the details—place of exchange, names, the whole thing—so we were able to nail Santiago and make it stick. But the informant was killed within hours after Zeke left him."

"By whom?"

"We haven't found out. We may never find out."

"Do you think the informant's death ties in with the attempt on me?"

"Who can say? It would help if you knew what your assailant looks like."

"There is somebody who's seen him. Unfortunately, she—"

"What are you waiting for? Bring her in. This may be the break we're looking for."

"If I can get her to come. She won't leave the mountains."

"We're not asking her to move! She'd just visit the office, look at the mug shots. When can you get her up here?"

"Good question."

*

SUMMER WEATHER came early to the mountains. Caitlin welcomed the opportunity to open her door and windows to the warm air. Her flower garden burst with riotous colors, as though to help lift her spirits.

Late one May afternoon, Caitlin entered the clearing where her cabin stood. She was weary, not only physically, since she had gotten little sleep the night before, but emotionally, because she had been sitting beside the bed of a woman old in years, but young in heart. And yet Caitlin had seen the peace that stayed with the old woman until the end.

The evening rays of the sun followed her through her cabin door, lighting the shadows and illuminating the figure in front of the fireplace.

"I told you I'd be back," Adam said quietly.

Caitlin burst into tears.

He was beside her in two long strides. Scooping her into his arms, he walked over to the bed and sat down, holding her close. "What's wrong, my love? Tell me."

His soft words only made her tears flow more freely, and she gave herself up to him, holding him tightly as though afraid he would disappear. When the tears began to diminish, she leaned back to see him more clearly.

The weeks away had obviously done him good. He looked fit—tanned and healthy.

"Oh, Adam," she finally said. "I didn't know if you would really come."

"You should know I always do what I say." He glanced down at her arms, still locked around his shoulders. "I have the feeling," he said with a slight smile, "that you're glad to see me."

She smiled and nodded, and with a hesitancy that she found endearing, he kissed her softly on her lips.

Adam seemed to be trying to memorize her, his hands roaming up and down her back, as though reassuring himself that she really did exist.

He eased back on the bed until they were lying side by side, their mouths still clinging, enjoying the taste and touch of each other.

His hands lightly traced a line from the hollow in her neck down between her breasts to her waist, then paused.

She seemed so relaxed with him, as though for the first time she no longer fought her true feelings.

Caitlin began to pop open the snaps on his shirt so that her hands could find the smooth surface of his broad chest.

Her fingers touching his bare flesh caused him to quiver. Surely she understood what that was doing to him, but she didn't seem to care.

When he found her breasts with his fingertips, he felt her jump in response, but rather than pull back from him, she merely deepened the kiss. Adam could feel his heart racing.

Her blouse lay open, exposing her breasts, and she leaned

closer to him so that they touched his bare chest. He groaned, unable to fight the feelings that were rapidly overtaking him.

"Caitlin, love—"

She looked into his eyes, seeing the love and burning desire, feeling the same emotions within her.

"I love you, Adam," she murmured.

With those words, Adam smoothed her blouse off her shoulders so that her upper body was revealed to him. Her skin glowed with a satiny sheen, her translucent coloring in deepest contrast to her fiery hair.

He traced the scar that followed the line of her shoulder, pleased to see that it had healed well. Then he leaned over and kissed it.

She was so beautiful, even more beautiful than he'd remembered.

He felt her heart fluttering when his mouth rested on the pink tip of her breast. He watched her body's response, gazing down at her with a possessiveness that seemed to scorch her with its warmth, while leaving her feeling shy and uncertain. Without saying a word, he slipped off her pants and shoes, and she felt the cool evening air against her bared skin.

Adam picked her up, pulled back the covers of the bed, and slipped her between them. After quickly undressing, he crawled in beside her.

Her body responded to his touch while he gave her slow, intoxicating kisses, reassuring her on the deepest level that he would never hurt her.

By the time he was poised above her, Caitlin watched him with fascinated eyes, her breathing ragged, her skin warm from his touch.

Adam slowly lowered himself to her and was not surprised to discover that no one had been there before him. He'd been aware of her innocence on some subconscious level. He touched her lightly, so as not to frighten her.

Her eyes widened at the unexpected pressure and the sensation of him, so intimately pressed against her.

"It's all right, my love," he soothed. "Just relax."

When he took possession of her body, Caitlin discovered

that he was right. Because of his loving concern and his patience, she was ready for him. Once the initial discomfort was past, Caitlin was swept away with the sense of release.

She had never experienced anything resembling the feelings Adam aroused in her. He was so much an extension of her own being that for the first time, she realized what it meant to be one with another person.

He seemed to know how to increase the pleasurable feelings that were sweeping over her, and Caitlin seemed to know instinctively how to respond to him. She met each of his movements with one of her own, delighting in what her responsiveness did to him. Suddenly there was no more caution or patience. He caught fire, causing her to burst into flames, as well.

By the time Caitlin could comprehend what had happened, Adam was drawing slow, deep breaths, his head resting on the pillow next to hers, his body slumped to her side. She felt bemused lying in his arms—as though it was the most natural place in the world to be.

When his eyes finally opened, she was surprised to see the rueful, contrite expression in them.

"Will you forgive me, love?"

She leaned closer and kissed him lightly. "There's nothing to forgive."

"You probably won't believe I didn't plan this."

"I know."

He stroked her back. "I came back to convince you that I love you. I wanted you to know that you can trust me." He shook his head ruefully.

"Why do you want me to trust you?"

"Because I have a favor to ask of you."

"All right," she responded calmly.

"You told me you saw the man who drove the car the night I was almost killed. And that he was also the gunman who shot you."

"Yes."

He paused. "I need you to identify him for me. I need you to go to San Antonio with me, look through the tons of photos

on file and see if he's in our records.'' He watched her face
for some reaction.

Caitlin was quiet for several minutes, knowing that her decision would have an irrevocable impact on her life.

Adam softly kissed the palm of her hand. ''I know how you
feel about leaving here. But I would be with you, love. These
last few weeks have been hell without you.''

I know only too well what it's been like without you, Caitlin
silently answered. *I'm not sure I'm strong enough to allow
you to leave me a second time.*

''I love you, Caitlin. I want to marry you.''

Not marriage, Adam, she protested silently. *We can't take
that risk.*

''Would you at least give our relationship a chance? I promise to bring you back if you want to come.''

What could she say? She wanted to find the man who had
tried to kill him. Until he was apprehended, Adam wouldn't
be safe. Caitlin couldn't live with that thought.

''When do you want to leave?'' she finally asked.

THE GENTLY rolling hills of central Texas were already baking
in the sun, although the calendar insisted summer wouldn't
arrive for a few more weeks.

Now that they were nearing the ranch, Caitlin could feel
herself growing nervous. She refused to dwell on the fact that
Adam wanted to marry her. One step at a time.

The frustrating part about her ability was the way her emotions interfered with her reception of messages. Seldom could
Caitlin visualize how things would work out in her own life.
It didn't seem fair, somehow, since she felt more afflicted than
blessed with the awareness in the first place.

When they pulled into the ranch yard, Caitlin looked around
in dismay at the size of the place.

The two-story house had been built in another era, when
labor and material were cheap. A long porch wrapped around
three sides of the house. There was also a large barn, and other
outbuildings. The ranch looked almost as large as the small
village where she traded for supplies.

As the car stopped, the screen door of the house flew open, and a young woman came out. Caitlin immediately recognized Felicia. Adam hadn't mentioned that Felicia was pregnant.

With his arm around her shoulders, Adam walked Caitlin to the house.

"Caitlin, this is my sister, Felicia." He leaned over and kissed Felicia. "Here she is, sis."

Felicia's smile reminded Caitlin of Adam, and she said so.

Felicia laughed and hugged her brother tightly for a moment. "I consider that a compliment, Caitlin." She motioned for them to go into the house ahead of her.

Caitlin peered into open doors along the hall as they went by. She saw a long living room, dining room, a den and office, then found herself in the kitchen while Adam held out a chair for her.

Felicia poured each of them a large glass of iced tea, then sat down at the table.

"I'm so glad you came, Caitlin. Adam was worried you wouldn't."

Caitlin glanced at Adam. He was leaning back against his chair, looking relaxed and happy.

"I'm glad, too," she agreed softly.

"I've put you in my old room. It's got a nice view of the place. Later on, I'd like to take you over to see the house Dane and I are building. It's about two miles from here, on the river." She glanced at Adam. "It would probably never occur to Adam to reassure you that if you decide to settle here you won't have to share your home with a bunch of relatives."

So Adam had told Felicia he wants to marry me, Caitlin realized. She cast around for a way to change the subject, and she remembered Felicia's pregnancy.

Her mind filled with images, and she knew that Dane and Felicia were delighted. They wanted a family. Impulsively she leaned toward her.

"I know Dane wants a boy, Felicia," she said with a grin, "but he's going to love his daughter very much. The boys will come later."

Adam and Felicia stared at her in stunned silence. Adam

spoke first. "Uhh, Felicia, I did forget to mention one thing about Caitlin. You see, she, uh—"

"You already know I'm going to have a girl?" Felicia interrupted him.

Caitlin could feel the tension begin to build behind her eyes. She'd already managed to create a problem.

She met Felicia's startled gaze. "I seem to have the ability of knowing things like that," she explained.

Felicia clapped her hands in delight. "But that's wonderful!" She turned to Adam. "Why didn't you tell us? What an amazing gift. Have you always had it?"

Caitlin gazed at Felicia in surprise. She didn't seem to be shocked or upset. She was sincerely interested, and was waiting for Caitlin to respond.

Caitlin soon found that for every question she answered, Felicia had three more. And Caitlin felt accepted as she was slowly drawn into the loving circle shared by Adam and Felicia.

When Dane walked into the room, he found his wife and brother-in-law chatting with a glowing young woman with bright red-gold hair cascading over her shoulders, her face animated and her eyes sparkling. He had no trouble understanding why Adam had fallen head over heels in love. The man had taste.

"It looks like the St. Clairs are at it again, both talking nonstop." Sauntering over to Felicia, Dane kissed her, then held out his hand to Adam.

Felicia said, "Oh, Dane, I want you to meet Caitlin Moran. Caitlin, this is my lord and master, Dane Rineholt."

Dane pulled a chair out and sat down. "You can't appreciate the irony in that statement yet, Caitlin, but when you get to know her better, you will."

The men grinned at each other, and Caitlin felt the love that was shared here. She had a sudden yearning to be a part of their magic circle. Was it possible?

DINNER that evening was a hilarious affair. By unspoken agreement, no one brought up the planned trip to San Antonio or its purpose. Instead Dane and Felicia told Caitlin all about Adam as a boy and a young man. He retaliated by describing the relentless war waged between Dane and Felicia before they acknowledged the love that had been between them for years.

By the time Caitlin prepared for bed that night, she knew that she could be very happy living in this house with Adam, with Felicia and Dane nearby.

Her years on the mountain had given her enough time that she no longer felt intimidated by the knowledge that seemed to flow through her at unexpected times.

Now she was going to put that knowledge to use.

ADAM'S MOOD was cheerful and teasing during the trip to San Antonio. Caitlin found it contagious. Her weekend at the ranch had brought back memories of how she'd felt as a young girl—full of fun and high spirits.

"I hope the weekend wasn't too much for you," Adam said. "You haven't spoken since we left home."

"Oh, no. I enjoyed it very much. Dane and Felicia are very special people."

"They enjoyed you, as well."

"I was just thinking…that it might be nice to be married at the ranch."

The car swerved before it continued down the highway.

"You pick a hell of a time to accept a marriage proposal, lady. At the moment, I can't do a damn thing about it."

Caitlin looked over at him, her face glowing. "What do you want to do about it?"

"I'd much rather show you than tell you."

Admitting that she wanted to marry him seemed to lift a weight off her shoulders. Somehow she had to believe that what they felt for each other was strong enough to weather whatever life presented to them.

Adam insisted they go shopping and buy her a ring before going to the office. Once in town, he called Rob from a pay phone. Afterward, he laughed and caught her in his arms.

"Rob said a few hours wasn't going to make that much

difference and if I'd managed to talk you into an engagement, I'd better get the evidence on your finger.''

By the time they reached the Agency office, Caitlin felt her thoughts almost whirling. Glancing down at the large diamond solitaire, Caitlin could scarcely believe how quickly Adam had gotten organized once she'd accepted his proposal.

The man striding down the hall beside her was a definite force to be reckoned with. After the introductions, Rob McFarlane motioned for them to be seated. ''I'm very pleased that you agreed to help us out, Miss Moran. Has Adam explained what was happening at the time of his disappearance?''

''No. I never asked.''

''He had made friends with Felipe Santiago under the guise of helping to distribute drugs on this side of the river. Santiago was the middleman between the South Americans and the distribution up here. After a few successful operations, Santiago had learned to trust Adam.''

She looked at the men in dismay. ''You mean you were actually distributing the drugs?''

''We brought them in and impounded them. But Santiago wasn't aware of that. Adam had asked to meet his contact from South America, and Santiago arranged it. That meeting was aborted by a message Adam received just before he left his hotel, although Santiago never knew that.''

Rob continued, ''Adam got a call telling him the meeting was a trap, that Santiago was trying to bypass him. The caller said he could give him the evidence he needed without risk if Adam would meet him in the mountains.''

''Only he never kept his appointment.''

''Correct. What we want to know is who knew about the appointment in the mountains. Was it Santiago, or is someone else involved? The bottom line is—does someone know that Adam is an agent, or were they just trying to get rid of competition? I can't send him back over there until I know for certain. That's where you come in.''

''If I can identify the man for you, you'll know why he was trying to kill Adam?''

"That's what we're counting on, yes."

"I see. I appreciate your explaining all of this to me."

"If you were merely a witness, I wouldn't have. But as Adam's future wife I wanted you to understand the situation. He didn't have the clearance to give you the details. I do."

Caitlin followed Adam to another office where two desks were pushed together.

"Zeke and I share this office whenever we're in town, which isn't very often," Adam explained. "Have a seat, and I'll bring in the albums."

She sat down and looked around. "Where's Zeke now?"

"Mexico, as far as I know. He rarely comes out anymore. He's been with the Agency for years and has developed a damned good cover down there."

He leaned over and kissed her. "I'll be right back."

Hours later Caitlin finally had to call a halt to the progression of photographs. "I'm sorry, Adam. This is getting to be more than I can handle."

Adam took one look at her face and realized he'd been pushing her. She was very pale. "Damn. I wasn't thinking. I'm afraid I get carried away with something like this. You must be exhausted."

"I am, but it's because these people carry such a charge on them." She pointed to one. "He's in prison now and filled with hate." She indicated another. "He's extremely dangerous. Kills for the excitement of it." About a third, she said, "I think he's dead."

Adam stared at her in surprise. "I guess I hadn't given it a thought—how all of this would affect you." He stood up and held out his hand. "Come on. I'll buy you dinner and ply you with wine. That's bound to help you relax. Then back to the hotel."

He was as good as his word. By the time they walked into the hotel room, Caitlin felt much more relaxed and more than a little sleepy.

She kicked off her shoes and unbuttoned her blouse while Adam adjusted the drapes. When he turned around, she wore only her panties and a bra. She walked into the bathroom and turned on the shower.

"I'll stop by in the morning so we can have breakfast together," he said.

Caitlin glanced around in surprise. "You aren't staying with me tonight?"

"I know you're tired and—"

"That doesn't matter. I'd like to know you're nearby."

He wondered if she had any idea how enticing she looked. "You don't understand, Caitlin. I love you too much to spend the night without making love to you, especially now."

She calmly unfastened her bra and stepped out of her panties. "No one's said 'no,' Adam." With a lingering glance over her shoulder, she stepped into the shower.

Caitlin looked around in surprise soon after, when the shower door slid open. Adam stepped in, wearing only a grin.

"Are you enjoying the convenience of a shower after all those years without one?" he asked as he took the soapy washcloth away from her. He began to lightly stroke her arms, her shoulders and, with ever widening circles, her breasts.

Caitlin felt a shiver race through her at his touch. He had such a strong effect on her.

"Am I disturbing you in some way?"

She looked up at him. "What do you think?"

His hands went around her, pulling her closer until her soap-slickened body pressed against him. He meticulously soaped her back from shoulder to hip, but his touch felt more like a caress.

When Adam finally leaned down and kissed her, her knees gave way, and she would have fallen if he hadn't held her even tighter. She twined her arms around his neck and returned his kiss, her uninhibited response making it clear she felt committed to him, and their future. He hadn't thought it possible to love her more than he did, but now his heart threatened to explode with the joy that flooded over him.

She insisted on taking her turn at bathing him and took such an excruciatingly long and loving time to soap his body that he thought he'd lose his mind.

When he'd had all he could take, Adam turned her toward the water so she could rinse off, then gently pushed her out of the shower. After quickly rinsing off, he followed.

After a couple of careless swipes with a towel, he picked her up and strode into the other room. "I've had all the teasing I intend to take from you, young lady," he said, dropping her on the bed.

"Who says I was teasing, Mr. St. Clair?"

His breath caught in his throat when he took in the picture she made, and with a feeling bordering on reverence, he knelt and began to kiss her—starting with her neck, then her breasts, and slowly downward, pausing to nip her with his teeth and stroke her with his tongue.

She felt as though her body had caught fire. "Oh, Adam—"

"Do you love me?" he asked between kisses.

"Oh, yes."

"Do you want me?"

"Desperately."

There was nothing gentle about their lovemaking this time. It was an expression of powerful love mingled with need. Neither one of them could get enough of the other during the ensuing hours. Their murmured whispers spoke of their joy with each other, their hope for the future, their unquenchable love.

*

SOMETHING WOKE HER from a sound sleep, and Caitlin sat up in bed, alarmed. She felt a niggling in the back of her mind— a warning about something.

Getting out of bed carefully, so as not to awaken Adam, she slipped on her robe, then got a glass of water. Back in the bedroom, she went over to the window and quietly opened the curtains. Eventually she sat down in the large chair by the window and leaned her head back.

While she sat there, pictures began to form. She saw the man whose picture she had tried to find today and now she understood why she hadn't seen him.

Other people came in and out. Scenes were enacted, and slowly she began to piece the sequence of events together. It was a story of deceit and betrayal, of greed and malice. Pain began to build up within her. Pain for Adam...and for herself.

Now she knew. And in order to protect Adam, she must tell him. Would he accept the truth? Was there any way she could prove to him that it *was* the truth?

CAITLIN WOKE to the smell of coffee, and opening her eyes, found Adam holding a cup and sitting on the bed.

"I was wondering if you intended to sleep all morning. I didn't mean to wear you out last night." His grin was full of mischief. Adam was so full of life, so loyal to those he loved and trusted. It was that loyalty she had to disturb this morning.

Trying to gain some time, she asked, "What time is it?"

"After ten. Breakfast is here. I went ahead and ordered."

"Oh." She glanced over at the table, all set up. "I'll be ready in a few minutes." She would tell him...right after breakfast.

Caitlin dressed and sat down across from Adam whose face shone as with a thousand candles. Conversation was limited while both of them ate. Caitlin didn't realize how expressive her own face was until Adam finally said, "Are you going to tell me what's wrong?"

"What do you mean?"

"Something's bothering you. Dammit, don't leave me out of your thoughts. Share them with me."

"I know who is trying to kill you."

For a moment Adam just stared at her.

"You're in considerable danger," she added.

He tried to lighten the situation by joking. "If I didn't get the message the first time, the gunman convinced me of that. So who is he?''

''The gunman isn't important. He's a hired killer. You don't have him booked because he's never been to the States.''

''Do you know who hired him?''

This was the hard part. ''A friend of yours.''

He laughed harshly. ''Right. A friend.''

''I mean it, Adam. He's a man very close to you, and he's betrayed you, not once, but many times.''

His stomach clenched as he stared at her. ''Who?''

She was quiet for a few minutes, her eyes closed. When she began to speak, it was in a clear, detached voice. ''He's tall, but not quite as tall as you. American but with dark hair and eyes. He can pass as a Latin. He wears a closely trimmed beard...quite a ladies' man.'' She opened her eyes and looked at him. ''You work together.''

Adam stared at her in disbelief. That description fit only one man, the one that it couldn't possibly be. He was stunned. He'd trusted Caitlin's abilities, but this was so absurd that he had to discount everything.

''Zeke Taylor?''

''Taylor. Yes. That fits.''

''Well, love, I'm afraid your psychic powers led you astray on this one, but that's all right.''

''You don't believe me.''

''Oh, I'm sure you believe what you're saying is the truth. You're just wrong, that's all.''

''Am I?''

She sounded so aloof, not like the warm woman he'd held so close to him the night before.

Adam stood up and walked across the room, then turned around and faced her.

''There's no way you could know this, but Zeke and I have been working on this case for as long as I've been with the Agency. My God! He trained me. I never made a move down there that he didn't know about. Caitlin, why would Zeke Taylor want me killed?''

"Because you found out too much about what was going on down there. You got too close to him."

"That doesn't make sense."

"You remember the man you were to meet that night? Taylor killed him."

"That's a lie!" He strode over to her. "Zeke Taylor met the man after I disappeared and got the information that led to Santiago's arrest. Zeke solved the case!"

Caitlin stood and walked over to the window. Lifting her chin slightly, she turned and faced Adam. "No. Taylor already knew about Santiago, Adam. He sacrificed Santiago. Taylor had to decide who was expendable." She walked back to the table and stood there. "The man died because he intended to tell you about Taylor's involvement in the operation." Restless, she turned and faced him again. "Taylor has kept the smugglers informed of the Agency's movements for years. Periodically he throws someone to the Agency to keep them happy."

Adam watched her wander back to the window. She explained as she paced. "Santiago was actually a bored businessman who enjoyed the excitement. Zeke used him to front his own involvement. Zeke's the one who vouched for you to Santiago. Zeke needed you where he could keep an eye on you.

"Zeke doesn't know how the man you were supposed to meet found out about him," she explained, "but when you called him that night about that anonymous phone call, he knew he had to do something fast." Adam's face remained without expression. "He got to the man first but lost his temper and killed him before he found out how he got the information."

Once again, she looked out the window. She had no choice but to tell it all.

Turning to Adam, Caitlin said, "That's when Zeke realized he would have to eliminate you before you found another source that would lead you to him." She walked over to him. "Zeke Taylor has a flourishing business in Mexico, one that he doesn't intend to jeopardize over a little thing like friend-ship." Wishing she could soften it, she continued, "He likes you, Adam, but you've become too much of a threat to him. As long as you're alive, he won't feel safe." In a musing tone she added, "He still can't figure out how you survived. He saw a picture taken of you at the scene of the crash and thought you were dead. Later, when he discovered your body was gone, he sent his gunman up in the mountains to look for you."

Adam felt almost numb with shock. His world seemed to have broken into small, unrecognizable pieces. Zeke Taylor? Impossible. Zeke had taught him everything he knew. Took him under his wing when he first started. He and Zeke had become good friends. Zeke wanted him dead?

"I'm sorry, Adam."

He could feel the pain and frustration pulling at him. "Why didn't you tell me this at the very beginning, when I regained consciousness? If you're so damned psychic, why did you wait until now?"

Caitlin stood up. "I didn't pick up on Zeke Taylor before because I wasn't trying to solve anything, Adam. I had no desire to find out who was trying to kill you or why. I was just trying to keep you from dying."

She walked over to the window and stood there looking out. With her back to him, she said, "You understand now, don't you? Why I can't live around people? Why I can't have close friends or close ties of any kind?"

When he didn't respond, she continued, her voice husky. "I know what you're feeling right now, you see. You're feel-ing betrayed and angry and hurt. And you resent the fact that I knew, as though you have no privacy at all, no place to retreat until you can come to terms with what you're feeling.

"This is why I was so uncertain about marrying you. No one should have to live with someone like me."

Adam felt overwhelmed with emotions. He had to get away. Moving toward the door, he said, "Look, we're both upset right now. I need some time to think. I'm sure you do, too.

Why don't you do some sight-seeing? I'll be back later and we can talk then.''

She turned. ''I'll be fine, Adam. Go ahead and do what you need to do.''

He nodded and walked out the door.

Caitlin sank down into the chair and stared out the window. Then she went and packed the few things she had taken out of her suitcase the night before.

Glancing down at her ring, she carefully slipped it off her finger, placed it in a hotel envelope, then in Adam's bag. He'd see it when he packed.

Caitlin left the room. She would go to the airport. Get a plane to Monterrey. Hire a car to take her to the village, hike back to her cabin.

Rebuild her old life.

ADAM WALKED for several hours. He knew he'd overreacted. Caitlin hadn't been to blame. Even though he didn't understand her perceptions, he did know that she was sincere and had only been trying to help.

That was the key, he was sure. Because she wanted to help so much, she had forced some sort of ''pick up'' that she had misread...something.

He glanced at his watch. Three o'clock. Rob expected them in before now, but Caitlin wouldn't be in the mood to look at any more photos. Neither was he.

When he arrived, Rob's secretary smiled. ''You're supposed to go on in whenever you show up.''

Adam tapped at the door, opening it at the same time.

The man seated across from Rob wore a Mexican shirt, faded jeans and Mexican sandals. His wide smile flashed white in contrast to his close-trimmed beard. He stood up, threw his arms around Adam, and hugged him. ''Well, *mi amigo*, Rob tells me congratulations are in order. I can't believe it, you old reprobate.''

''Hello, Zeke, what brings you back to the States?'' Adam asked in a neutral tone that clearly surprised the others.

"Don't tell me you've already had your first quarrel," Rob asked.

"Something like that," Adam said, sitting down. "So what's up?"

Rob shrugged. "I was just filling Zeke in on things at this end."

"Yeah. I'd heard you managed to get yourself out of Mexico. That was a miracle, *amigo*. Why didn't you let me know you survived?"

"I wasn't in any shape to contact anyone."

"You were damned lucky. Rob tells me the woman who nursed you back to health is your fiancée?"

"That's right."

"And she also saw the man who tried to kill you."

Adam was finding himself more and more reluctant to continue the conversation. He didn't believe what Caitlin had told him, but his emotions had just gone through a wringer.

"Yes, but she couldn't identify him from any of our mug shots."

"That's too bad. Is she in our office now? Maybe I'll go on back and introduce myself." Zeke stood up.

"No, I didn't bring her today. She was tired."

"Where are you two staying?"

"At the Hilton."

"Good choice." He turned to Rob. "Well, guess I'll check my desk. I'll talk to you guys later." He left the room.

Adam looked over at Rob. "Why did Zeke say he was up here? I didn't catch that."

"Oh, said he was checking out some leads. He was very interested in everything that had happened to you. Says you're one of his most valuable men. He was quite upset when he thought we'd lost you."

Damn Caitlin for planting doubts in Adam's mind.

"How well do you know Zeke, Rob?"

"Hell, I don't know. As well as I know you. Zeke was here when I transferred in from Washington about eight years ago. Why?"

"I just wondered. He's been with the Agency a long time, hasn't he?"

"Fifteen years."

"And he's spent all his time in Mexico?"

"That's right. Is there some point to all of this?"

"Isn't it unusual that he hasn't been promoted?"

"He's turned down numerous promotions. Says he likes fieldwork. What the hell is this all about?"

Adam sighed. "Rob, only two people knew I had a meeting that night—Santiago and Zeke. I didn't make the meeting with Santiago's contact, and Zeke was the only other person who knew I would be going out into the mountains."

"What are you saying?"

"I'm not sure. All I know is that I'd swear I wasn't followed. Whoever came up behind me was waiting. They knew where I would be going."

The two men sat across from each other. Each knew what the other was thinking. Their salaries were good but couldn't compare with the kind of money generated by drug dealing.

If Zeke Taylor had succumbed, he wouldn't be the first agent to be lured away. Or the last.

But if he were straight, how could Adam ever face him again? He didn't know what to do.

"I'm not telling you you're wrong, Adam," Rob said slowly. "But Zeke's the one who pulled this one out of the fire for us. He nailed Santiago."

"Yeah, I know. But just for the sake of argument, let's suppose that Zeke *is* involved. If that's the case, he'd already have had that information.

"Suppose the information I was to get was something else...something about Zeke. But the informant turned up dead, right after Zeke saw him."

"You're saying Zeke killed him?"

"I don't know. I'm just thinking out loud."

The men sat there in silence for a time.

"I could do some investigating," Rob finally said. "Check on his bank accounts, that sort of thing. He couldn't hide that much extra income, although with him living in Mexico, we haven't kept tabs like we could if he were here.''

"I don't know what to say, Rob. I just have this sick feeling in the pit of my stomach. And I can't help but think about Caitlin's predicament if Zeke had anything to do with what happened to me.''

"What do you mean?''

"She can identify the driver. And we filled Zeke in on everything. If we can find the driver, and he can point the finger at Zeke— Look, let's just remember that no one else knew where I was going. Is that enough to start watching what Zeke is up to? Do we really know what leads he's following up here? Is it possible I'm one? And now Caitlin?''

Rob pushed the intercom button. "Would you tell Zeke I'd like to see him?'' Then, "Oh?'' he said. "When did he leave?'' He frowned at Adam. "I see. No, no problem.'' He hung up.

"He's gone?''

"Yeah, said he probably wouldn't be back today.''

"Which could be perfectly in line with his job.''

"Yeah.''

They both sat there for a few moments.

"Where's Caitlin?'' Rob finally asked.

"I'm not sure. We had words earlier, and like an idiot I stormed out.''

Rob stood up. "Why don't you get back to the hotel and make up? I'd feel a hell of a lot better if you didn't let Caitlin out of your sight for a few days, at least until I've had some things checked out.''

BY THE TIME she heard the announcement that her flight was canceled, Caitlin felt numb, which she considered a blessing. All she wanted to do was get home.

She couldn't get Adam out of her mind. She still felt his pain and confusion, but also his guilt at his behavior toward her. However, she wasn't ready to face him again.

"When is your next flight to Monterrey?" she asked the harried airline official behind the counter.

"Tomorrow afternoon at 3:30."

Now what was she to do?

She wished she knew.

ADAM FELT a distinct sinking sensation in his stomach when he returned to the room and saw that Caitlin's suitcase was gone.

Adam called the front desk, knowing there was only a slim chance that someone had seen her leave.

The desk clerk told him, "I came on at three today, sir. Her key was already here."

Great. She left before three. There was only one place Caitlin would go. He called the airport.

"What airlines fly to Monterrey?"

When he was given the name of the only airline, he called their number, but there was no answer. He glanced at his watch. It was almost seven.

He paced the floor, trying to decide what to do. Did he go out and walk the streets, go looking for her? And if so, where?

Adam decided to call Rob at home.

"Caitlin's gone," he told him.

"That must have been one hell of a fight you had," Rob said. "Well, that's just great, isn't it? If what we think is true, she's going to be a sitting duck."

"I don't know what to think at this point. All I know is I have royally messed up this relationship."

"Take it easy. If what you suspect is true, your deductions may have cracked this drug ring wide open."

"They weren't my deductions, Rob. That's the point."

"What are you talking about?"

"The fight I had with Caitlin. She's psychic, clairvoyant...whatever. She picked up on the man, gave me his motivation, and I blew up at her. Wouldn't believe her."

Stunned silence greeted him. Then Rob asked, "If you didn't believe her at first, what made you change your mind?"

"I'm not sure. I probably wouldn't have if he hadn't been in the office. Today I watched him as I would any other suspect, and I picked up on things."

"Such as?"

"Mannerisms, body language, eye contact. That warm, friendly greeting I got looked great, but his eyes were cold, Rob. He was studying me, trying to figure out what I knew. I could almost feel it."

"Maybe you're psychic, too." Rob chuckled.

"You know as well as I do that our intuitive abilities get overworked in this business. And mine kicked into overdrive during that session, Rob. Now I've just got to find Caitlin and convince her that although I'm a complete clod I love her to distraction."

"I just wish we had something concrete to hang on him," Rob pointed out. "I made some phone calls to Mexico City. At the moment we can't trust any of our usual pipelines. I explained the urgency. We should be hearing something soon."

"Thanks, Rob."

"Well, I won't pretend that I don't hope you're wrong."

"I feel the same way."

"Call me when you hear something from Caitlin."

Sighing, Adam dropped onto the chair by the window and gazed out at the night.

CAITLIN HAD LOST track of time. She felt as though she'd spent days at the airport, but when she caught a taxi back downtown, she realized she'd been gone for only a few hours.

Adam's love seemed to surge around her in heavy waves as though he were sending messages to her. By the time she got into the taxi, Caitlin knew that she had to return to the hotel and face him. Perhaps that plane hadn't taken off for a reason. She'd been given another chance.

There were a great many cars and taxis in front of the Hilton, and she had her driver let her out nearby. But as she started down the street toward the main entrance, a sense of unease settled over her, and she paused. Something was wrong.

Without analyzing her feeling, Caitlin knew that she must bypass the lobby area. She went into a boutique with entrances both on the street and inside the hotel. From there, she quietly went toward the lobby.

What was wrong?

The lobby was filled with people, probably conventioneers. She felt no threat from any of them.

Then her mind's eye clearly focused on a man across the lobby, talking to a bellhop—a man with dark hair and eyes and a closely-trimmed beard.

Zeke Taylor.

She knew without a doubt that he was looking for her. Hastily stepping back, she took the stairway to the next floor, then the elevator to the floor where she and Adam had spent the night.

Caitlin hadn't stopped for her key, and so could only pray that Adam was in the room. Pausing, she tapped lightly on the door and waited, forcing herself not to hold her breath.

Adam heard the soft tap and sprang from his chair. Few people knew he was there. Zeke was one of them. He had his pistol in his hand when he asked quietly, "Who is it?"

"Caitlin."

Adam threw open the door, grabbed her and hauled her into his arms. Kicking the door closed, he held her tightly against him.

"Oh, God, Caitlin. I've been so worried. Where the hell have you been? I've been out of my mind!"

Not giving her a chance to answer him, he began to kiss her, then he remembered that he still held his pistol and he paused, looking down at her.

"Do you have any idea how much I love you, lady?" he asked.

"I love you, too, Adam. And I don't blame you for your doubts. I'm just so afraid at the moment."

He'd laid the gun down by the bed and gathered her in his arms. "Don't be. Everything's going to work out all right."

"Adam?"

"Hmm?"

"I know how you feel about Zeke and all. I just think you should know he's in San Antonio."

"Yes, I know. I saw him— How did you know?"

"He's downstairs in the lobby."

He immediately dropped his arms and walked away.

"I know he's your friend, but I'm afraid of him."

"Yeah, well, I can understand that."

"Do you think he's coming up here?"

"There's a strong possibility. I told him where we were staying, and he said he'd like to meet you."

She felt a shiver run over her spine.

"Don't worry. I have no intention of letting him see you."

There was a knock at the door, and Adam put a finger to his lips, then called, "Who is it?"

"Zeke."

Adam picked up Caitlin's bag and placed it in the bathroom. He motioned for her to get into the shower, then went and opened the door.

"Well, hello, Zeke. I didn't expect you. Come on in."

Zeke wore the same clothes he'd had on earlier. He walked in, glanced around, then sat down.

"Where's your fiancée?"

"Good question. I guess I made her madder than I thought this morning. When I came back, she was gone."

Zeke laughed. "Some ladies' man you are, St. Clair. Thought I'd trained you better than that."

Adam shrugged and sat down. "So what are you up to?"

"Oh, nothing much. Thought I'd take you guys out for a drink, meet your lady love. Where do you suppose she went?"

"Probably back to the mountains."

"You never did tell me where you were for all that time. Those mountains are pretty vast."

"To be honest, I couldn't tell you, myself."

Zeke looked around the room again. "So. How about you and me going for that drink?"

"I don't think I'm up to it tonight. I still get tired easily, and I'm feeling pretty beat."

Zeke stood up. "Sure. I guess I'll see you tomorrow."

"I'm thinking about asking for a leave of absence. There's work to be done around the ranch."

"You thinking about giving up your Agency work?"

"The thought has crossed my mind. I don't know how you've managed to stay with it so long."

"Oh, it gets in your blood after a while. You get so you can't live without the excitement."

"Better you than me." Adam walked him to the door. "I'll see you tomorrow."

Zeke gave a casual wave and walked out. Adam put the night latch on and listened at the door until he heard the clang of the elevator doors closing. He turned to find Caitlin standing in the bathroom doorway.

"You know about him, don't you?" she said softly.

His eyes met hers. "I do now." Adam walked over to her and began to unbutton her blouse.

"What are you doing?"

"Getting ready for bed."

"Adam, we need to talk."

"I know. I find I can talk better horizontal."

"I'm sorry for running out that way—"

"I'm sorry for being a complete fool when you were trying to save both of us," he replied, peeling away her blouse.

"Adam—"

He unfastened her skirt and let it fall to the floor, then pushed her remaining undergarments down. Picking her up, he put her on the bed.

"Adam, I know how you must feel—"

"Good," he muttered, stripping out of his clothes, "then I don't have to explain my intentions."

"No, I mean about Zeke and... Oh, Adam."

His mouth had found her breast, and he tenderly touched

his tongue to the peak, his hand gently squeezing the other one.

"I love you, Caitlin," he murmured.

"Oh, Adam, I love you, too."

"Don't give up on me yet, love. Give me some time to get used to all of your talents and abilities, okay?" His mouth had touched her intimately, and she could no longer think. She could only feel.

By the time he raised himself above her, Caitlin felt reduced to a mass of sensations, knowing that Adam was the only man in all the world who could fulfill her. His possession of her was more than physical. It was as though their very spirits were entwined, and they became lost in the sharing.

Whatever happened, they would face it together. Each had something to teach the other—about life, about love.

They had a whole lifetime in which to learn.

ADAM AND Caitlin fell asleep in each other's arms. They clung to each other, as though aware of how close they had come to losing what they had.

The phone rang several times before Adam answered.

"Good news," Rob McFarlane said cryptically.

Adam blinked and turned on the bedside light.

"My inquiry detonated a powder keg down south. Seems they've been working on something similar, but through different sources. The evidence has been mounting up, but they couldn't put a name or face to it. Until tonight. We've got him, Adam. Got him cold."

"Why can't I feel better about that?"

"He almost succeeded in killing you, Adam."

Adam glanced at Caitlin lying next to him, asleep. Her hand rested under her cheek, and for the first time he realized she wasn't wearing his ring.

"When are you going to make the arrest?"

"In the morning. There's some paperwork to get done. And I've got to make sure he can't get out on bail. If he does, and he were to get across the border, he'd be gone."

"Are you going to need me for anything?"

"No. You deserve some time off."

"Thanks. I need it."

"I expect a wedding invitation, you know."

"You'll get one," he replied. *If there's a wedding.*

Eventually Adam dozed, sleeping fitfully, but he was so aware of Caitlin that he knew the moment she woke up the next morning.

He opened his eyes and looked at her. "Good morning," he said, trying to read her expression.

She smiled. "Did I hear the phone ring last night, or was I dreaming?"

"It rang. Rob called to say they had the evidence to pick up Zeke."

"Oh." She propped herself up. "I know how badly you must feel."

There were degrees of feeling badly, he thought wryly. Losing a friend was tough. Losing your love was a hell of a lot tougher.

"Looks like the case is wrapped up," he offered. "So there's no reason to stay here."

She sat up and stretched. "Did you mean what you said to Zeke last night? About getting out of the business?"

"I've given it some thought. Why?"

"I just wondered."

"So what do you want to do now?" Why did his heart rate seem to pick up just because he'd finally asked?

"Go back to the cabin, I suppose."

Well, he had his answer. Funny that he'd thought all of his fears were behind him. What could he say to that? He couldn't hold her captive on the ranch. Having previously agreed to marry him didn't lock her into anything. That's what engagements were for. A testing. And he had flunked the test.

"Do you want me to drive you back?" He was proud of his voice. He sounded carefully neutral.

Caitlin paused from sliding out of bed and looked at him, really looked at him. Why did he ask such a question?

"Don't you want to take me back?"

His eyes looked wintry. "Shall I be polite or honest?"

"Okay, so you don't want to make another trip down there. But how do you suggest I get everything moved from down there to the ranch?"

He sat up straight. "The ranch? You're moving to the ranch?"

Caitlin looked at him, worried about his mental condition. Maybe this latest news had been too much for him. She walked around to his side of the bed and sat down. Taking his hand, she lovingly stroked it.

"Adam. Most new marriages are begun under a considerable strain. I'm sure ours won't be an exception. But we really need to be together to make it work."

He slid his hand behind her neck and pulled her mouth over to his. "Is that your way of trying to tell me that you'll marry me, after all?"

She blinked. "What do you mean, after all?"

His mouth clamped tightly to hers in a hard, possessive kiss that left no doubt in her mind that he was perturbed about something. However, it also made it quite clear that he wanted her very badly.

"Where is your ring?" he finally said.

"My ring? Oh! I forgot." Scrambling off the bed, Caitlin hurried over to Adam's suitcase and delved into it. She took the ring from the envelope, slipped it on her finger and returned to the bed. "There." She smiled at him.

"Why did you take it off?"

"You know why. I thought our engagement proved how unsuited we were and that it proved how right I'd been all along not to get involved with anyone."

"And now?"

"Now I know that you'll hate it when I know what you're thinking, but the only thing that really matters is that we love each other. That's what counts."

He pulled her down on top of him. "You are a very wise

lady, Caitlin Moran. Now, I was thinking maybe we'd spend some time today planning our honeymoon."

"You mean this isn't it?"

He pulled her down beside him, and began to untie her robe. "No, ma'am. This was just a preview."

Caitlin ran her hands along his back and smiled. "Then I can hardly wait for the main event."

RETURN TO YESTERDAY

Annette Broadrick

Felicia St. Clair stared out the small window of the plane, watching the dark, swirling clouds surround the wingtip. As the plane descended from its long flight from Los Angeles to Austin, the local weather made itself felt. Driving rain beat against the aircraft.

Felicia glanced down at her hands, which were gripped tightly together in her lap. She felt strange returning home to Texas. Whenever she had tried to imagine a homecoming, she always visualized her brother, Adam, there to greet her. Adam, with his contagious grin and sparkling eyes.

Five years her senior, he had been the hub of her life as a young girl. He'd taken the place of the father she'd never known. After their mother had died, when Felicia was twelve, Adam had become both parents and brother.

Thinking about him made the hollow feeling in her stomach more pronounced, the same feeling she'd had since Dane had called to tell her that Adam had disappeared somewhere in Mexico.

Please, God, don't let anything happen to him.

Adam had always been there when she'd needed him. And never had Felicia needed him more than now, when she would soon be forced to see Dane Rineholt again and pretend he was just a family friend.

The Fasten Seat Belts sign flashed on and Felicia hastily checked her appearance in a small compact mirror. Her sun-streaked blond hair was fashionably shaped in a long, straight bob that flipped under at her shoulders. The face staring back at her looked considerably different from that of the naive young woman who had left the state five years before, convinced her heart was broken because Dane didn't love her.

At least she had a few more hours before she would have to face him. She hadn't told him she was coming, but had reserved a rental car at the airport. The drive to the ranch would give her time to prepare for their meeting.

Would Dane recognize the well-dressed, young executive as the girl who had followed him and Adam around the ranch for years? She hoped not. Felicia hoped that girl, with all her foolish dreams, had been put aside.

After disembarking from the plane she searched for the rental car sign. She spotted Dane as she reached the doorway to the terminal. He stood head and shoulders above the rest of the crowd.

How had he known she'd be on that plane? Or even that she would be coming? She hadn't told him. His news had left her so shaken that she barely remembered hanging up the phone.

Dane's piercing gaze met hers over the crowd and she mentally acknowledged that, like it or not, she now had to deal with the feelings he stirred within her. His steel-gray eyes seemed to see deep inside her, reading her thoughts and sensing her emotions.

Felicia was swept along with the jostling passengers until she reached Dane. His impassive gaze never wavered. Whatever his thoughts, he kept them well hidden. Whatever emotions were aroused by seeing her after five years were his own private feelings.

She fought the urge to throw herself into his arms like a child needing to be comforted. Instead she asked him, "Have you heard anything from Adam?"

He shook his head, lightly grasping her arm just above the elbow and piloting her down the concourse to the baggage claim area. "Nothing."

With one touch, Dane took control—of her and of the situation. The years seemed to drop away and Felicia shook her head to dispel the sensation.

"How did you know I was coming in?"

He glanced down at her and with a slight quirk of his well-shaped mouth, he murmured, "I've known you a long time, Felicia," as though that explained everything.

"Does anybody have any idea what might have happened to him?" she asked, returning to the subject of her brother.

"The authorities have spoken to the personnel at the hotel in Monterrey where Adam stays. No one could pinpoint the exact time he was last seen there. When I talked with him last Friday, he said he intended to return home no later than yesterday morning. When he didn't show up, I called down there and discovered he hadn't slept in his room since Thursday night."

They both were silent, then Felicia finally asked, "Why had he gone to Mexico?"

"On business," was Dane's terse reply.

"Ranching?"

"He and I have several other interests."

His response emphasized the strained relationship between them. Felicia had deliberately cut herself off from any knowledge of the ranch in general and Dane Rineholt in particular. She could hardly complain now that she didn't know anything about his and Adam's shared activities.

While they stood waiting for her luggage, Felicia noticed the admiring glances from females that Dane's tall, lean figure drew. He'd had that effect on women as long as she'd known him.

His fleece-lined denim jacket clung to his shoulders, emphasizing their breadth, then narrowed to his flat, slim waist. Long, muscled legs were outlined by snug Levi's. He didn't need the added height his custom-made boots gave him.

Dane Rineholt was the epitome of the Texas rancher. Even in February his face was deeply tanned, except for the line on his forehead from the Stetson he wore. He held the hat loosely in his hand now, slapping it against his hard thigh as they waited.

"I didn't expect to see you here," Felicia finally said.

"Didn't you?" His sardonic response surprised her. "I knew you wouldn't take my advice and stay in L.A. This was the first flight you could have caught after I called."

"I didn't realize I was so predictable."

"You are to me."

Felicia didn't like the sound of that at all. She had hoped that as she'd grown older she had learned to hide what she was thinking and feeling. Of course Dane knew how close she was to Adam, so his guessing her actions this time wasn't too surprising.

She was an adult now, she reminded herself, an editor on a prestigious women's magazine. She had a life of her own, a career. What more could she want?

Dane nodded toward the baggage carousel. "You'll have to point out which ones are yours," he said in his husky drawl.

Placing his Stetson on his head, he then picked up her bags and headed toward the door. Felicia followed reluctantly.

She thought of her intended rental car and regretted the loss of freedom. Instead she would have to borrow whatever was available at the ranch to drive to Mexico.

Of course, there was always the chance that by the time they reached the ranch Adam might have called, explaining his delay and apologizing for the scare.

Dane set her luggage down by the door while he studied the blowing rain. "Wait here while I bring the car around." He thrust the door open and strode toward the parking area, arrogantly knowing she would obey.

Felicia smiled slightly at the memories his tone of voice provoked. A picture of Adam flashed in her mind and she knew he would be amused to think of them together without him around to referee. *Oh, Adam, please be all right,* she thought with a pang.

A late-model automobile drew up and Dane stepped out, placing her bags in the trunk while she climbed into the passenger's seat.

"This isn't a very good advertisement for the sunny South," Felicia said lightly.

"We need the rain," he stated as they pulled away.

"That's what Adam said last time he called."

"When did you speak with him last?"

She thought back. "About two weeks ago. Why?"

"Just wondered."

"What's going on, Dane?" she asked quietly. "You know more than you're telling."

"Now what's your vivid imagination cooking up, Tadpole?" he asked.

Tadpole. How she had hated that nickname. Felicia let her eyes focus on the rapidly moving windshield wipers, glad after all that she wasn't the one having to drive. Visibility was poor. The streets and highway were flooded.

Yet she felt safe. Dane had always made her feel that she could depend on him, even when she was the most irritated by his autocratic manner.

Resting her head wearily against the cushioned headrest, Felicia allowed her eyes to drift closed. She hadn't been able to rest since Dane's phone call the night before. But now the rhythmic swish of the wipers lulled her into a restless sleep.

FIFTEEN-YEAR-OLD Felicia St. Clair stepped off the school bus at the end of the lane. A hot breeze caused a dust swirl to greet her.

How she hated Texas. The heat, the dirt, Adam's constant concern over water and the state of the cattle. He was too young to have to deal with the ranch, yet he'd assumed full responsibility at the ripe old age of seventeen when their mother had died three years ago.

She sometimes wondered how he stood it. Of course Pete had been there. Otherwise Adam would never have managed the two years of college at Texas A & M, driving home every weekend to help where he could. But Adam hadn't bothered to go back this year.

Pete had been their father's foreman, and had stayed on these fifteen years, looking after the ranch and his best friend's family. But Adam had grown up too fast. He'd never had a chance to be a carefree boy.

After their mother had died, he'd hired a housekeeper to look after them. Millie had done all she could to make the orphaned teenagers feel like they had a family.

Felicia gripped her schoolbooks tighter and began the long walk to the house.

Lately Adam had spent his evenings poring over the account books. There had been little moisture the previous winter and she knew he was worried.

Felicia's daydreams carried her far away from the dusty track. She was a famous writer living in a penthouse apartment in New York. Or Paris, London, Rome. She was busily working out how much money to send Adam each month for the ranch when Prince, their dog, came bounding up to her.

"Oh, Prince, you fool. Get down. You'd think I'd been gone for years." She was laughing at his antics and walking backward, scolding him, which was why she didn't see Adam and the stranger standing on the porch, until she turned to start up the steps.

The man was several inches taller than Adam, but they were similar in build: broad shoulders, slim waist and hips, long legs. They were even dressed similarly. But where Adam's open expression made him look even younger than his twenty years, the stranger's face was closed, his eyes slitted against the bright sunlight, his hat pulled down low. He seemed much older than Adam.

Felicia felt all knees and elbows as she gazed up at the man leaning gracefully against the porch rail. A hollow place seemed to form somewhere just below her ribs and she unconsciously placed her hand there, wondering why the stranger had suddenly made her aware of what she looked like. She had never cared before.

"Hi, sis," Adam said. "I want you to meet Dane Rineholt."

Felicia tentatively smiled. "H'lo."

Adam continued. "Dane, this is my sister, Felicia, one of the best ranch hands we've got."

"I'm the *only* ranch hand you've got, besides Pete," she pointed out.

"Well, that's going to change. Dane has agreed to become a partner on the ranch."

Felicia stared at the other man. "You mean you are now part owner of the St. Clair ranch?"

Dane slowly straightened. "That's right." His tone made it clear the subject wasn't open to debate.

Felicia could feel her heart racing. She had a sudden instinctive feeling that nothing in her life would be the same again.

She glanced at her brother. "Does that mean he's going to live with us?" she asked in a low voice.

A sudden, slashing smile caused Dane's face to take on an entirely different look. Felicia could only stare at the transformation.

"That's what it means, all right. But you don't need to worry. I'm no threat to a tadpole like you, honey."

BY THE TIME she was a senior in high school, two years later, Felicia knew there would never be another man in her life to compare with Dane Rineholt.

She couldn't understand the flurry of confused emotions that came over her whenever he was around. She hated being so aware of him and tried to cover up her reactions—not that her behavior toward him seemed to matter. Dane treated her the same way Adam did, with a casual familiarity, so that Felicia bristled at everything he said and did. Particularly the odious nickname Tadpole.

Perhaps she had been in the transition between child and adult when he'd first met her, but two years had brought changes. Slowly but surely the angular parts of her body had begun to fill out, becoming firm and rounded.

Her mirror told Felicia that she was not ugly. Wide-spaced gray-green eyes stared back at her, framed by long, thick lashes. High cheekbones gave her face an elegant shape. And her tanned skin made the light color of blond hair even more noticeable.

The boys at school had taken to hanging around the ranch in their spare time, which was little enough, because they, too, had work to do at home.

Adam enjoyed teasing her about her following, but Dane never said a word. He just sat there watching her, amused mockery in his eyes.

Until the night Blaze was sick.

Dane's presence had meant there was money enough to buy more stock, including horses, as well as hire additional help. And when one of the mares had a colt, Adam had allowed Felicia to keep it.

She never gave up her dreams of leaving Texas and becoming a writer. Yet she also enjoyed being outdoors and working with the horses. Especially Blaze. So when he became ill she was beside herself.

"I don't think it's anything too serious." Pete tried to comfort her. "Probably something he ate."

She hoped he was right, but she was still prepared to spend the night in the barn in case he became worse. She was kneeling beside the horse, murmuring softly, when she looked up to see Dane.

"I don't see any reason for you to stay out here tonight, Tadpole. Blaze is looking much better."

"He seems to rest easier when I'm here. Every time I get up he starts stirring."

"You're spoiling that damned horse, you know."

"I don't care."

Dane knelt down beside her. "That horse is all you care about, isn't it?"

She glanced up at him, startled. "Of course not. I care about Adam and Millie and Pete. And you."

He grinned. "Well, I'm glad I made your list, anyway. Sometimes it's hard to tell with you."

"If you didn't tease me so much, I'd probably be a lot nicer to you. Did anyone ever tease you?" she asked, stroking Blaze's neck.

"Are you kidding? With two older brothers?"

"How old are you, Dane?"

He lifted one brow. "How old do you think I am?"

Trying not to smile, she offered, "Oh, forty or so."

He grabbed her by the shoulders and lightly shook her. "You know better. I haven't reached thirty yet."

"But you're still years older than I am."

"Ten years, but well preserved." He grinned.

"I suppose. Some people might find you attractive."

"Some people, but not you, I take it?"

"For an old man you aren't too bad."

He threw back his head and laughed. After a few minutes, she said in a quiet voice, "Thank you for checking on us tonight."

"No problem. Look. He's doing much better. Why don't we go back to the house?" He stood and pulled her up beside him. Blaze never stirred and Felicia admitted to herself that he seemed much better.

They crossed the area between the barn and the house in silence. A full moon cast mysterious shadows and Felicia paused, gazing up at the sky with a pleasurable sense of belonging.

Her view was suddenly blocked as Dane leaned down and kissed her softly on the lips. Pulling back, he said in a low voice, "You look like a fairy princess standing here bathed in silver light. I couldn't resist."

She stared at him in wonder, realizing that he had just given her her first kiss.

"I'm sorry. I didn't mean to offend you."

"You didn't," she managed. "You just surprised me."

"I take it you aren't used to being kissed."

"On the contrary," she said loftily. "I'm just not used to *you* kissing me, that's all."

Felicia was glad he couldn't know how her heart was racing as he pulled her into his arms and said, "Oh, then you won't mind if I kiss you again."

Before she could offer a reply, his mouth had found hers once more. However, this kiss was very different from the first one. This time his arms were firmly around her, pulling her close to his hard body. His mouth felt firm and she gasped with surprise. Taking advantage of her parted lips, he ran his tongue along the uneven edge of her teeth, lightly forcing his way inside her mouth.

Felicia couldn't think as new sensations swept over her. She felt hot and cold at the same time and her knees would not have supported her weight. But Dane stood with his legs braced, holding her against him as he slowly explored the depths of her mouth.

Feeling the urge to touch him, Felicia placed her hands around his waist and began smoothing the material that covered his muscled back. She could feel his heart pounding and she realized that this was better than any of her fantasies.

Dane's hand moved slowly up and down her spine as though memorizing it. A tingling sensation followed everywhere he touched and she found herself wanting to get closer to him somehow. She moaned slightly, unaware that she did so.

Dane lifted his head abruptly. She never knew for sure why he stopped, only that he did. She couldn't see his eyes because his face was in shadow.

"I'm sorry, Felicia, I shouldn't have done that." He shook his head as though trying to clear it, and stepped away from her.

"You don't have to apologize," she managed to mutter. "It's okay."

"I'll see you tomorrow." He turned to walk away, then paused and said, "I promise I won't do that again, Tadpole. I never meant to take advantage of you."

"You didn't."

He shrugged. "Good night."

Felicia spent a very restless night, trying to come to grips with the feelings Dane had invoked in her, trying not to feel rejected because of his actions after the kiss. One thing she knew—she would have to hide her feelings from Dane even more so now. She was sure he would make fun of her if he thought she cared for him. He still saw her as a child.

But Felicia no longer felt like a child. Dane's kiss had introduced her to the burning ache of adult emotions.

*

THE RAIN was getting worse and Dane was forced to slow down for safety's sake. He glanced at the sleeping woman beside him in the car.

He had honestly thought he was over her. After all, five years was a long time and there had been many women willing to take the place she had occupied in his mind and heart.

He still remembered the first time he'd seen her. She couldn't have been more than fifteen, with a coltish quality about her he'd found instantly endearing.

She'd been walking up the lane from the county road, playing with the dog, her smile so radiant that it practically lit up the countryside.

He'd forgotten that there was such innocence in the world. After the years he'd spent overseas, and later in his special investigative field, he'd returned to Texas to try and establish a quiet, ordinary lifestyle.

He had met with Adam St. Clair several times, working on the partnership agreement, before he finally saw Felicia. He hadn't given much thought to what it would mean to share the home of a young girl slowly blossoming into womanhood. Until he saw her that day.

He glanced over at her now. Knowing how close she was to Adam, Dane couldn't have kept his disappearance from her. He had also known she wouldn't be able to stay away.

Dane frowned. If there were only some kind of clue to follow. Adam knew that the work was dangerous and Dane felt responsible for having recruited him. But Adam had been a natural. He enjoyed the intrigue, but didn't take unnecessary chances. In the four years they had been working with the government, they had managed to stop some major sources of drug smuggling between the States and Mexico.

Now Dane was afraid Adam's luck had run out.

On the surface he was a tourist-businessman who had mysteriously disappeared while visiting a foreign country. But the covert authorities on both sides knew this could be more sinister. Adam wouldn't be the first agent to disappear and never be heard of again.

The question was what to tell Felicia. Adam had casually mentioned after one of his trips to L.A. that what they were doing had been made easier by the fact that she was far enough away not to ask questions. Adam had never told her about their activities.

Their contacts across the border had no idea Dane and Adam worked together. They had independently infiltrated unrelated drug operations. But if some news didn't turn up in the next few days, Dane would jeopardize his cover and go down there to use his own sources.

Once again he glanced over at Felicia.

He would never forget how she'd looked a few weeks before she'd graduated from university. At twenty-two she was one of the loveliest women he'd ever seen.

For four years he had worked hard to give her the impression that he was serious about someone else so that she wouldn't practice her budding feminine wiles on him. He lived with her and yet wasn't a relative. There was no way he'd betray Adam's trust by taking advantage of her innocence.

The situation improved somewhat after she left for college, even though she came home occasionally for a weekend. He planned his weekends so that he was seldom there when she was.

After four years of that routine he'd been lulled into a sense of false security, until he'd felt there was no longer a problem. Then she had asked him to escort her to one of the graduation festivities, and like a fool he agreed to go.

Dane showed up at her dorm at the appointed hour and got his first glimpse of the woman she'd become while he wasn't looking.

She took his breath away.

Felicia wore a floor-length gown of the softest blue-green he'd ever seen. Her eyes glittered, their color enhanced by an iridescent green underslip that shimmered through the sheer surface of the softly swirling material.

Her hair had been cut so that feathering curls framed her face, drawing attention to the patrician line of brow, high cheekbones and dainty nose.

She looked like a princess, and Dane knew he had been fighting a losing battle over his feelings for her.

He and Felicia had never danced together before. Dane couldn't deny that he enjoyed holding her in his arms during the few slow numbers, but that created its own problems. He didn't know which was worse—holding her close and forcing his body not to react to her nearness, or watching her stand in front of him during the upbeat numbers, her face flushed and smiling, her body dipping and weaving in unconsciously provocative movements.

Dane felt relieved when Felicia suggested they leave.

They were in the car returning to her dorm when she asked, "Are you driving home tonight?"

"No. I'm staying at a motel."

"Oh. Will I see you again before you leave?"

"I hadn't planned on it. Why? Did you want a ride home?"

"Oh, no. I still have another week at school before I can go home."

They lapsed back into silence.

"Would you like to get something to eat?" Dane asked finally. "I think I saw an all-night restaurant near the motel. Or do you have to be back right away?"

"I have plenty of time, Dane. I just don't want to delay you anymore. I really do appreciate your coming to Austin to take me to the dance." The smile she gave him almost caused him to miss his turn.

Dane sat across from her during their meal, fascinated by her ever changing expressions as she told him hilarious tales of life in the dorm and on campus.

When they left the restaurant Felicia asked if he would show her his room, explaining that she'd never been inside a motel room.

"I find that hard to believe," he responded, reluctantly walking her across to the motel.

"It's true. We never traveled."

"And no man has ever coaxed you in to one?" he asked, opening the door.

She grinned. "I didn't say they haven't tried, Dane."

His room was a standard style, with a king-size bed taking

up most of the space. A sliding glass door spanned the width of the room. Felicia parted the draperies slightly.

"Oh, look. You have a pool!"

"Most motels do."

She spun around with a mischievous sparkle in her eye. "I know! Why don't we go swimming?"

He sat down, her youthful exuberance suddenly making him feel his added years. "Felicia, use your head. Neither of us brought anything to swim in."

She glanced back at the window, then at him. "Nobody would see us swimming now, you know. Couldn't we swim in our underwear?"

He studied her for a moment, then slowly shook his head. "I don't think Adam would approve."

But something in his voice told her he was weakening. She disappeared into the bathroom. "I'll keep a towel around me in case anyone is watching. Come on, Dane. It'll be fun."

She had echoed his thoughts and while she was slipping out of her formal, he quickly undressed, finding a pair of Levi's to wear. When she reappeared he silently opened the sliding door and stepped outside.

The night was hot and muggy, typical of Texas in late spring. Indirect lighting gave a soft glow to the pool area.

Dane unfastened his jeans and pulled them off, revealing navy blue briefs that could pass for swimming trunks.

Felicia tossed her towel on a nearby chair and he had to admit there was nothing childish about the body revealed to him. Her lacy underwear was probably more than adequate for today's swimwear styles. Gone were her coltish lines and in their place, a slender young woman with curving breasts and thighs, and a waist that made him want to wrap his hands around it.

He forced himself to look away, waiting until he heard her splashing around.

"Come on in," she said gaily, "the water feels great."

At first he stayed the pool length away from her, swimming laps to keep his mind off her and how she looked in the moonlight.

Eventually she came gliding through the water to join him at the deep end of the pool.

"Don't you ever just relax and enjoy the water?" she asked. "You act as though you're training for the Olympics!"

He ran his hand through his hair, flicking water over them both. "Just getting rid of some excess energy."

"I see," she said, and moved closer, placing her hand beside his on the tile rim of the pool.

"Dane? Are you upset about anything?"

He eyed her warily. "No, why?"

"I don't know. You just seem jumpy. I thought a swim might help to relax you."

He lifted one brow slightly. "Oh, you did, did you? My, the sacrifices you're prepared to make for out-of-town guests."

Her predictable temper got the better of her and she suddenly hit the water with both hands, causing a wave to break over him. Then she swam underwater toward the other end of the pool, but Dane was waiting for her. Giving her only enough time to get a mouthful of air, he pushed her back under.

No matter where she tried to go, he was waiting for her, until they were both panting from the exertion.

"Give up, Tadpole. You can't win," he said between breaths.

They were in the middle of the pool. Dane was able to stand, but the water was over Felicia's head. He heard her labored breathing and, without considering the consequences, pulled her into his arms. The buoyancy of the water floated her closer to him. Her legs entangled with his until he realized she was straddling his thigh. He felt the warmth of her as her thighs clamped around him in an unconscious invitation.

Dane glanced down at her as Felicia slowly raised her head. Succumbing to the overwhelming temptation, he placed his lips on hers in a soft kiss. They felt cool and moist. Her mouth opened beneath his—so naturally, so inevitably, that he let go of the side of the pool to pull her even closer. The water provided a warm cocoon of sensation as her body glided smoothly against him.

It was only when Dane realized he couldn't breathe that he kicked them back to the surface. This time he found his footing in shallower water.

Once again they were both gasping for air, but when their lungs filled this time their mouths blindly searched for each other again. Dane forced himself to raise his head and looked down into Felicia's upturned face. Her eyes were closed, her lips slightly swollen from the pressure of his kisses. He could feel her breasts against his chest while she took quick, shallow breaths.

Never before had Dane come so close to losing complete control of himself.

"Felicia?" he whispered. "I think we've done enough swimming for one evening, don't you?"

"Oh, yes," she agreed and continued to hang on to him as he moved toward the steps in the shallow end of the pool.

Dane slipped his arms under her thighs and shoulders. Once out of the pool, he lowered her legs and reached for the towel she had left on a chair.

Back in his room he refused to look at her. Instead he handed her a shirt.

"Get out of those wet clothes and put this on. Then I'll drive you back to the dorm."

Felicia disappeared into the bathroom without a word and Dane grabbed a towel and hurriedly began to dry off. He pulled on a dry pair of briefs, then his Levi's.

He was towel-drying his hair when he heard the bathroom door open. He glanced around. His shirt hung to her knees. The lightweight material could not conceal that she no longer wore a bra. If she'd followed his directions, she no longer wore panties, either.

How had he gotten himself into this situation?

"Are you ready to go?" he asked gruffly.

Felicia's eyes glowed. "No. I don't want to go. I want to stay with you." Her smile made his heart pause in its rapid beat. She placed her palms on his bare chest, and Dane knew at that moment that he had lost the battle. Blindly he reached for her, wrapping his arms around her and pulling her tightly against his aroused body.

*

THE RHYTHMIC swish of the wipers provided a steady undertone for the sound of the hard driving rain. Forcing her eyes open, Felicia realized that night had fallen.

"Where are we?" she asked Dane.

"About a mile out of Mason," he responded. "I thought we'd stop and eat before going home. I told Millie not to bother fixing anything for us."

"How is Millie?"

"Same as usual."

"Hasn't thrown up her hands in disgust trying to look after two crusty old bachelors, huh?" Her light tone broke into a husky whisper.

"He's okay, Felicia. Who knows? He may already be at the ranch by now."

"You don't really believe that, do you?"

He was silent, watching the road. "I thought we'd eat at The Homestead. It's a restaurant built on one of the old places. I think you'll like it."

They drove up a lane that didn't seem to be marked with any signs, through a gate standing hospitably open, and she saw the restaurant, warm light shining from several windows. As Dane opened the door for her, Felicia caught the scent of wood burning and saw a massive fireplace at one end of the room.

A blond woman with a cheerful smile greeted them. "Well, hello, Dane. I didn't expect we'd see you out on a night like this." She led them over to one of the small tables in front of the fireplace.

"Charlotte, this is Adam's sister, Felicia St. Clair."

If anything, Charlotte's smile grew broader. "I'm so pleased to meet you, Felicia. I've heard so much about you from Dane and Adam.'' She took their orders and headed for the kitchen.

In the car Felicia could pretend she wasn't with Dane, had even managed to sleep. But in the soft lamplight of the restaurant she was forced to look at what her heart had never forgotten.

If possible, Dane had grown more handsome. At thirty-seven, his thick, black hair was beginning to show flecks of silver around his ears. It was still hard for her to believe that he had remained single.

Perhaps he preferred to play the field. The only thing she knew for sure was that he didn't want her. He'd made that extremely clear five years ago and she would do well to remember that. He was her brother's partner. That's all.

"I intend to go to Monterrey," she said after Charlotte had served their meal and left once more.

Dane's head jerked up. "The hell you are. Why?"

"To find Adam."

"It's too dangerous," he stated in a flat tone.

"People go down there all the time. There's nothing dangerous about it."

"Even though Adam might argue the point?"

She didn't need to be reminded. Perhaps it was dangerous, but that wasn't going to deter her. She continued to eat, determined not to let him upset her.

The rain had slackened some by the time they left.

"You aren't serious about going to Mexico, are you?" Dane asked once they pulled up in front of the house.

"Yes. I'm very serious."

"What about your job?"

"I explained that it was a family emergency. My assistant can handle the routine things. If not, she's to call me."

He got out of the car and came around to open her door. He wished to hell he knew how to keep her out of Mexico. He knew better than to try to use threats. Once she got the bit between her teeth, there was no controlling her. He knew that as well as anyone.

In the house, Dane found a note on the kitchen table listing his phone messages. But no word about Adam. Dane crossed the hall to the living room to turn off the lamp Millie had left on for them. Felicia was standing in the middle of the room.

"It all looks so familiar," she said with a catch in her voice. "I don't know why I expected it to change." She ran her hand along the bookcase. "He saved all my books."

Tears glistened as they ran down her cheeks. "It's just as though I left this morning. And Adam will come stomping in from the porch any minute now."

He couldn't stand to see her pain. In two long strides Dane reached her side and pulled her roughly into his arms. She stiffened at his touch, but he didn't let go, and gradually he felt her relax.

God, she felt so good to him. How long had it been since he'd held her? Too long. How had he found the strength to let her go? The truth was, he'd had no choice. She wanted no part of the only kind of life he could live.

Felicia gave up battling her tears and let them flow. She had missed her home. And even though she talked with Adam frequently and saw him at least twice a year, she had to face how much she missed him.

The most traumatic truth Felicia faced during the past few hours was how she felt about Dane. He was so much a part of her past. And she loved him.

His hands slowly stroked her back and he murmured, "He's going to be okay, love. He'll be home soon."

If only she *were* his love. Fighting for some control over her emotions, she loosened her hold around Dane's waist. He slowly dropped his arms and stepped back.

With calm deliberation, Felicia met his gaze. "I intend to leave tomorrow."

"If you insist on going to Mexico, I'm going with you," he replied.

His tone of voice made it very clear that he had no intention of changing his mind.

Part of her reason for leaving so soon was to get away from Dane. So much for that idea. However, she hadn't looked forward to making the trip alone, either. Despite the pain of being around him, Felicia knew there was no one she'd rather have on her side if the going got rough.

Nodding in acceptance, she went upstairs to her old room. The furniture gleamed in the soft lamplight and she ran her hand across the crazy quilt that her mother had made from scraps of the clothes Felicia had outgrown.

Feeling totally drained, she tossed back the covers and wearily crawled into bed.

Perhaps it was being home again that triggered old memories that helped form her dreams. In particular she kept recalling her senior year at the university, when she'd finally gotten up the nerve to invite Dane to escort her to one of the graduation dances.

If anyone had asked her that spring what her hopes and dreams were, she could have readily listed them. She wanted to marry Dane, return to the ranch that had always been her home, help with the local paper and try her hand at writing a novel. Since Dane had not announced any engagement by her senior year, Felicia had begun to hope that he'd been waiting for her to finish school.

The question was, did he love her? And if he did, did he want to marry her?

It was no wonder she was nervous when she came downstairs at the dorm to meet him. And later, while they were swimming, Felicia began to hope that all of her dreams were about to come true.

Dane didn't kiss her as though he still saw her as a child. And there was no way he could hide from her his physical reaction to their closeness.

She couldn't control the shiver of anticipation that ran through her when she walked out of the bathroom and found Dane standing there, wearing only a pair of jeans. When his arms wrapped around her, she knew she was where she wanted to be. His mouth came down on hers in a desperate possession, one that she was willing to allow. How many years had she dreamed of this moment with this man?

His kiss was even better than she remembered. She loved the feel of him so close to her and she felt her knees give way. Without taking his mouth from hers, he carried her to the nearby bed.

Both of them fell across it, arms entwined, mouths still touching. The shirt she wore had ridden up on her hip and his hand found her bare skin and gently rubbed across it, back and forth, until she thought she would cry out with the intensity of the feeling.

She couldn't resist touching his chest, something she had often yearned to do. And as he ran his hand softly from the top of her rib cage to where her thighs met, her stomach muscles tightened.

Felicia pulled back slightly, trying to get her breath. She gazed into his blazing eyes and reminded herself that this was Dane and anything he did was all right.

With probing fingers he caressed her, touching her gently. She wanted to touch him, and slid her hand into his jeans, feeling the hardness there—a smooth hardness that she found fascinating.

Dane lowered his head, nudged the shirt aside with his mouth, and found the tip of her breast. His tongue caressed the point until the nipple grew taut. Then his lips slipped over the pebblelike hardness and coaxed it into his mouth.

Felicia thought she was going to explode with the intensity of her feelings. Tears ran down her cheeks.

Dane shifted on the bed, one leg thrown across her thighs as he gathered her closer.

One moment he was kissing her passionately, his tongue imitating the erotic rhythm of his fingers, the next moment he froze.

Pulling away slightly, he looked down at her.

"What's wrong?" she asked breathlessly.

"You're a virgin," he stated in a flat voice.

"Yes," she agreed, bewildered.

"I didn't realize. I thought you had some experience."

"And now that you know I don't?"

"I'm not the one who's going to give it to you."

"But you wanted me!"

He glanced at her, then reached over to pull the shirt she wore down, covering her thighs.

"You're a very attractive woman," he admitted.

"But you don't love me. Is that it?"

"Love has nothing to do with what almost happened tonight."

Felicia felt a sharp pain in her chest, as though a doubled fist had hit her. "You really are a bastard, aren't you, Dane," she managed to say after a moment.

"Maybe I am, but I don't accept virginal offerings from young ladies eager to learn about life."

Felicia scrambled off the bed. "I hate you."

"I'm sure you do. At the moment, anyway. Tell me, was this some sort of bet you made, to see if you could seduce me tonight? For the record, you almost won. Another few minutes and I would have been unable to…"

"You don't need to lecture. You've made your point. I don't know why I ever thought I was in love with you. I must have been out of my mind to think I'd ever be happy married to an arrogant—"

"Married!" Dane almost flinched.

"Don't worry, Dane. I don't intend to blackmail you into marrying me, even though Adam might be curious about my being here with you tonight."

"I did not invite you here, Felicia. Tell Adam whatever suits you, so long as you keep your facts straight."

Felicia had never felt so humiliated in her life. All her dreams had been shattered. Dane Rineholt didn't love her— never did and never would. The sooner she accepted that, the better.

THE SOUND of a phone ringing finally broke through Felicia's consciousness. Groping for the switch on the lamp beside her bed, she threw back the covers and stood up. By now, the ringing had stopped. She looked at her watch. It was almost three a.m.

She quietly opened her bedroom door and listened. Faintly she heard a voice downstairs. It sounded like Dane.

As quietly as possible, Felicia descended, pausing in the doorway of the office where Dane stood, clad only in jeans, listening on the phone. He had his back to her.

"She's insisting on going down there," she heard him say, and realized he was talking about her. "I can't tell her anything. You know that. It's too dangerous."

A sudden spurt of adrenaline shot through her body at his words. Adam was in danger and Dane knew why!

"Thanks for the report," he was saying. "Yeah, I wish the news had been better myself." A long pause ensued. "I'll just play it by ear. Hopefully you'll find him before she gets too involved. Then it's up to him to decide what to tell her." He nodded. "Talk to you later."

He turned to hang up and saw Felicia standing inside the doorway.

For the first time she was aware of her very skimpy nightshirt and the chill of the hardwood floor on her bare toes.

"You're going to catch cold coming downstairs like that," said Dane. "I turn the furnace down at night."

She glanced at his chest, then down to his bare feet. "I could say the same about you."

He smiled slightly, but the smile never reached the watchful intensity of his eyes.

"Who called?"

He shrugged. "Just a business associate."

"Did he have anything to do with Adam's disappearance?" she asked calmly.

He stared down at her in silence for a moment. "What's that supposed to mean?" he finally asked.

She crossed her arms, trying to hide the trembling that had overtaken her, partly because of nerves.

"I want to know what's going on."

He shook his head. "You know as much as I do, Felicia."

"And that's a lie," she responded swiftly. "I want to know what Adam was doing in Mexico, who he went to see and why."

He rubbed the tight muscles in his neck, studying her determined face. "I don't suppose we could postpone this discussion until morning, could we?'' he asked. Her gaze never wavered, and soon he said, ''I guess not. But I'm going up to put on a shirt and some shoes. I suggest you do the same. We might as well be comfortable.''

By the time she'd returned, Dane had coffee made and a fire going in the den. He sat in one of the large overstuffed chairs in front of the fireplace, sipping from a large mug while gazing into the fire.

Felicia poured some of the brew into a cup and joined him in front of the fire.

''Do you think Adam is alive?'' she asked.

Dane's gaze met hers. ''I hope to God he is. If not, I'm responsible for his death.''

There was so little expression in his voice that for a moment she missed the import of his words. When they registered, she almost flinched.

''Go on,'' she finally said.

''I've been working with a government covert operation for years—ever since I was in the service—on the drug problems that have plagued the United States. I became more active about five years ago when drugs seemed to be pouring across the river at an increased rate.'' He paused to sip his coffee. ''Because of my increased absences from the ranch I had to tell Adam what I was doing. I don't suppose anyone can understand why a person would be willing to get involved in tracking down drug smugglers unless he's seen what addiction does to a person. My brother Johnny got involved with drugs and almost died.

''Our group is always understaffed, and when Adam offered to help I wasn't firm enough in my refusal to have him involved. That was four years ago.''

''So you think his disappearance is drug related?''

''There's a strong possibility.''

''Do you know who he was going to see?''

''No. He was following up some leads of his own. We tended to work independently of each other, so he had several contacts down there I knew nothing about. The authorities had a couple of leads to follow, but that call tonight was to let me know they'd turned up nothing so far."

Felicia stared blindly into the fireplace. "I've got to know," she murmured, her voice barely audible.

"Believe me, I can understand your feelings. We'll be the first they notify when anything turns up."

She looked over at Dane. "I'm still going down there," she stated firmly.

The corner of his mouth tilted up slightly. "Now why doesn't that come as a surprise to me?" He stood.

She stood, too, facing him. "I don't care about the danger," she said. "All I care about is finding Adam."

"I know. And I'm going with you."

"I suppose we'd better get some sleep," she said. "It will be light soon."

He nodded. "We'll make plans later this morning."

*

LOOKING OUT the window, Dane studied the sky. The rain had stopped, but the wind was cold and blustery and he didn't look forward to the drive south—partly because he didn't know what they would find. He wished to hell Felicia would change her mind about the trip. She had no idea what they were dealing with and he saw no point in going into graphic detail about what these people did to those they felt had betrayed them.

He hoped she never had reason to find out.

Dane heard Felicia coming down the stairs, and went out to meet her. She wore woolen slacks and a bulky turtleneck that brought out the color of her eyes. Those eyes had haunted him for years.

He helped her with her jacket. Then, shrugging into his own, he picked up her bag.

Stepping outside, they were hit by a strong gust of wind and Felicia staggered under the impact. Dane pulled her into the shelter of his arms, using his body to block the wind. She was breathless by the time she settled into the seat next to him, but tried to convince herself the weather was to blame.

Their trip together was going to be every bit as uncomfortable as she had feared. She shivered.

"Are you cold?"

Felicia looked at him in surprise. "No, why?"

"I saw you shiver."

"Oh. No, I was thinking about Adam."

"I know this is hard on you, Felicia. Just try not to let your imagination run away with you."

"You're right, of course. But it's hard not to think about him. After all, that's why I'm here."

"Oh, I've never had any doubt about that," he said dryly. "You made it clear you were kicking the Texas dust from your feet five years ago when you left."

"I had something to prove—to myself and to you and Adam."

"Oh? What was that?"

"That I could make it on my own."

"Honey, there was never a doubt in our minds that whatever you went after, you'd get."

"Not everything," she murmured.

He smiled. "You were quite a handful back then. I'm surprised Adam and I don't have more gray hair than we do."

"You never seemed to have trouble dealing with me."

"You think not? I distinctly remember a few times that you got the best of me." He shook his head. "There was one time in particular, but I doubt you'd even remember."

"Try me."

"That night I was foolish enough to take you back to my motel room in Austin."

"You would have to bring up the most embarrassing evening of my life," she muttered. *And the most heartbreaking,* she silently added.

"Embarrassing?" he repeated thoughtfully.

"Yes. You made your position quite clear. You didn't intend to waste your time on an inexperienced woman."

"You couldn't be more wrong," he responded. "I wanted

to make love to you that night more than I've ever wanted anything in my life.''

His quiet statement sent an electrical jolt through Felicia. "Then why didn't you?''

"Because one of us needed to hang on to his sanity. I figured that because I'm older, it had to be me.''

"But you were willing enough at first, until you discovered I'd never been with a man before.''

He remembered that moment as though it had just happened. He could almost feel her body pressed against him, taste the warmth of her mouth.

"That brought me to my senses, thank God. I needed something to remind me that seducing you would end up making both of us miserable.''

"How do you figure that?''

"You and I couldn't be more different if we tried, Felicia. We want different things from life. If I'd made love to you that night, we would have been married the next week. There would have been no job in L.A. No chance to spread your wings. You'd still be living at the ranch.''

Remembering the devastation she'd felt that night, Felicia wanted to scream at him that he hadn't understood at all, that nothing would have made her happier than to have married him five years ago. Instead she said lightly, "Surely you don't expect me to believe you offer marriage to every woman you take to bed, Dane. If so, a lot of women must have turned you down over the years.''

"I didn't say that. Besides, there haven't been all that many women.'' *Particularly after you came into my life*, he added silently. "You were different.''

"I know. Inexperienced. Oh, well, that's all in the past now. Five years makes a difference.'' She was thinking about how her perspective had changed. What she had assumed to be Dane's rejection of her had been a reflection of his sense of caring and responsibility. From her new vantage point, she could better understand his concern.

Dane felt a sharp pain in the region of his heart at her words. *Five years makes a difference.* He wondered why her comment should hit him so hard. He had always been aware of Felicia's passionate nature. She threw herself into everything she did with utmost abandon. Lovemaking would be the same way. She had been eager for him to show her that aspect of life. He had known at the time that once he made love to her, he'd never be able to let her go. No doubt she had found other men who weren't quite so primitively possessive.

His decision not to make love to her had been proven right. Too bad he didn't feel better about it. He'd spent many a long, lonely night imagining what would have happened if he hadn't stopped when he did, how she would have responded, how it would have felt to possess her.

There had been a time a couple of years ago when he'd come close to flying out to see her, to confront her with his feelings. But he hadn't.

Now she was back and they were being thrown into a situation of intimacy that he wasn't sure he could handle. Just sharing the car with her, having her nearby so that he caught the scent of her perfume, so close that he could touch her, played havoc with all his good intentions.

After a long day of driving, they found a vacancy at a large motel in Laredo. Their rooms were located on the same floor, down the hall from each other.

Over dinner Felicia tried to draw Dane out. "The drive must have been tiring for you," she offered.

"Why do you say that?"

"You've been so quiet."

He took a swallow of the bourbon and water he'd ordered from the bar, then replied, "I was just now remembering you being so excited to see a motel room because you'd never been in one before."

She chuckled. "Yes, I was very green back then. You must have found me very boring."

"I found you adorable." His quiet statement caused a warm color to flow over her cheeks.

"Hardly that, I'm sure. I was pretty headstrong."

"Was?" he repeated.

She grinned. He seemed to be coming out of his mood. "I

know I used to give you a bad time, Dane, but I didn't know how else to handle the way I felt about you."

He sat back in his chair slightly and studied her. "Was that what your rebellion was all about?"

She smiled. "Most of it."

"Well, the finished product was well worth it. You've turned into a pretty special person."

"Thank you, kind sir."

"I missed you," he said huskily. The tone of his voice and words tugged at her heartstrings.

"Is that why you called and wrote so much?"

"You know me better than that. I never wrote a letter in my life."

"You could have called."

"And said...what? I miss you, please come home?"

Taking courage, Felicia said softly, "If you had, Dane, I would have been home on the next flight."

Dane felt as though a sledgehammer had just hit him. He could only sit and stare at her in silence.

She took a sip of her wine, watching him. Dane looked stunned. Felicia felt a certain amount of satisfaction at having caught him so unaware. Following up on her advantage, she asked him, "Why have you stayed single all these years?" Would he even answer her?

"I think you know," he said after a moment. "You have kept me single."

She tried to think of something light to say.

Dane signaled the waiter to bring him another drink. "You've never had a clue about how I felt about you, have you?"

"I thought I did, when you refused to make love to me that night. I now realize you have some very strong protective instincts where I'm concerned."

"That's true. I loved you too much to take advantage of the situation. Too much to allow you to walk out of my life once I'd made love to you."

"And how do you feel about me now, Dane?" she asked, trying to hide the trembling deep inside her.

"My feelings have never changed."

So now she knew, Felicia thought in wonder. And here they were, once again in a motel together, both consenting adults. What were they going to do about it?

Probably nothing, thanks to Dane's code of honor. But was she ready for anything more? Loving him had become such a habit that she hadn't considered what it would mean to have her love returned.

A light seemed to come on within her at the thought. To have Dane love her in return was a pleasure she needed to grow accustomed to. Knowing he loved her changed her perception of many things.

*

BY NINE O'CLOCK the next morning they were across the border and headed south. The drive to Monterrey along winding mountainous roads was tedious and tiring, but the scenery was breathtaking.

When they arrived, Dane drove to the hotel where Adam had been staying.

The hotel clerk greeted Dane by name and he introduced Felicia as Adam's sister.

"Ah, yes, Senorita St. Clair. We were so sorry to hear about your brother's disappearance." He handed their keys to a young man. "Take their luggage on up, Jaime."

Jaime paused before two doors side by side. He opened each of them with a flourish and Felicia saw the connecting door, invitingly opened, into Dane's room as she walked into her own.

"We shouldn't be disturbed by any street noises here," Dane said, looking out at a patio that resembled a fairyland of tropical flowers and greenery.

"No."

He glanced around. "I don't know about you, but I'm ready to get some sleep."

She nodded. "That's a good idea for both of us, I think. Tomorrow is soon enough to make the rounds."

He looked so tired, and she loved him so much. She walked over to him and slid her arms around his waist. She held him for a moment, needing to feel his warmth.

Slowly he placed his hands on her back, as though his reluctance were being overcome by a compulsive need to touch her. They stood there in silence for several minutes, absorbing each other. Then Felicia went up on tiptoes and kissed him softly. "Good night, Dane. I hope you sleep well." Slowly she pulled away.

His arms tightened around her. "Don't go." His voice sounded harsh.

She knew what he was feeling because she felt it, too. How could she walk away? All the years they had known each other had led to this moment.

She had to let him know that he was more important to her than anything else. She loved him. She was more than willing to show him that love in its most physical form.

With an almost soundless sigh, Felicia put her arms around his neck and kissed him. Dane needed no more encouragement than that.

Their urgency swept them onto the bed. Dane couldn't get enough of the taste of her, giving her long, mind-drugging kisses that reached inside her soul.

His iron self-control had deserted him, and as he tugged her clothes away from her, his mouth found new places to kiss, to touch, to taste.

Felicia felt as though she'd been caught up in a whirlwind of sensation. Everywhere he touched set off electrical charges that set her to quivering.

He paused, his hand brushing against her cheek. "Oh, Felicia. I never meant it to be this way." His ragged breathing stirred her.

"It's okay, Dane. It's okay."

His mouth found hers once again, cutting off her words, and his hands began to memorize her body.

She felt his weight on her, pressing her into the bed, and

she opened herself to him, holding him close as he made his entry.

A sharp pain shot through her, then was gone, to be replaced with a wonderful sense of completion, of wholeness—what she had yearned for all these years.

She brought her thighs tightly around him, locking him into a fierce grasp that urged him to take her with him into the world of sensual satisfaction.

His uncontrolled movement deep within her sparked flames that soon became infernos and Felicia cried out with the sudden riches unfolding before her. It was as if showers of color rained down around them, lighting the room.

And when Dane's arms tightened around her, a sudden spasm of deep contractions shook them both until they were limp.

Dane rolled onto his side, pulling her with him so that she remained firmly clasped in his arms, their legs still intimately entwined.

"I'm so sorry, love," he whispered. "So sorry."

"For what?" she murmured.

"For finally going over the edge…losing control…I didn't mean to."

"I'm glad you did." She reached up and smoothed the line between his brows.

"But it was your first time."

"Yes."

"You should never have been rushed and—"

"It's okay, Dane. Really."

His eyes drooped close. "I haven't slept since you came back," he murmured. "I haven't been able to get you out of my mind since that night I almost made love to you. And, now…" He was asleep.

Felicia lay there, wrapped closely in his arms, and thought about what had just happened.

Dane had finally made love to her. And it had been even more wonderful than she had imagined.

Her eyes shifted shut and she, too, fell asleep.

BRIGHT SUNLIGHT beamed through the windows of the room and Felicia blinked against the glare.

Glancing around, she realized she was in her bed, alone. The door that separated the rooms was closed.

Dane must have brought her in here. She had no recollection of coming to bed. Forcing herself up, she went in and showered, taking her time, trying to come to terms with the adjustments that would have to be made in their relationship.

Dressing carefully, she made sure she looked her best before knocking on the connecting door. She heard Dane's voice.

"It's open."

He sat on the side of his rumpled bed, fully dressed, listening on the phone. "Okay, then give me what you have," he said.

Felicia watched as he took down whatever he was being told. Her eyes were drawn to the bed.

"All right. This will get us started," Dane said. "Felicia wants to put an ad in the paper, offering a reward for information." There was a pause, then he spoke again. "I know. But we've got to get some action. If this is all you've turned up in a week, we're in trouble."

When he hung up he stood and looked at her with an intent gaze. "How are you feeling?"

She smiled. "I'm fine."

"We need to talk about last night, but not now. There's too much to do. But I do want you to know that you don't have to worry about anything. I'll take care of what needs to be done."

What was he talking about? Before she could ask, he said, "Are you ready for breakfast?"

"Yes."

At the table, Dane pulled out the notes he'd made.

"I've been given the name of a man who is one of the best agents in the Mexican operations. He's difficult to trace, but if anyone can help us, it's Alvarez."

"So what do you suggest?"

He looked at her for several long moments. "Felicia," he said finally, "the people I need to contact will not meet me with you along. I must go by myself. I'd feel much better if you'd wait here until I get back."

"How long do you think it will take?"

"I can't predict, but I'll try to get back by midafternoon."

"Isn't there anything I can do? I could at least go to the paper, talk to the police."

He thought for a moment, then nodded. "All right. See what you can find out. But be back here no later than noon, okay?"

"I'll do my best."

He sat studying her. Then with something like resignation he said, "I know you aren't going to like this, but I want us to get married as soon as I can make the arrangements down here."

Surely there had been more romantic proposals.

Felicia merely murmured, "Do you?"

He seemed to relax at her calm response. Taking her hand, he said, "It's the best way I know to protect you at the moment. You said you love me, and I believe that. You know how I feel about you. Under normal circumstances we wouldn't be in such a hurry, but after last night, I don't want to take a chance that you might be pregnant. If anything should happen to me, you'd have the protection of my name."

She studied him gravely. "Are you afraid something is going to happen to you?"

"I'm certainly not counting on it. But we're into something dangerous now. Once we find Adam and get out of here we can have the marriage annulled if you aren't pregnant. You'll be free to go back to L.A. and continue your life there."

"And what will you do?"

"That part doesn't matter. The main thing is, you'll be okay, no matter what happens."

Dane's intent gaze seemed to swallow her. He had always protected her. Why was she surprised at his attitude now? But she didn't need his protection. She wanted his love. *He's giving you that, too,* she reminded herself.

"So what do we do now?" she asked.

He smiled. "Let's go find out how to get married."

Dane knew his way around the city. Within an hour he had

obtained the necessary papers and a local official who promptly married them. Then he whisked her back to the hotel, saying, "I'll see you this afternoon."

Well. The new bride has been escorted to her suite and abandoned. Felicia looked around and realized that they no longer needed two rooms. After informing the front desk, she moved her things in with Dane, made sure the connecting door was locked and headed out.

First, she went to the newspaper office, where she found someone to help her draw up a notice. Then she went to the police station.

After waiting almost half an hour, she was shown into the office of Lieutenant Delgado.

"How may I help you, Senora Rineholt?"

She loved the sound of that name.

"My brother, Adam St. Clair, was staying here in Monterrey last week and he is now missing."

"St. Clair. Yes, I remember. Excuse me." He spoke into the phone in rapid Spanish. Soon after he hung up, a young woman walked in, handed him a file, then left. He studied it in silence. When he looked up, his expression was grave. "Do you know why your brother was here in Mexico?"

"I was told he was here on business."

He glanced down. "Ah, yes. Business. I'm afraid it's a very dangerous business your brother is doing."

"Yes, I know. I found out after he'd disappeared."

"Another agency in our government has taken over the investigation. They will keep us informed, but—" he shrugged "—I don't think I am going to be able to assist you, senora."

Felicia stood up and held out her hand. "I appreciate your courtesy in seeing me, Lieutenant. If any news does turn up, please contact us at our hotel."

"Certainly." His voice was grave and she shivered. He didn't expect to have any news. Not any *good* news.

Felicia hurried back to the hotel. She was so caught up in her thoughts that she didn't see the man until he stepped up beside her.

"Senorita St. Clair?"

Startled, she glanced up. "Yes?" She stared into the man's dark eyes. Without another word he grasped her arm and shoved her into the back seat of a limousine parked at the curb.

The wide seat easily held its three passengers. With as much dignity as possible, Felicia sat between the other two occupants.

She could not remember ever having been so frightened. "Who are you?" she asked, wishing her voice didn't sound so shaky.

"No es importante," was the answer.

It might not be important to you, she thought, *but I'd like to know what's going on.*

"Where are you taking me?"

Her question was greeted with silence.

She looked out the window, trying to get her bearings. The car was moving away from the central part of the city into the residential area. Was it possible she was being taken to Adam? At least she would know he was all right.

The limousine turned into a driveway and waited while a wrought-iron gate opened slowly. Then it followed a winding driveway through trees and around hills, stopping before a house that was so large it seemed to sprawl over several acres.

Her escorts ushered her from the car to a room that was large enough for a football scrimmage, nodded and left, closing the double doors behind them.

"Come in, Senorita St. Clair."

A slight, elderly man rose from a chair behind a majestic desk and strode across the Persian rug.

"Please, won't you sit down?" He motioned to a comfortable chair. "Would you like some coffee, perhaps, or tea?" His face was a deep teak color; his hair, an iron gray. He looked very distinguished.

"Who are you?" she finally managed to say.

"I am Felipe Santiago. I thought, of course, that you would know that, or you would never have accepted my invitation to visit."

"I didn't receive an invitation, Mr. Santiago. Your men forced me into a car and brought me here."

He frowned. "There must be some mistake. Please forgive me. I asked them to deliver a message to your hotel that I would like to speak with you regarding your brother."

"Do you know where Adam is?" she asked eagerly.

"Unfortunately I do not. However, I do know your brother quite well."

"Did you see him on this trip?"

"Yes. We had dinner the first evening he was here."

"Did he tell you where he was going?"

"Not really, but I would not worry about him if I were you, Senorita. I believe he can take care of himself."

"I know. But I've been so worried."

"That is understandable. How long do you intend to stay here in Monterrey, Senorita St. Clair?"

"Actually, my name is Rineholt, Mr. Santiago. My husband and I may stay until we can find Adam."

"Dane Rineholt is your husband?"

She smiled. "Yes. Do you know Dane?"

"No. However, Adam often speaks of him. They are partners, I believe. But he has never mentioned that the two of you are married."

"There was no reason to, I'm sure."

"No," Felipe agreed thoughtfully, "I don't suppose there was." He was silent for several minutes, then, as though coming to a decision, he stood. "Well, I could not have Adam's sister and partner remaining at a hotel. Both of you must stay here while you are in Monterrey."

Felicia also stood. "Oh, no. We can't do that. As a matter of fact, I'm sure Dane is quite worried by now. I was supposed to have met him several hours ago."

"Nonsense. I insist. I will call your husband and have him meet us here for dinner."

"But—"

"Please do not feel you are imposing. I have more than enough room. Come. I will show you."

Felicia slowly followed him, to find him waiting by the

ornate stairway to the second floor. Lightly grasping her elbow, he escorted her up the stairs.

She couldn't decide what to do. He was being polite, yet she felt he was no friend of Adam's, no matter what he had to say.

At the end of the hall, Felipe opened a door and motioned her into an enormous room with windows on two sides. An oversize bed occupied only a small portion of the room, part of which was a sitting room. "It's beautiful," she said.

Felipe nodded graciously. "Thank you. I believe you will be most comfortable here, senora. I'm sure you must be tired. If you would like to rest, feel free."

Did she have a choice? She walked a few steps inside and heard the door close behind her with a distinct click.

Her kind host had just locked her inside the room.

DANE HAD gotten a great deal of information in a few hours. There was no doubt that Adam had been involved in a big drug buy. Playing himself, he had convinced the necessary parties that his position as a rancher was a perfect cover for dealing in large quantities of drugs.

Adam's disappearance could have been caused by several different factions.

Dane would need to follow up some of the leads before he was sure the group he was currently working with hadn't been the ones responsible. He didn't know what he was going to tell Felicia. The news was not good. Since no one had seen or heard from Adam since the day he'd disappeared, chances were good that he had been killed the same day.

Dane opened the door to his room, not too surprised to find it empty. But the other room was empty too, and none of Felicia's things were there.

What the hell?

He called the front desk.

"This is Dane Rineholt. Where is Miss St. Clair?"

"I do not know, sir."

"None of her things are in her room."

"No, sir. She said she would no longer need it."

"I see," he said, and hung up. He should have known. She had been too docile this morning, agreeing to the marriage, then agreeing that he should check on his leads alone.

But where could she be? He went into the bathroom for a drink. Reaching for a glass, he froze. Her toiletries were neatly set out next to his.

He walked back into the bedroom. Her suitcase was behind his. Dane took a deep breath and relaxed. Of course. She had moved into his room. He'd been scared she had left him.

He laughed, the sound loud in the quiet of the room. But where the hell was she?

He paced the floor, wondering whether to go look for her or stay at the hotel.

The sudden ringing of the phone startled him. He grabbed it before it could ring again.

"Rineholt."

"Are you interested in seeing your pretty wife again, senor?" a voice said softly.

Dane's worst fears had just been put into words. He felt as though a giant hand had squeezed his heart. "Yes," he said.

"Then you will follow my instructions."

*

THE DIRECTIONS were detailed and obviously set up to be sure that he was not being followed. When Dane got to the designated area, he pulled up and parked, then switched off his headlights. Checking the time, he realized he was early. Did they intend to bring her to him?

A car approached slowly. When it was even with his car, it stopped and the window was rolled down.

"Dane Rineholt?"

"Yes."

The back door opened. "Get in."

He didn't need a second invitation.

The car seemed to get lost in a maze of streets, finally turning into a curving driveway. He noted that wrought-iron gates closed behind them as soon as they passed.

Dane was escorted inside a white adobe villa and left in a wide hallway with a curving staircase. Was Felicia here?

A young man in dark pants and a white coat appeared, carrying a large tray of food.

"Senor Rineholt?"

"Yes."

"Follow me, please."

Dane followed him up the staircase. "Whose home is this?"

"Senor Santiago's, senor."

Dane had never heard the name.

The man paused at the end of the hallway, shifted the tray to his shoulder and unlocked the door. "Your room, senor," he said.

Felicia stood by a far window, looking out.

"Felicia!"

"Oh, Dane!" She threw herself into his arms, and he held her as though he never intended to let her go. Neither of them heard the door close behind the young man.

Cupping her face in his hands, Dane let his eyes wander over it. Then his mouth found hers in a searing kiss that left them both shaken.

"Dear God!" Dane managed to mutter in a husky voice. "I've never been so scared in my life. Are you all right?" he asked with concern, brushing a wisp of hair off her forehead.

She nodded. "Now that you're here."

He glanced around the room, then back at her. "How did you get here, anyway?"

"I was on my way back to the hotel when a man called my name, then pushed me into a car. When I arrived, Felipe Santiago introduced himself as a friend of Adam's. Then he started asking me about his disappearance."

"Did he say why he kept you here?"

"No. But when I told him we were married, he insisted we stay here with him."

"Did you tell him how long we'd been married?"

"No. Something gave me the feeling that our being married didn't fit in with his plans."

"I hope that works in our favor," Dane said, bringing her fingers to his lips, where he slowly kissed the tip of each one. "So far the marriage hasn't been much of a protection for you."

"It has if that's the reason you're here," she responded. "How did you know where to find me?"

"I didn't. I got a phone call."

"Did you find out anything about Adam?" Felicia asked.

"Nothing encouraging, I'm afraid."

"What do you mean?"

"I mean that as soon as we can get away from here, we need to get back across the border fast."

"Dane! Does that mean…?"

"There's no way to know, Felicia. But our being in Mexico isn't helping anything. We've stumbled into a real mess and I want you out of here."

He walked over to the window. "What were you watching earlier?"

"The dogs. I saw three of them. Dobermans."

"I had a hunch they wouldn't be Chihuahuas. So even if we get out of this room, we still have to get off the property in one piece."

Felicia joined him at the window. "I don't think Santiago intends to hurt us, Dane. He seems to be trying to find out how much we know about Adam being down here."

Dane pulled her next to him and she rested against his long length. "Other than the locked door, he's treated me with courtesy. He invited me downstairs for dinner, but I told him I wasn't feeling well, so he had dinner sent up."

Dane glanced over at the table. "Shall we eat?"

Felicia's gaze followed his. "I'm not all that hungry, are you?"

He shook his head. "But I could use a shower. Is there one available?"

Felicia smiled. "Oh, yes. We have all the conveniences of

home.'' She walked over and opened a door, revealing a luxurious bathroom with a large shower stall and tub.

Dane needed no more encouragement. He disappeared into the other room and turned on the water.

Felicia walked over and looked at the tray of food. Then she glanced over her shoulder toward the bathroom.

Succumbing to impulse, she stepped out of her clothes and wrapped a towel around herself like a sarong. Then she walked into the bathroom and opened the shower door.

Dane glanced around, startled, then grinned as she dropped the towel and closed the door behind her.

''I got lonesome,'' she explained solemnly as she began to soap his back.

''I understand the feeling.'' He smiled. Turning around, he took the soap from her and began to lather her body lovingly, from neck to thighs, with a gentle touch that soon had her trembling.

The warm water smoothed the lather away, leaving them both glistening with moisture. Dane's gaze seemed to burn her skin wherever it touched. Without taking his eyes off her or saying a word, he reached over and turned off the water.

Opening the shower door, Dane stepped out, picked up her towel and began to dry her. She stood there before him, already aroused by his touch, and watched him as he dried himself. Then he carried her into the other room.

When Dane reached the bed he stood her on her feet and smiled. ''This time I intend to do this right.'' He pulled the covers down to the foot of the bed. Then he picked her up and placed her in the center.

''This is our wedding night, you know,'' Felicia murmured.

''I'm very much aware of that fact,'' he replied. He propped himself up on one elbow beside her, studying her expression, and she smiled—a slow, tantalizing smile that increased the beat of his already racing heart. Dane placed his hand on her cheek and stroked it lightly with his finger, then began to trace a trail along her body, circling her breasts, then her navel, moving down to the short curls below her abdomen.

She reached out and caressed his chest, then slowly let her

fingers slide down until they touched his aroused masculinity. Felicia heard him catch his breath and smiled.

As though he could no longer tolerate what she was making him feel, he held her against him as he rolled over onto his back, so that her body blanketed him. "Oh, Felicia. I'll never get enough of you—your touch, your presence or your love in my life," he murmured, hungrily searching for her mouth.

Their slow, relaxed lovemaking escalated into a fiery need. Dane's hands wrapped around her waist in a firm grip and he lifted her slightly, fitting her to him, before surging upward, deep inside her.

Felicia almost cried out with the wonder of his aggressive possession. He felt so good to her, strong and hard, and she luxuriated in the feeling that they belonged together. They had waited so many years for this magic, but it had been worth the wait.

She could hold her own with this man now. They were equals. At the moment she enjoyed the sense of being in control, even if for a few moments, as she set a pace for them in the ancient ritual of lovemaking.

Dane could take only so much before he pulled her down to his chest and hung on to her while he rolled over, placing her beneath him. She smiled up at him, noticing the tiny furrow between his brow, the slight dampness of his face, his look of concentration that caused her to lose what little control she'd salvaged.

She clamped her thighs tighter around his hips, meeting each of his movements with one of her own. Then she was lost to everything but sensation. She felt as though she were in the midst of a celestial collision, with thousands of stars spinning out of control.

Dane's final lunge seemed to carry them away from earth's gravity, causing them to drift in utter contentment before falling into an exhausted sleep.

Yet during the night Dane reached for her again and again, to touch her hand and feel the ring on her finger, to stroke her breast, to kiss her slightly swollen lips and to ignite the flame within her once again.

WHEN DANE woke up the next morning, he glanced around the large, airy room, then saw Felicia sound asleep a few inches away.

God, how he loved her! And he was going to do everything he could to protect her. Moving carefully so as not to wake her, he crawled out of bed. After a quick shower he put on the clothes he'd worn the day before.

He decided to try the door, and discovered that it wasn't locked, so he went in search of his host. From the dining-room doorway, he watched as a gray-haired man stood up at the table and said, "Good morning, Senor Rineholt. I trust you slept well. Won't you join me for breakfast?"

Was this affable man the same one who had abducted Felicia and spirited him to his home?

Felipe poured another cup of coffee and set it at the place to his left. "My name is Felipe Santiago. I happen to be an old friend of Adam St. Clair's."

"So Felicia said. He's never mentioned your name."

"Is that so? I'm surprised. He often speaks of you."

Dane took a sip of the coffee. It was excellent. "Look, would you mind telling me what's going on?"

Felipe's face sobered. "Senor Rineholt. You and your wife have no business down here at the moment. In my own way I have tried to protect you. You are asking questions in places where the answers are fatal. Rather than try to reason with you, I chose to bring you here."

"Do you know where Adam is?"

"No. But I have reason to believe that he is dead."

Hearing the words spoken with such certainty was like a blow. "Did you kill him?" Dane managed to ask.

"Of course not. We were doing business together. Working with Adam, I stood to make a great deal of money. I am afraid someone caught a scent of that money."

Dane realized that Santiago didn't know Adam was an agent, which meant that he must be a dealer. How ironic that they should get protection from him.

"What makes you believe Adam is dead?" Dane asked.

"Otherwise he would have contacted me. I feel certain that

he was double-crossed by someone he trusted—someone, perhaps, we both trusted.''

"Where does that leave you?"

"Without a means to sell what I am holding, but I have
other avenues to pursue, as you well know.''

"What do you mean?"

"I know who you are, Senor Rineholt. Your name keeps
coming up whenever I am looking for another distribution
source. I thought perhaps we could talk business while you
are visiting with me.''

"I wouldn't mind if my wife weren't here. She knows nothing about all this, and I want to keep her out of it.''

"I don't understand why you brought her.''

"She wanted to find her brother.''

"She won't find him.''

"I believe you. So I intend to take her home.''

"You're a very intelligent man, Senor Rineholt.''

Dane held the other man's gaze. "If you'll help me get back
to the hotel, we'll be headed for the border by noon.''

Felipe nodded. "If you will give me your car keys, I will
have the car delivered to the hotel. And my car will be available at your convenience.''

Dane stood up. "Thank you. I appreciate your concern for
our safety. Other than that initial scare, we've had a very
pleasant stay with you.''

WHEN THEY walked across the lobby the clerk motioned to
them. Dane guided Felicia over to the desk.

"Your car keys were delivered a few moments ago, Senor
Rineholt. Your car has been serviced for you.''

"Thank you.'' He dropped the keys into his pants pocket.

When he unlocked the door of their room, he pushed it open
and allowed Felicia to pass him, then stepped in and closed
it. Their suitcases were where they had left them. Dane figured
that as soon as they packed their toiletries they would be on
their way.

He heard Felicia gasp, and spun around. In the far corner
of the room sat a dark-haired man.

"I understand you have been looking for me," the stranger said. "My name is Alvarez."

The drapes had been closed and he sat in shadows.

"How long have you been here?" Dane asked.

"It doesn't matter." He looked at Felicia. "You are Adam St. Clair's sister?"

"Yes. Do you know where he is?" she asked.

Alvarez slowly shook his head. "He was scheduled to meet a man who was hiding in the mountains, and who had the proof we needed to nail the person who controls the drug route in this area."

"Felipe Santiago," Dane said.

Alvarez straightened in his chair. "You know him?"

"We've just spent the night as his guests."

"How did you meet him?"

"He found us," Dane replied. "But what about this man Adam was supposed to meet?"

"We can't find him. But we did find Adam's car."

Felicia jumped up. "Where?"

"In the mountains. It had been pushed over the side, but there was enough left to identify it."

"Was there any sign of Adam?" Dane asked.

"No."

The three sat in silence for several minutes. Finally Alvarez spoke. "What do you intend to do now?"

"I'm taking Felicia back home."

"That's a good idea. At present we are still searching for the man Adam hoped to contact. If we can find him, we may still be able to accomplish what Adam set out to do."

The two men looked at each other, silently communicating. Dane held out his hand. "Thank you for coming. I know how dangerous this has been for you."

"I'm sorry there isn't more." Alvarez stepped behind the drapes and they heard the window being raised. "Good luck," he said in a low voice.

"You, too," Dane responded.

"Is this yours?" Felicia asked, as Dane turned around. She held an envelope. "It was lying here by the phone."

"Maybe one of the maids put it there."

Felicia opened it, and when a slip of paper and a photo fell out, she leaned over to pick them up.

Her sudden cry seemed to pierce him. He strode to her side just as her legs gave way. She had fainted.

Carefully placing her on the bed, Dane picked up the contents of the envelope.

The note contained two words: "Go home." The photo told its own story. A body lay in a crumpled heap on a mountain road near a car. He recognized the car. He also recognized the body.

It was Adam.

*

WARM APRIL sunshine flooded the Texas countryside. Spring showers had turned the grass and trees a vibrant green. Everywhere she looked Felicia saw signs of growth and rebirth.

She felt as though she had been through a long, serious illness and was only now beginning to heal. Her grief for Adam had been an illness of sorts and she wondered if it would ever completely go away.

Sitting down in the porch swing, she gave a slight push that started it swaying gently. Felicia had learned a great deal about life in the past two months.

She barely remembered the long trip home from Monterrey. Felicia had cried until there had been no tears left. By the time of the memorial service she had escaped to the numbness that had protected her from more pain than she could handle.

The official word was that Adam had been killed in an automobile accident. No one needed to know why he had been willing to risk his life.

Thanks to men like Alvarez and Lieutenant Delgado, Adam hadn't died in vain. Working together, they had pieced together his last few days. Santiago had been correct—Adam had been double-crossed. The authorities found the man he had gone to meet, and enough evidence to have Felipe Santiago arrested without ever revealing Adam's part in the investigation.

Adam would have been pleased.

DANE SAT on a stone outcrop that overlooked the river and the ranch, staring out at the surrounding hills. He'd gotten into the habit of coming up here, trying to come to terms with all that had happened.

Adam was gone. He could no longer hide from that fact. Dane had thought he was prepared for the possibility, but seeing the photograph had shown him differently—particularly when he knew that if he himself hadn't been involved, Adam would not have been.

Dane also blamed himself for pushing Felicia into a hasty marriage. He hadn't been fair to either one of them. With Adam gone, Dane had to stay on the ranch, but he had promised Felicia that they would work out something regarding her career and his. The only solution he could come up with was to let her return to California without him, and he wasn't sure how he'd be able to deal with the separation. Dane glanced at his watch. It was almost noon.

DANE'S TRUCK bounced up the driveway and came to a stop in front of the house. Felicia's heart began to beat faster at the sight of him.

Dane stood in the kitchen doorway and watched Felicia as she brought a large pitcher of tea from the refrigerator. "Are you ready to eat?" she asked.

Dane nodded and went down the hallway to the bathroom.

When he returned to the kitchen he picked up a serving dish and began to fill his plate.

They ate in silence, each rehearsing what they wanted to say to the other. Felicia cleared their places and served peach cobbler and coffee before sitting down again.

"Felicia? I, uh, was just going to ask if you'd talked to your boss lately."

Here it comes, Felicia thought sadly. "No, I haven't, but I need to."

"I suppose you've extended your leave about as long as you can, haven't you?"

"I suppose so," she murmured.

"So what are your plans?"

She stared at him helplessly. "What do you want me to do, Dane?"

Dane threw down his napkin. "Damn it, Felicia, you're not being fair. I want you to be happy. I know your job's important to you—"

"Not as important as you are, Dane. I can always find another job. A husband is a different matter."

"Are you saying you want to stay here—with me?"

"If you want me."

He got up so quickly his chair fell over. He was beside her in two strides. "Of course I want you. I've always wanted you." He lifted her in his arms and started up the stairs.

"You didn't finish your dessert," Felicia managed.

"The peach cobbler can wait. I've got other plans for dessert."

Dane carried her into his room and lowered her onto the bed, then stood there watching her while he unfastened his shirt. He wasted no time in ridding himself of the rest of his clothing and joining her on the bed. With practiced ease he began to remove her clothing.

"Dane, I think we need to talk."

"Talk," he replied, and removed her remaining garments.

"Are you sure you want to...I mean...are we even legally married?"

He stopped abruptly and looked down at her. "Would you rather not be married to me?"

She brushed her hand against his chest. "I want very much to be married to you."

"That's good to know," he growled softly, "because the marriage was quite legal." He lowered his head until his lips touched hers. His kiss was warm and possessive, as his tongue traced first her top lip, then her bottom lip, before plunging into her mouth. She shifted restlessly and he caught her thigh between his, clamping it firmly so that she could feel him pushing against her.

He began to kiss her from her nose to her knees—soft kisses, nipping kisses—touching her with an expertise that drove her wild. Then he started a path of kisses that began on the inside of her knee and continued up her inner thigh.

"Oh, Dane, please don't do this to me…"

His touch was like setting off a charge of dynamite inside her and just when she thought she could no longer stand it, Dane lifted himself higher and buried himself deep inside her.

Her arms and legs wrapped around him, holding him to her in a convulsive grip as Dane set the pace, never losing control.

The fire deep inside her raged, then exploded with a cascade of sparks that caused her body to release all its tension. Then the white hot flames turned into soothing tongues of tranquility.

Dane felt her body explode and he could no longer control his reaction. He quivered with the force of his excitement as he felt first the heat of the fire, then the soothing coolness of the aftermath of their passion.

They lay there in a tangle of sheets, their overheated bodies damp with perspiration.

After a few minutes Dane said quietly, "Are you sure you want to give up your job?"

Felicia turned her head on the pillow. "I'm sure."

"Won't you be bored staying at home?"

"I don't think so. I intend to try writing a book, and besides, I'm going to have quite enough to keep me occupied, since we didn't waste any time getting started on our family…"

"What?" Dane jackknifed into a sitting position. "Do you mean…?"

She nodded. "I mean just what you think. I had my suspicions, so I had some tests run. They called with the results this morning."

He grinned. "I'm delighted about our baby." He gave her a long and very possessive kiss.

"I love you," she told him when he straightened slightly.

"I love you, too."

The ringing of the phone was an unwelcome intrusion. She stirred, reluctant to move away from him. He said, "Let it ring. Whoever it is will call back."

"I can't do that. It drives me crazy not to know who's calling." She reached for the phone.

"Felicia? Is that you? What are you doing at the ranch?"

Felicia felt as though she were going to faint. The voice on the phone couldn't be—

"*Adam!* Is this Adam?"

She heard his laugh, Adam's special laugh that no one could possibly duplicate. "You bet it's Adam. Where is Dane? I need to talk to him."

"Dane's right here. Where are you?"

"I'm in Del Rio, trying to get home. I'm a little short on transportation, and having trouble proving my identity. I don't have any papers on me."

"Oh, God, Adam, you're alive," Felicia said, tears pouring down her cheeks.

"Adam! Is it really you?" Dane said, taking the phone.

"You'd better believe it's me, although everyone around here keeps telling me I'm dead."

"Don't let a little thing like that upset you now. Where the hell are you?"

"Del Rio. I got as far as the border and was taken into custody, which is a laugh, isn't it? How about coming down here and bailing me out?"

"There's nothing I'd rather do, partner. We'll be there as soon as we can get there."

"What's Felicia doing in Texas?"

"That's another story. We'll have time to fill each other in once we get you home."

A WEEK went by before Adam felt like doing much more than eating and sleeping. His body demanded recuperation time. Dane kept busy on the ranch and Felicia tried to keep herself occupied, but it was hard. She would find herself tiptoeing upstairs to make sure Adam was all right.

He caught her doing that one day. "I feel like a fool, lying in bed and letting Dane do all the work around here."

"Don't worry about it. As soon as you're on your feet, Dane and I will take off on that honeymoon we never had and let you run things for a while, okay?"

"Sounds good to me. God, it's good to have you back home, sis."

"That's exactly what I was thinking about you."

"Do you miss your job in L.A.?"

"Not like I thought I would. Besides, I'm with Dane."

"I always thought you put up quite a front where your feelings for Dane were concerned."

"I would probably never have given in to them if you hadn't gone missing. I flew home to find you." She grinned at him for a moment. "What happened, Adam?"

"It's a long story. One of these days I'll sit down and tell the details to both of you. But the important thing is that I made it to hell and back."

"At least you don't have any reason to return."

He lay there looking at her in silence for a while. "A baby, huh?"

"Yep."

"That's just like you. Jump in and start a family first thing. You always were headstrong."

"Dane is rapidly taming me, believe me."

"Good for Dane." He grew thoughtful. "You never know why things happen the way they do. I believe you and Dane have discovered what I learned during the past two months. Loving someone and sharing your life with a person can add a powerful dimension to your existence."

"You talk as though you've discovered what love can do."

"I have. I've always known how I felt about the two of you, but I need to tell you that I'm going back to Mexico when I'm fully recovered. There's someone there who not only saved my life, but my soul and my sanity. I told her I was coming back for her—and I'm going."

"She sounds pretty special."

Dane suddenly appeared at the doorway. "Just as I suspected. Here you are entertaining my wife in your bedroom again. We'll have to have a talk.''

Felicia walked over to him and going up on tiptoe, she kissed him, her heart overflowing with love.

''I don't think you'll ever have to worry, cowboy. I've got my hands full trying to take care of you.''

Dane hugged her to him, then looked over at Adam, who exchanged a glance of silent communication.

The St. Clair ranch was back in full operation—everyone was home.

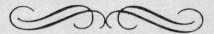

EVERYTHING BUT TIME

Mary Lynn Baxter

The door chimes pealed loudly and insistently.

"Damn," Danielle Davis muttered under her breath. Seven o'clock. It was much too early in the morning for a casual visitor and much too early for bookstore customers, she thought, fighting back the twinge of fear that twisted through her like a dull knife.

She pivoted on her heels and rushed out of the room. She had just stepped on the top step of the carpeted staircase when a chirpy voice called up to her.

"I'm up, I'll see to the door."

Thank goodness for Jusie, Danielle thought as she turned away from the stairs and poked her head around the door on the right. If it weren't for Justine Evans, who was both friend and housekeeper and at times guardian angel all rolled into one, Danielle would not be able to survive, much less work, in her bookstore full-time or teach night classes at the university.

Danielle tiptoed across the room and peered down at her two-and-a-half-year-old daughter, Ann, who was sleeping dead to the world.

Tears burned the back of her eyes as she took in the long, thick eyelashes that fanned over deep green eyes, complementing a silky mop of black curls. If only she weren't her father made over.... No! Don't think like that, she berated herself. Don't think about *him!*

Sighing deeply, she leaned over and grazed Ann's cheek with her lips before hurriedly exiting the room.

She met Jusie at the head of the stairs.

Her housekeeper's almond-shaped brown eyes were pensive and a frown wrinkled her forehead. "There's a man to see you. If I didn't know better, I'd say he looks like he's one of those FBI agents or Internal Revenue dudes," she whispered.

Danielle tried to smile, but it was impossible; her lips were too stiff. Why now? After all this time.

For the past three years, Danielle's life had settled into pattern. She loved her work, owning and managing a small but lucrative bookstore in the quaint East Texas town of Nacogdoches. Adding to her pleasure was the convenience of having her business in the same building as her home. It was an ideal setup, allowing her to be close to Ann while she worked.

To Danielle, creating a home filled with love and security for her daughter and herself was the most important thing in life. Having been reared in an orphanage, she'd had a hard life. She had learned at an early age that she could count on no one but herself.

Smoothing her hands down her corduroy skirt, she breathed deeply and began a slow but determined descent down the stairs. Without hesitation, she twisted the knob and opened the door that screened the stairs leading up to her private apartment. For once she did not pause to glance at the racks of paperback and hardcover books. She marched through the maze as though someone had a gun pointed to her head.

The door to her office was open. She paused long enough on the threshold to view the tall stranger standing in front of the bookshelves decorating one complete wall of her office. He was casually thumbing through the pages of a book when he looked up and saw her standing in the doorway.

"Good morning, Ms. Davis. I'm Tony Welch from the U.S. Marshal Service."

Danielle had to squelch the urge to turn and run. But somehow she managed to stand reed straight.

"Does it always get this cold in East Texas?" He smiled, obviously trying to put Danielle at ease. "It's a helluva lot colder here than it is in D.C. The minute I stepped off the plane, the chill cut clear through to my bones."

Suddenly she could not wait another second to find out why this man had intruded upon her life. "Mr. Welch, I'm sure you didn't come all this way just to discuss the weather. So if you don't mind—" She halted in midsentence.

Suddenly Tony Welch hated himself and his job for having

to bring more pain down on those fragile shoulders. But he had to do it. If not him, someone else....

"You're right," he said gruffly. "You're needed in Washington. Immediately." He tried to ignore the way she flinched as though he'd struck her. "I'm here to take you back with me."

"Why?" The simple word was barely audible.

"The Russian agent that has escaped the FBI's clutches for the last three years is finally in custody." He paused and eyed her closely. "Or at least we think he is. You're the only one who can identify him."

Her legs felt as though they were made of jelly. She felt herself begin to slowly unravel on the inside, a feeling she had hoped never to experience again. When the government had taken over her life three years ago, it had done so with a swift precision. But then they had disappeared, leaving her to live a normal life. Fool that she was, she had begun to think that she would never hear from them again....

How could she possibly endure returning to the place that had brought her so much heartache? But then she bitterly reminded herself that she had no say in the matter. The die had been cast a long time ago.

MARSHAL Luke Cassidy's office was on the fourth floor of the district court building. When she entered his office, he hastily circled the desk, his hand held out to her.

"Good afternoon, Ms. Davis. Have a seat, won't you? I've never been one to beat around the bush, so I'll speak bluntly." He sat down and then leaned forward, looking at her, a hard glint reflected in his eyes. "Unfortunately there's been a change in plans."

For a moment Danielle's eyes brightened. Dare she hope that this ordeal would be over before it had even begun?

"The Russian agent is no longer in FBI custody." His mouth had tightened into a bitter line.

She lifted a hand to her throat. "Where...where does this leave me?"

"There's more," he continued bluntly. "We have strong

reason to believe that your cover has been blown, that the agent and his counterpart can identify you.''

Danielle's bag clattered to the floor.

"I'm sorry," he said. "It's a damned mess."

"It can't be true," she whispered.

"I've got the proof right here—in this folder." He picked up the manila envelope and slapped it against his leg before pitching it back on his desk. "But we know that Letsukov is still in the D.C. area. We've launched a full-scale manhunt for him and his partner, Zoya." His eyes glistened dangerously.

"Oh, my God," Danielle whispered, sinking forward, as the blinding tears came with a rush. "What about my daughter? Is—is she in danger, too?"

"We're sending a deputy marshal to stay with your child and housekeeper until this mess is cleared up."

In spite of Danielle's effort to hold her chin steady, it began to wobble again uncontrollably. "Please...can't I just go home?"

Cassidy acted as though she hadn't spoken. "Our top man is on his way up. You'll be under his protective custody in a retreat in the mountains of Virginia while the FBI is combing the area." He paused, the insistent knock on the door claiming his attention.

"Come in," he bellowed.

Danielle heard the door open but didn't turn around.

"Dammit, Cassidy, I told you to get someone else for this assignment!"

It had been over three years since she'd last heard that voice. Oh, God, no! It couldn't be.

She turned around, positive that her exhausted mind had failed her. But it hadn't. Eyes that were the exact replica of her daughter's stared back at her.

Then his harsh words effectively sliced the silence.

"Dammit to hell, Cassidy, what kind of game are you playing? This woman's not Danielle Davis, she's Erin Richards!"

Keir McBride's rise in the ranks of the U.S. Marshal Service had been swift and sure. He had gained the reputation of being tough as nails and always in charge. But the sight of this woman was almost his undoing.

Her hair was the same. Its fine silvery strands had always reminded him of trapped moonlight and still did. And the graceful lines of her slender body were unmistakable, the way her blouse outlined the gentle curves of her breasts....

Oh, God, why now? he groaned silently. When he had discovered that she was missing three years ago, he had hired the best private detective in the area to track her down. Nothing. She had vanished as though the earth had opened up and swallowed her, leaving a dead silence and a hole in his heart as big as the Grand Canyon. Damn her to hell!

"McBride, sit down," Luke Cassidy barked, effectively cutting into the heavy silence. "If you'd read her damned file, you'd know what was going on." Then his eyes narrowed shrewdly. "I won't take the time to find out how you two knew each other. That's not important now. But what *is* important is getting Ms. Davis out of the Washington area."

By sheer force of will Keir removed his eyes from Danielle's face. "Who the hell had a chance to look at a file? I was told to report immediately. I was given the bare facts and nothing more. If you'll remember correctly, you promised me two weeks off." He paused. "And if you'll also remember, I was to have gotten married this week."

Cassidy actually looked disconcerted. "Er...sorry about that, but I promise I'll make it up to you and Natalie when we have that Russian bastard back in our clutches."

Danielle could not head off the horrified moan that escaped through her trembling lips. Questions with no answers began swirling around in her head, making her feel dizzy and disoriented. Surely Keir McBride, the rich playboy and the only son of a renowned senator, could not be a U.S. Marshal? It was ludicrous! Unbelievable!

She had reconciled long ago that she would never lay eyes on this man again. After all, wasn't she a totally new person with a new name, a new life, a new identity? The vision of Ann's tiny face leapt in front of her face. *Oh, God,* she thought in silent agony, the baby. *Their baby!* The only good that had come out of their affair was the perfect child they had created. She was blinded by sheer mindless terror. What would Keir do if he ever found out about Ann? He must never know....

Keir swung on his heels, his eyes zeroing in on his superior. "Replace me, Luke," he clipped savagely. "Get someone else to take care of Er—I mean..."

"Dammit, man," Cassidy growled, "her name's Danielle. Danielle Davis. Don't forget that again. Surely I don't have to remind you how dangerous a slip like that could be?" Luke Cassidy's eyes narrowed as they bounced back and forth between Danielle's pale figure and Keir's grim, unyielding one. "I don't know what the hell's going on with you two. And furthermore, I don't give a damn. But what I do give a damn about is Ms. Davis's safety." His eyes shifted to Keir. "You're the best man for the job. It's that simple. And I have to think I can depend on you to put personal feelings aside and do what you've been trained to do." He paused. "I'm afraid you two are stuck with each other."

*

SHE WAS sitting beside Keir in a blue unmarked Chevrolet on their way to the undisclosed destination in the mountains of Virginia. They had gotten off later than planned, but they'd had to wait for Cassidy's secretary to go shopping and buy Danielle several more articles of clothing. Also Keir had had to make arrangements for the heat to be turned on in the cabin and food to be delivered. She was aware of him with every fiber of her being.

She shuddered just thinking about the moment in Cassidy's office when Keir had walked into the room. How she had managed to hold herself together was beyond her. Even now she could still hear the violent curses that had followed her out the door and into the adjacent room where she had phoned Jusie and explained her change of plans.

Jusie had been upset, but had assured Danielle that everything would be fine, that Ann was fine but missed her mommy. Having to explain the presence of a U.S. Marshal invading their home had been a different matter altogether. Finally, she convinced Jusie that it was just a precaution and nothing more. And she had prayed that it was true.

With a sigh, she sat forward and began pulling off her coat. It was stifling in the small car. Suddenly a hand shot out behind her and latched onto the collar of her coat while she struggled out of it. She kept her gaze averted, but she felt rather than saw him flinch as his arm grazed her breast.

She had a ridiculous impulse to burst into tears; it was like a nightmare. It couldn't be happening to her. For she had known the minute she saw him, even after three long years, that she had never gotten him out of her system.

A brittle silence settled between them. Against her better judgment, she ventured a look in his direction. The grooves around his mouth were deeply carved, meant to endure. But the strong defiant chin, square jaw, the black unruly hair now interwoven with silver threads were unchanged. And those same startling green eyes still had the power to drive through her, straight to her soul.

"Why didn't you come and ask me for help?"

Danielle was shocked by his unexpected and startling question. She answered before she thought.

"How could I?" she choked. "You were off on another of your jaunts, taking care of, and I quote, 'important business.'" She made no effort to mask the sarcasm that punctuated each word she flung at him.

Keir sighed deeply. He rubbed his hand wearily across the back of his head. "I only know what Tanner told me when he summoned me to Cassidy's office this morning, and that wasn't much, just the hard cold facts, and he showed me pictures of the Russian agents."

"Oh, Keir, I don't know," she said. "I...I still have terrible dreams, awful nightmares about that horrible day." She twisted her hands together. Her tongue felt weighted with lead. "I...I had decided to stay and work late," she began, her voice low and shaky, "the night after you...you stormed out of my apartment."

She kept her head averted, not wanting to see the dark cloud that she knew would have settled over his face at the mention of that night. "I...I was on my way to the office of my boss, John Elsworth, to get a file. I heard muffled voices. I was about to knock and let my presence be known when I heard Mr. Elsworth say, 'This highly classified information was just sent over this morning. It's hot stuff and your government had better be willing to pay through the nose for it.' I must have gasped, because both men whirled around and saw me. The...the last thing I remember before turning and tearing back down the hall was the murderous glint in both their eyes."

She paused again, this time to try to control the violent tremor that was racking her body. She sucked her breath deep into her lungs.

"I don't remember ever having been so frightened in my life—*except when I was having your child all alone,*' a hyper little voice inside her head whispered—as I was when I grabbed my purse and raced out of the building only minutes ahead of Elsworth. I jumped into the nearest taxi and told the driver to take me to an out-of-the-way motel. There I registered under a fake name and bolted myself in the room."

She paused a brief second and worried her bottom lip with her teeth. "Every time I heard the slightest noise, I just knew it was Elsworth coming after me. The next morning I went straight to the FBI's office without returning to my apartment. Elsworth had been under surveillance for months on suspicion of selling high technology secrets and endangering the security of the United States. My secret testimony to the grand jury would have put both him and the Russian agent, Letsukov, behind bars for life.

"However, the Russian managed to elude the FBI and suddenly my life was in immediate danger. After that, it was a living hell." For a moment her voice faltered. She pressed her knees together to stop their shaking. "I decided to cooperate with the FBI and the U.S. Marshal's office, agreeing to disappear with a new identity—a new name, a new job and a new place to live.''

"God, Erin…''

"Don't call me that,'' she hissed, swinging around to face him.

"Old habits die hard,'' he said harshly. "Why didn't you call me?''

She laughed without mirth. "It was over between us, remember? You had slammed out of my apartment the night before.''

"Only because you all but kicked me out.'' His jaw was clenched to the breaking point. "God, you have no idea what my life was like when you disappeared. I called you the moment I got back to the States.'' He ignored her whimpered cry and went on, "When the detective I hired was unsuccessful in tracking you down, I chucked everything and went to work full-time for the government as a U.S. Marshal doing undercover work.''

"What do you mean, full-time?'' she asked, unable to mask her astonishment.

"The times I pulled my disappearing act, as you called it, I was on special assignment for the government.''

Oh, God, she had thought there might be another woman. And for one crazy moment, she had wondered if he was in trouble with the law. But a spy. Never.

"What good is dredging up the past? All we're doing is making matters worse.''

If only things could have been different, she agonized silently. If only she hadn't overheard that conversation that had changed her life so completely. If only she had known he had called her that fateful day. If only he wasn't getting married. If only she wasn't harboring the secret of having borne his child. If only…if only….

THE SNOW was coming down thicker and faster now. It took all of Keir's concentration to keep the car on the slick road. The miles from D.C. to his cabin stretched interminably. Not only were the close confines of the car hard to endure, but coupled with the presence of Er...no, dammit, he reminded himself brutally, Danielle.

He turned and looked at her. So soft and pale and lovely, he thought. Was she asleep? Or was she feigning sleep in order to mask her own chaotic emotions?

He forced his eyes back on the winding road. Suddenly his mind became a wilderness of memories and impressions. God help him, but he still could not think of her as Danielle. When he had first met her she had been Erin....

He remembered his father's party as though it had been yesterday. It had been a bore. Too many people crowded into several small rooms.

He ate absently, his eyes moving over the faces—some overly animated, others empty—before coming to rest on a woman in a black dress in the far corner of the room by the door. She stood listening to a tall, earnest-looking man. Every so often her eyes left the face of the man and searched space for an exit she might discreetly slip through.

She looked soft, Keir thought. Her hair was a fine silvery color, swept away from her face, flattering and emphasizing her exquisite features. She was perfect, Keir decided. He felt less isolated now, having someone to focus on.

The effects of his meeting with his father earlier in the day still clouded his mood. His father, glowering at him from under bushy gray eyebrows, saying, "You're thirty-five. Don't you think it's about time you settled down and quit hopping the globe and got a real job? Dammit, I want to retire, and I want you to take my place in the senate chamber."

Keir's temper was still boiling just thinking about that conversation. It made him furious to think that his father thought he never did an honest day's work in his life. His air-cargo business netted over two million dollars a year. And he enjoyed being the free spirit that he was. His job allowed him to travel all over the world. But more important, it served as a cover so that he could adequately perform his special assignments for the government. A fancy word for spying, he added with a grim twist to his lips. But he could not tell Raymond McBride about these top-secret assignments. He could tell no one.

He shuddered. Why the hell had he given in and come to this party, anyway?

He carelessly thrust aside his empty plate, and when he shifted his gaze, the woman's eyes were on him. Even from a distance he could read the sadness that tinted their startling blue color. She appeared unhappy, out of place. He'd guess her to be anywhere from twenty-five to thirty years old. She had a graceful neck, narrow waist and hips, lovely slender calves. She fascinated him.

Someone touched him on the arm. He swiveled and when he looked back the woman was lost in the crowd.

He'd had enough. Keir made his way through the crowd, spying the bar, suddenly needing a refill. And after that he planned to go home.

It was the perfume, a rich, heady scent, and then his arm inadvertently pressing into a woman's breasts that alerted him. Raising his eyes, he found he'd collided with the woman in black.

"Sorry," he said. "I didn't spill anything on you, did I?"

"No...no, not as far as I can tell," she answered, dipping her head to glance at the front of her dress.

His pulse suddenly elevated. "Sometimes a man will do most anything to break the boredom, even go as far as sloshing a drink on a lady's dress."

She lifted perfectly arched eyebrows. "And is that what you did?"

Keir laughed, both embarrassed and elated. "No, actually it was an accident, but I'm awfully glad it happened, nevertheless."

There was a faint upturn at the corners of her mouth. Adrenaline pumped through his veins like liquid fire, giving him courage.

"It's given me the golden opportunity to talk to you," he said bluntly.

For a moment, she looked disconcerted, then she gave him a begrudging smile. "At least you're honest."

Her smile dazzled him.

"By the way, I'm Keir McBride," he said, a boyish tilt to his lips.

She hesitated a moment as though weighing the consequences of telling him her name.

"I'm Erin Richards," she said.

"Glad to know you, Erin Richards." He smiled at her again. "Are you with someone?" he asked.

She shook her head, lifting the glass to her mouth. "No, that was my boss I was talking to a moment ago."

So she'd been aware of him looking at her. That was a good sign, he told himself. "What brings you to this party?"

"Actually, I had no choice," she answered softly. "I work for the law firm that's hosting this affair and I was told to be here." She appeared suddenly uncomfortable. "But I hate being closed in with all these people."

"My sentiments exactly. Would you like to leave?" he asked, glancing around.

"Yes," she said simply, although she avoided his eyes.

"Tell me all about yourself," he said as they walked down the front path a short time later.

She shrugged, turning her blue eyes on him. A man could lose himself in those eyes, he thought.

"There's not much to tell."

He smiled. "Let me be the judge of that."

She began fingering the strand of pearls around her neck. "Well...I grew up in an orphanage just outside the city." She paused as though to test his reaction to her confession. When he showed none, she went on. "After leaving the home, I worked my way through college, finally getting a degree in business law. The Elsworth law firm gave me my first job. That was four years ago. I've been there ever since." She smiled. "See, I told you my life was unexciting. I'm a homebody, but I'm happy."

"That's all that counts," he said, looking again at her eyes, and then her mouth.

"And you?"

He sighed, shifting his gaze. "My life's as different from yours as night and day."

She appeared surprised. "Oh, how's that?"

"I'm the controlling partner in an air-freight company, which means I travel a great deal." A grin spread slowly over his mouth. "It's in my blood. I can't seem to settle down for very long at a time."

She frowned. "I couldn't handle that. As I said before, I like my home."

"You sound like my mother. If she and my father had their way, I'd be married with two kids and campaigning for the U.S. Senate seat my father hopes to turn over to me in the near future."

Her frown deepened. "Is Raymond McBride your father?"

"The one and the same."

"I'm impressed. He's a powerful man."

Keir laughed. "He'd love to hear you say that."

She moved like liquid flowing from one point to the next. He wanted to spend time with her and knock down that wall of reserve. He wanted to hold her slim, soft body and listen, with his eyes closed, to her voice gently breaking the darkness. He wanted someone to relax with, to laugh with, to love.

The next day was the first of many days they spent together. Somehow he had managed to persuade his partner to make his runs, thus freeing him to be with her. He wooed her with flowers, phone calls and long, intimate dinners at her apartment and his.

Then the night he planned to woo her into his bed, he received the dreaded phone call. He left that same day for South America.

The days dragged by, each seeming longer than the other. He thought that he would never get back to her, and when he finally did, he was unsure of his reception.

"Oh, Keir, I thought you'd never get back. I missed you so much," she whispered, tears darkening her eyes.

He crushed her to him, dizzy from relief at having her in his arms. It was pure magic.

"Please...promise me you won't ever leave me again."

He smoothed her silky curls. "Shh, let's not talk about that now. We have something much more important to take care of."

He took her hand in his and led her gently into the bedroom. She looked up at him, her eyes misty; he thought he had never seen anything more beautiful.

With graceful precision, they undressed one another, fondling the clothing, the snaps, the buttons, as though everything were flesh.

Her soft plea filled his mouth as he bent toward her. Her body was small and tight around him. He whispered, "Easy, easy," as he felt her muscles relaxing in order to bring him in.

"I...think I'm falling in love with you," he murmured, feeling his carefully built defenses and control systems going haywire.

"I know I love you," she said clearly before moans of pleasure claimed them both, rendering them speechless.

The months thereafter were perfect. Again Keir postponed as many trips as he could in order to be with her. They spent their time loving, laughing and talking, learning about each other.

It was only after he began fulfilling his obligations to his company and to the government once again that their relationship began to deteriorate.

She could not understand why he was gone for long periods of time, and he could not tell her. She always stopped short of nagging him, though she showed her displeasure by retreating into her cold shell, closing him out. She wanted him to give up his air-freight business and get a nine-to-five job. He, on the other hand, wanted her to trust him, to share his life with him the way it was.

He walked into her apartment one evening after he had been gone for two weeks on a dangerous assignment. He was exhausted, yet hungry for the sight of her, hungry to hold her, to make love to her.

She was standing in front of the window, her back to him as the door closed behind him with a click.

"Darling..."

She swung around. He knew the minute he saw the mutinous expression on her face that something was wrong.

"Keir...I don't want you to stay." She clamped down on her lip to still its trembling.

"What...what the hell does that mean?" he demanded harshly, taking a step forward. "Don't do this....God, we only have tonight as it is." He paused, his breathing hoarse and uneven. "I have to leave again in the morning."

"No! I don't want to hear it." She wrapped her arms around herself like a shield. "I'm tired of sharing you with your work, of never knowing where you are, when you'll be home. I...I can't take it anymore."

"Are you telling me you don't love me?" He closed his eyes, his jaw rigid as a spasm of pain flitted across his face. "Erin," he pleaded, his hand coming toward her. "Dammit, don't do this to us!"

She shrank back against the wall, biting her lip. She shook her head. "We're so different...I'm afraid..." Her voice stopped in her throat. Finally she said quietly, "Sometimes love just isn't enough."

He swore then; violence burned in his voice. "She doesn't want to get involved," he whispered menacingly. "Because it's disturbing. She might have to give up something, make a sacrifice, take a chance. You're a damned fake, Erin."

She turned away. "Please, just go...."

"But then, why should I waste any more of my life on someone who's afraid to love, to take a chance? May God help you," he said quietly, almost as if he were talking to himself.

He turned and walked out the door and out of her life without another word.

SOMETHING alerted him, drew him sharply out of the chasm of his dark thoughts. He raised his eyes and peered through the rearview mirror. Lines of worry ruled his forehead as a seething oath flew from his lips.

Suddenly he ground down on the gears without mercy. The

car lunged forward and around a curve at a daring rate of speed.

Danielle's eyes sprang open. She stared at him, wild-eyed, fright pounding through her veins. "What's wrong?" she cried.

Ignoring her cry, Keir's arm reached over and frantically released the lock on the glove compartment. Danielle watched in shocked disbelief as he pulled out a gun.

She panicked. "Keir, for God's sake!"

"Be quiet and get down." His voice was as cold as steel and just as hard. "We're being followed."

She tried not to stare at the gun, but her eyes were pulled toward it like a magnet. She shivered before slinking down lower in the seat.

If he had kept his mind on his business, he would have spotted them earlier, an inner voice taunted. He shifted his gaze back to the rearview mirror, purposefully blocking from mind Danielle's chalky face and bloodless lips.

He reminded her of an animal, sharp-witted and cunning, who seemed to spring to life when he scented danger. In his own way, Keir was as dangerous as the persons following them.

"Who do you think it is? Letsukov?"

"More than likely, or someone he's hired to do his dirty work."

The lump in her throat seemed to grow larger with each passing second. "What...what are we going to do?" she asked, though how she managed to push the words through her swollen throat was anybody's guess.

Keir did not answer for a moment, but she could feel the sudden tension in him.

Then he spoke grimly. "Try to lose them, if at all possible. I know this highway, and the roads that jut off from it, like the back of my hand. There's a shortcut through to the other highway a few miles ahead, and if I can keep enough in front of them, I can take that cutoff. Between the approaching darkness and the thickening snow, we're certain to be invisible."

"Whatever you think best," she said, twisting her head to

stare out the window. Keir was right, the snow seemed to be growing thicker, but thank goodness it wasn't sticking to the road—yet. That would have brought them to a virtual standstill. She watched as it swirled around the headlights like white rain.

"Tighten your seat belt," he ordered crisply, slamming the gun under his leg with his right hand. Then suddenly he pushed down on the gears, doing an intricate dance between brake and accelerator. The car went into a violent skid turn. Then Keir felt a shudder as the wheels suddenly righted themselves and regained their hold on the highway. He shifted again, building speed, feeling confidence grow with every second.

He had made up his mind in a matter of seconds. He reasoned that it was now or never. He had to lose the car before he reached the cutoff or it would be too late. Damn the blasted snow, he cursed silently as the car slid along the wet, uneven track. But he held his speed, gripping the steering wheel so tightly that every bone in his body felt jammed.

But it paid off. When next he looked in the mirror, the twin beams of the chase car were gone.

"Thank God, we've lost them," Keir said, keeping his eyes glued to the mirror.

Turning toward him, Danielle searched for his shadowed profile. She was amazed at how calm and composed he was. This was a side of Keir McBride she never knew existed. But then, she reminded herself, he had changed. There was a coldness, a hardness within him that had not been there before.

Suddenly Danielle was jarred out of her reverie as Keir made another sharp turn, the car lurching and bumping over potholes.

"Won't they figure out that we've turned off somewhere when they can no longer spot us in front of them?" she asked, trying to ignore the eerie darkness surrounding them while trying to control her rising fear, which refused to be suppressed.

Keir shifted down to a lower gear. "Probably, but there are other roads and cutoffs on both sides of the road. So by the time they turn around and come back to look for us, we'll be long gone.''

''What do you think the chances are that they'll find the cabin?'' There was a feverish edge to her voice as she sought frantically for his reassurance.

''Slim,'' he said, bringing the car to a sudden halt. ''And you'll see why when we get there. It's easier to get into Fort Knox than anywhere around the cabin.'' He turned his head around and began craning his neck, looking back toward the highway.

They sat silently listening for the sound of a passing car. Then they heard it, the faint, steady purr of that other car, as it cruised past them.

''What…what do we do now?'' Danielle whispered, unable to stand the quiet another moment.

''Pray that the snow still isn't sticking so that we can get through here to the other highway. Hold tight.''

He changed gears and nosed the car deeper onto the primitive mountain road. It was a nerve-racking experience. The ground was painfully uneven, strewn with rocks and dotted with branches from fallen trees.

How long they continued on their nightmare journey through the darkness, Danielle could not have said. Suddenly it all seemed to her painfully symbolic of what her future life would be. Barren, lonely, empty, no security, just endless suspense and struggles and misgivings. Certainly no love to brighten the darkness.

''Not much farther now,'' he said. His voice was deadly calm and matter-of-fact.

She almost hated Keir McBride. How could she have ever felt guilty about keeping Ann a secret from him? This cold, hard, cynical man was not father material. How could he have changed to the point that she hardly recognized him?

Her eyes felt as though someone had thrown a handful of sand in them. Oh, God, she thought, if only she were home with Ann….

''You might as well get some sleep,'' Keir said at length.

"It'll more than likely be dawn now before we reach the cabin, provided we don't run into any more trouble, that is."

Danielle did not bother to answer him. How could she even think about sleep with danger lurking around every corner and her mind a seething caldron of emotions? But she soon found that her battered body had other ideas. Her eyelids began to droop as the warmth enveloped her like a cocoon....

Keir knew when she had fallen asleep. He was glad. No point in both of them having to suffer a sleepless night.

He shifted his weight in the seat and massaged the tight muscles at the base of his neck. So far so good, he thought, seeing the main road coming into view.

His stomach tied in knots as he eased the car slowly down the deserted stretch of concrete, his ears alert to the slightest unusual sound and his eyes searching through the inky blackness for any signs of company.

He began to analyze the situation, turning it over in his mind, looking at it from every angle. Were they truly out of danger? Was the cabin as impenetrable as he thought?

*

DANIELLE jumped suddenly, as though an alarm had gone off in her brain, when the car's engine stopped. She sat up in the seat as if thrust forward by a spring. It took her a moment to realize where she was. But when she turned and saw Keir's haggard face and day's growth of beard, the horror of the past night returned to her.

"I...I take it there was no more trouble," she said hesitantly.

"So far, so good. I hope we've seen the last of our friends."

The house itself was nestled in the side of a mountain, tall pines flocked with snow surrounding it. Danielle knew immediately that this was no ordinary cabin; this was a luxurious trilevel mountain retreat aimed to please, with every conceivable comfort in mind. And it belonged to Keir's family. Was this where he had planned to spend his honeymoon? she won-

dered when they went inside, sudden nausea sending nasty
tingles through her body.

Her room was lovely, decorated in several shades of green
with its own bathroom. Out of the corner of her eye, she stared
at the bathroom longingly, wanting nothing more than to soak
her weary limbs and try to pretend none of this was happening.

"I'm going to scramble eggs and fix toast," he said. "I'll
call you when it's ready," he added.

Danielle stared down at her hands. "You go ahead. I...I
couldn't eat a thing."

"For God's sake, Danielle, be reasonable!" Keir cupped
the back of his neck with his hands as though it ached. Then
more huskily, "God, Danielle, you're nothing but skin and
bones. How long has it been since you've had a decent meal?"

How could she tell him that she'd never gained her weight
back after Ann was born? There had always been so much to
do...the responsibility had been so awesome....

He stalked out of the room, slamming the door behind him.

She shuddered in spite of the heat penetrating her limbs.
She was still finding it hard to believe that Keir had been an
undercover agent for the government before surfacing and becoming a U.S. Marshal. And she hadn't known it. How could
she have been so blind?

Would he be willing to change now, especially with a wife
in the offing? The muscles in her stomach contracted. She
would not think of things like that.

When she walked downstairs, he was sitting at the table
drinking a cup of coffee.

They had just sat down and were filling their plates when
the unexpected and jarring ring of the phone split the silence.
For a moment, they were both disoriented.

"I'll take it in the office." He shoved his chair back, looking down into her upturned face. His look sent the blood puls-
ing through her veins like warm, heady brandy.

Finally, he jerked himself upright. "Don't let your food get
cold," he said in a rough, unnatural voice, before turning and
walking out of the room.

Danielle let her breath out slowly. God, what was happening

to her? But she knew. She had wanted to touch him so badly that it made her insides shake.

She began concentrating on her food, desperate to banish the image of his long limbs entwined with hers throughout the long nights, their heartbeats as one....

She closed her eyes, fighting for her sanity. When they fluttered open again, he was standing in the doorway. Her heart jumped.

"You...you scared me," she stammered.

"That was Cassidy. Who is Ann?"

She simply gaped at him, soaking in the steely tension of his rigid jaw, the dark flush of fury staining his face. She held on to the table for dear life while she fought back the panic that threatened to suck her under.

When she finally spoke, it was a poor imitation of her own voice. "It's obvious you already know," she said defiantly.

"I want to hear *you* say it." His eyes cut into hers like ice picks.

The tilt of her chin remained firmly upthrust. "She's...she's my daughter."

Keir's sharp intake of breath pierced the air, shattering the moment's silence. He felt his heart twist. She had a child. *His child?* God! "Danielle..." His hands rose and fell in a terrible gesture of despair.

His reaction stunned her. She had never meant to hurt him, but she had. She had cut him to the core, and there was not one damned thing she could do about it. She could not risk telling him the truth. Ann was her life. She could face the agonies of dying a slow death easier than she could face losing her child—even to its father. Especially to its father.

She shut her eyes against the burning question in Keir's.

"Whose child is it?"

Her eyes flew open. "She's mine," she answered defensively, ignoring the erratic beat of her heart.

"I wouldn't advise you to play games with me." His voice had a menacing edge to it. "If she's not mine, then whose is she?" His face darkened, taking on a sinister glint.

"Mine!" Danielle repeated in an angry tone. She turned her back on him.

She was totally unprepared for the next attack.

"What did you do, run straight into some other poor unsuspecting bastard's arms and have the baby?"

Hot fury loosened her tongue. "You'll never know the answer to that question, will you?" she goaded, her voice rising with every word she uttered. "Because I'll never tell you! No matter what I said, you'd still blame me."

His eyes narrowed and cut into her like blades. Then with a muttered oath, he turned around, swinging his tough, rangy body as if it were on ball bearings, and walked stiffly into the den.

"Get out of my sight," he hissed, "before I do something that will cause us both to be sorry."

Danielle lost no time in making good her escape. But when she reached the top of the stairs, she stopped and turned around. Keir had not moved. His back was still to her, his shoulders hunched, seemingly more exhausted than she, as if his enormous strength had failed him.

Two days passed. It was as if a cold war existed between them, each fighting to come to terms with misery.

His hard, closed face followed her wherever she went. But what gnawed at her relentlessly was that she found herself *wanting* to know where he was, what he was doing. In spite of the tension between them she wanted to be near him.

With a disgruntled shake of her head, she pulled herself out of her musings and stood up, deciding that she had time to take a shower before going downstairs.

A short time later, her task complete, she was making her way back into the bedroom when the door of her room opened without warning and Keir stood on the threshold staring at her.

"What do you want?" she asked huskily, holding the sides of her robe together.

His hand was locked around the holster of his snub-nosed

pistol. Numbing terror washed through Danielle's body, threatening to stop her heartbeat. "What...what is it? Is it Ann?"

"It's John Elsworth. Cassidy says they found him in his cell this morning. He was murdered."

"Oh, no," she whimpered, putting her balled fist up to her mouth. Her insides began to shake. She was the only one who could identify Letsukov.

"It's not as bad as it sounds," Keir said softly, seeing fear pinch her features. "First thing, they don't know where we are, and the second thing, they have to go through me to get to you." His voice and eyes reminded her of cold steel.

She swallowed against the lump in her throat and nodded weakly.

Keir stared at her, taking in her pale solemn face. She looked so vulnerable, so haunted. He had never felt protective of a woman before, not even Danielle when he'd first met her. And certainly not Natalie; his attitude toward her was like that of an older brother. But there was nothing of that in his feeling for Danielle; there never had been. He wanted her so badly it was ripping his insides to shreds. *But you're not going to touch her, damn you! Get a hold of yourself. Do your job. Forget everything else.*

He inwardly railed at Cassidy for having gotten him into this fiasco, himself for having broken the first rule and becoming personally involved. Again. For whether he wanted to admit it or not, he *was* involved—had been since the moment he walked into Cassidy's office and saw her sitting there.

DANIELLE SAT straight up in the bed. It was the middle of the night and her heart was pounding wildly, her mouth was so dry that it hurt to swallow. Was it her own cry that had awakened her? Her shoulders shook violently as uncontrollable sobs pounded her body.

She wasn't even aware that she was no longer alone until she felt the mattress sag beside her. She jerked her head back and stared into Keir's deeply troubled eyes.

"Are you all right?" he whispered, a jagged note to his voice. "I heard you cry out."

Danielle shivered. "I…was dream-ing…a nightmare." She gulped. "It was awful. I…dreamed about John…." She couldn't go on.

"Shh, don't cry," he soothed, her tears cutting him to pieces. "It was just a dream, nothing more." For a moment, his hands closed over her bare shoulders. His groan penetrated the silence. He dug his fingers into the palms of his hands to keep from pulling her into his arms. "I'd better go now."

"Please…don't go." She swayed toward him. "I don't want you to leave me. I…know what it'll mean if you stay, but I don't care." She loved him, had never stopped loving him. And right now she thought that she'd surely die if he didn't hold her.

"Are you sure?" he asked. "Once I touch you…it'll be too late."

She put out her hand, and he caught it, turning her palm against his lips. The moist softness of his mouth against her skin set her insides on fire. It had been so long.

He closed both arms around her, the beat of their hearts throbbing in unison. He placed his mouth against her lips, softly, tenderly. She tasted of tears.

"Oh, please love me," she pleaded.

With quick, adept fingers he removed her gown, feeling her fingers pressing hard into his flesh. He lay down beside her, his body pressing warmly against her.

His mouth touched her everywhere. His hands caressed her sweetly, familiarly, following the hungry quest of his lips. She melted like hot wax against his aroused body, kissing him deeply.

When he entered her it was swift and frantic. She arched her back and began to move slowly, sensuously. He clung to her hips, joining her in her movement, lifting her, kneading her flesh as he accelerated to meet her in this extraordinary incidence of simultaneous timing. He knew in that moment that he had never stopped loving her.

They fell sideways, still joined, and lay panting, breathing in the air from each other's lungs.

"Oh, Danielle," he whispered.

She held on to him, unable to speak. He was her fortress where she could hide. His shoulders, chest and arms formed a shelter in which she could rest safe from her fears. She did not want it to end. Ever.

He held her tighter, spreading himself about her like a protective shell.

They slept. They pushed aside the danger that surrounded them, forgot that time was their number-one enemy.

*

IT WAS a truly incredible day. The heavens were an incredible blue, making the sky appear solid, the snow-covered mountaintops so sharp and vivid, the craggy outline of each rock and tree so distant.

"How does it feel to be a lady of leisure?" Keir asked, swinging the ax as though it were made of air instead of steel.

She smiled at the teasing glint in his eyes. He paused, supporting himself on the handle of his ax and looking at her.

"I'll just sit here on the porch, soaking up this wonderful clean air and sunshine and watch while you slave away." A smile teased her lips.

How long she sat there she didn't know. Keir showed no signs of tiring, nor did she tire of watching him. It was as though his big, brawny body were made of iron, the way he split one log after the other, stopping only long enough to stack them. She was mesmerized by his display of untiring strength. And he was so good to look at.

She never knew, could not remember later what made her suddenly turn and stare off into the distance. But it was that small unconscious action that saved her life.

Lurking on the mountainside adjacent to them, a man was scurrying around, a rifle wagging in his hand.

For a moment—stunned—she couldn't react. Then she raised wild, rounded eyes to Keir, stretched her arm toward him in a silent plea.

As if aware of her panic, Keir whirled around. It was then

that he caught his first glimpse of the metal flashing in the bright sunlight. He heard the brittle, echoing crack of a shot, heard wood splinter behind him on the tree opposite Danielle.

"Danielle! Get down!" he screamed, slinging the ax aside before ducking and crawling on his hands and knees, dragging his rifle with him. "Danielle! Are you all right?"

"I...think so," she whispered.

Keir reached for his rifle and cocked it, looking at his target, an evil glint in his eye.

"When I give you the signal, you crouch down and run like hell." He then rolled over on his stomach and began firing. "Now! Run!"

She ran.

Keir did not let up until he saw Danielle reach the side door of the lodge, frantically yank open the door and dart through it.

She was sobbing openly now, beside herself with fright for Keir. *Oh, God, please, don't let anything happen to him. Please not because of me.*

From where she was standing she could see Keir stop to reload.

He was alive! Thank God, he was alive. There were no more sounds of gunfire to disturb the uneasy, eerie silence that now filled the air.

THEY WERE huddled in front of the simmering fireplace, the sunlight having succumbed to the full moon and twinkling stars. It would soon be time to make their move. They had to get to the helicopter Keir's family kept at the lodge for emergencies and get away before their tormentor or tormentors returned. Keir had no way of knowing yet if he had fatally wounded the sniper. But there was no doubt in his mind that they were no longer safe in the lodge. He had gone to the phone to get an emergency coded message to Cassidy. But lifting it off the hook, he hadn't been surprised at what he'd heard: nothing. The lines had been cut. They were on their own.

Danielle's eyes dipped to the revolver lying on the hearth

only a hairsbreadth away from his right hand. Close to his heavy booted foot and resting on his thigh was a long-barreled rifle. Looking at those menacing objects, she was again reminded of the dangerous game they were playing. A game of cat and mouse with high stakes—their lives.

She recoiled, whipping her eyes away from the guns.

"It's time to go," he said. There was a brittle, controlled edge to his voice.

Getting up, Danielle marshaled every bit of self-discipline she possessed to keep her mind clear. She would not be a burden to him. But the thought of slipping through the inky blackness trying to get to the helicopter made her limbs knock with sheer terror. However, she let none of this show as she faced him.

Yet Keir was aware of her fear. It was so strong that it was almost tangible. He glanced at her, taking in the lovely picture she made standing straight as an arrow, her shoulders squared stubbornly.

"Atta girl," he said, his voice having suddenly gone hoarse. Then he touched her hand, and she followed him wordlessly out the door.

Danielle was positive that she did not breathe the entire time they stole through the dark, cloudy night. The moaning wind whipping through the bare treetops was the only sound between them.

It wasn't until Danielle slammed the door of the helicopter shut behind her that she breathed.

Wasting no time, Keir began flipping toggle switches on and off, checking needles and dials. He gave her a reassuring smile. A few seconds later the blades overhead began making a whop, whop, whop noise. The helicopter rose swiftly in the cold Virginia night.

"Are you going to try and contact Cassidy?" Danielle asked, her heart no longer palpitating.

Keir raked a hand over his hair. "I'm tempted, but I'm afraid to break radio silence. Once they realize we're airborne they'll tune in to our radio frequency. I'm going to fly us to our training camp where I know you'll be safe."

She kept telling herself that she was no longer afraid.

"Why do you think they weren't waiting for us?"

Keir looked grim. "It's my guess they're operating one man short now and have probably gone back to regroup."

Danielle shivered and fell silent.

A short time later Keir tightened his knuckles around the wheel, feeling them almost snap in two under the pressure. It wasn't his imagination; the controls were jamming.

"We're losing pressure!"

Danielle's features mirrored her disbelief. "We're going to crash?"

"No, but I'm going to have to set her down. Now!"

"But…but how? It's dark…the mountains…"

The terror had begun again.

He could feel the sweat beneath his arms, running down his sides. He knew that under the weight of the grip he was exerting on the lever, his hand was shaking fiercely. Quickly he adjusted his airspeed, at the same time checking the hydraulic circuit breaker. He was right. The sign flashed: OUT—hydraulic failure confirmed.

He switched to manual override. Next he reached over and flipped on the bottom landing lights, searching desperately for a place big enough to land.

"Keir, are we going to make it?" Her voice shook.

His face grew black with determination. "You're damned right," he snapped.

Danielle's eyes were glued straight ahead, her hands digging into the seat as Keir continued to fight the lever. It seemed like forever, but in actuality it was only minutes before he guided it onto a flat strip sandwiched between two mountains. Her heart was in her throat as she felt the helicopter make contact with the hard ground.

"Do…do you think they'll be waiting for us?"

He hesitated, his heart still knocking. "Probably," he answered honestly.

"SIR, ARE WE going to make our move now? Join the FBI?"

Luke Cassidy swung around. "We don't have any choice,

especially after what we've just learned." Cassidy's features were bleak. "A forest ranger sighted a chopper in the mountains not far from McBride's lodge. We wouldn't have thought about it except on the forest ranger's radio frequency they picked up a scrambled message from what sounded like two Russians. One was demanding help while referring to their target being in range."

He paused. "It's just been confirmed that McBride's chopper is definitely gone from the lodge. We're leaving at first light."

Cassidy walked to the door, yanked it open and turned around. "Meeting adjourned, gentlemen."

THE SHACK appeared deserted. All the same, he couldn't be too cautious.

Keir tromped carefully through the trees, glancing around him. Since he had found the shack, they could have, too, and since this was the only one nearby, they could have easily guessed that this was where they might come for shelter.

Up above Danielle was waiting. He had to hurry. Danielle couldn't make it much farther. From the moment they had left the chopper at dawn, stiff, freezing cold and hungry, they had been on the move.

He bolted over to the side of the shack, stopped, pressed himself flush with the building, peered around the corner, gun raised.

No one.

Then he placed his ears next to the shuttered window for any sound from there. Hearing nothing, he angled in through the door, gun ready.

Deserted.

It was a moment before he relaxed enough to move, breathing slowly. Then going to the door, he waved for Danielle to come down.

He met her halfway.

WHILE KEIR reached for a weak and trembling Danielle, three men with binoculars watched them from the top of the op-

posite mountain peak. And when the two weary figures turned
and made their way back toward the shack, one man let the
glasses fall to his chest and took a sip of cold coffee from a
cardboard container while watching the door of the shack
close.

*

THEY WERE both aware of the quiet darkness and of the sleet
as it continued to fall on the tin roof. A hint of something
hung in the air between them, a sense of waiting.

Three o'clock in the morning found them hovered around
the fire. Danielle's eyes were closed, her head resting in the
curve of his arm. He stared into her face, an ache around his
heart seized by love for her.

Her face. He could spend the rest of his life sitting here
looking at her face. Lovely woman with her delicate features,
fragile eyelids lined with the finest threads of violet, the curve
of her cheek, her jaw, her throat....

"Hey," he said suddenly, snapping his mind back to the
moment at hand. "Hey, don't go to sleep on me now."

With the dawn came the knowledge they were no longer
alone. Keir was never quite sure what followed—Danielle's
scream or the small explosion that blew apart the left front
window. Two bullets had whacked close together into the wall
beside him.

"Dammit, they're out there. Get down," he ordered before
crashing to the floor.

The wind was shrieking outside; snow was gusting in
through the shattered window, bullets splitting the air.

He flung his arms around Danielle, seizing her with all his
might, holding her crushed against his chest.

Her lips shook violently as she tried to speak. "What...
God...what are we going to do?" she whispered, clinging to
him.

Keir reached for his rifle behind Danielle, while slamming the pistol in her hand. His eyes found and locked on the back door that was in reaching distance of his foot. Deliverance. Maybe. Better than nothing.

Cupping her cold face between his hands, he forced her shocked eyes to meet his. ''When I shove open the door, I want you to take off. Whatever you do, don't stop shooting as you run toward the woods. I won't be far behind you.''

Positioning her hands on the trigger, still crouched, he slammed his boot against the door, shoving it open.

''Go!''

With her mind completely divorced from her body, Danielle darted through the door, struggling to fire the pistol. She battled the snow, spotting a clump of trees to her right. Sobbing, her chest heaving, bullets dancing through the air, she pushed on, sometimes stumbling, sometimes not. How long she ran she didn't know.

Then suddenly she stopped dead in her tracks.

Her heart slammed into her throat.

A man's booted feet blocked her path.

Fear rendered her motionless. *Oh, God, I'm going to die after all.*

She forced down the scream and, slowly defeated, she raised her eyes.

''Thank God, you're alive.''

She fell in a dead faint into Luke Cassidy's arms.

KEIR SAW the man follow Danielle's path, cutting across the snow. Keir halted, spun around, dropped to the ground, rifle aimed, and shouted, ''Zoya, take another step and you're dead!''

Then suddenly from another angle, a bullet whizzed by his head. Lunging to the side, Keir leveled his rifle and fired. Zoya dodged. His bullet only grazed the hit man. Stumbling, Zoya continued to follow Danielle's path.

An expletive flew from Keir's lips simultaneously with another bullet whining past his ear, forcing him to seek cover. Dammit, he cursed again silently. If only he could see where the shots were coming from or how many there were to contend with.

"Come out, McBride. You're covered," a heavily accented voice shouted.

Keir didn't bother answering. He slipped, slid and scrambled in the snow, hoping to circle to the rear. He thought of Danielle in Zoya's clutches and did not pause to catch his breath. With luck, he'd get one clean shot.

As soon as Keir spotted Letsukov, a beefy arm circled Keir's throat and lifted him high off the ground. He felt the tightening of that forearm on his windpipe. Kicking back, Keir smashed his heel hard into a kneecap. The goon fell with a thud as he released Keir.

Taking advantage, Keir spun and aimed his foot for the point of the man's jaw.

Crunch!

That one blow was all it took. The man lay sprawled facedown in the snow, out cold.

A sharp sting in his side doubled Keir over. Letsukov's laugh filled the air. Using the beefy man's inert body as a shield, Keir rolled over behind him, clutching his side. He scrambled for his gun, growing weaker by the moment.

He saw the feet before he saw the face.

"Surely you didn't think you could outsmart us, McBride." Letsukov's voice held an icy sneer. Raising his gun, he pointed it at Keir's head and laughed. "Too bad you won't be around to watch Ms. Davis suffer the same fate."

Reacting instinctively, a strangled cry erupting from his lips, pain blinding him, Keir came up and rammed against the man.

He heard it then. The sharp crack of a rifle. *Oh, God, please, not Danielle!*

Letsukov slouched on top of him just as he seemed to hear a voice, distant and high, and feel a hand on his shoulder, pulling at him....

He knew no more as a sweet darkness sucked him under.

*

DANGLING HER FEET off the edge of the bed, Danielle stared at the cream-paneled walls just as she had the day before and the day before that. An unbearable loneliness consumed her. Why couldn't she get hold of herself? Why couldn't she be thankful that she was back home with Ann and Jusie? Why couldn't she be thankful that her life had been spared? Why couldn't she be thankful that the nightmare was over, that she was out of danger?

But she *was* thankful, she argued. Thankful for everything, but— It was the "but" that was her problem, that was filling her days and nights with mental anguish and despair. She had not heard from Keir.

Since she had boarded the plane for home, she had lived in silent agony. Thoughts of Keir filled her heart and mind every single moment of every single day. Oh, she knew that physically he was going to be all right. He was recovering from his wound satisfactorily. Cassidy had assured her of that each time she had spoken with him by phone. And he had also assured her that both Letsukov and Zoya would never bother her again, nor would their sidekick. And that once she came to Washington and gave her deposition, she would never hear from the U.S. Marshal's office again.

Still, nothing relieved the pain of not hearing from Keir. Was she wrong? Had she just imagined that he still loved her? Had he gone home, married his fiancée? No. She would not, could not, believe that. She had seen the look in his eyes; she had seen love.

And when she did hear from him, what then? Would he forgive her when he learned the truth about Ann? And if so, would they be able to overcome their other differences? Would he be willing to change? To give up his dangerous job?

KEIR WALKED slowly across the grounds. He'd been at his parents' estate outside D.C. for a few days now. His stay in the hospital had turned into almost a month due to an unexpected bout with pneumonia. But he was stronger now, much stronger.

Cassidy was still clucking over him like a mother hen, as were his parents and...Natalie, until yesterday, that is. Had it been just yesterday that he had told her he couldn't marry her? The words simply spilled from his lips, and with them a heavy burden fell from his heart. Oddly enough, they had parted friends.

Yet his misery was immense. Even now, his aimless wanderings did nothing to help him. He thought distance would help. Distance, he expected, would make him free. But it hadn't. The merest thought of Danielle made his pulse race. She was inside him, in his head and in his heart.

DANIELLE FELT much better, her heart lighter, having unburdened herself to Jusie. She had told her everything, except of course those intimate moments she had shared with Keir. They were too private, too sacred to share, even with her beloved friend. Some things were better left unsaid.

It had been over a month. Could she have been wrong in thinking he still cared? No! She would not think about that. Not now. It was a beautiful day and she was headed home after shopping.

She parked the car in the driveway and scooped up her packages in her arms. Then carefully she made her way to the door, opened it and began climbing the stairs. "Jusie, Annie, I'm home," she called.

Silence.

Frowning, she crossed the threshold into the family room, only to freeze suddenly in her tracks.

"Oh, God!" she mouthed as the packages fell from her arms and scattered across the floor.

Keir, his massive body filling the rocking chair to capacity, was sitting by the fireplace rocking a sleeping Ann. The child's dark curls were tumbling across his muscled arm.

Keir looked up at her, tears clinging to his thick lashes. "Why didn't you tell me?"

She stood motionless. Seeing father and daughter together

for the first time, the likeness uncanny, it hit her squarely between the eyes what he must be feeling at this moment, knowing that he had been deprived of the first years of their child's life. The room began swaying.

"It's going to be all right, you know," he whispered, smiling through his tears.

"Oh, Keir," she groaned. Broken sobs began pelting her body, robbing her of speech.

Keir rose slowly, and clutched his precious burden against him. "Please don't...I can't stand to see you cry. Show me her room, and I'll put her down," he said. His voice trembled fiercely.

Wordlessly, Danielle preceded Keir out of the family room, down the hall to Ann's room. She stood by helplessly as Keir strode across the room and gently laid Ann's relaxed body on the bed.

"She's perfect," he murmured.

Danielle uttered a faint, choked sound as if she had attempted to speak and found her voice gone.

He left the room and she followed him.

In the den he stopped and faced her. "God in heaven, if only one could turn back the pages," he whispered, his voice raspy, broken.

"It's too late. One can never do that," she said gently, keeping her own tears at bay by the greatest of effort.

They looked at each other; Danielle's heart began to throb, Keir's hands closed until the knuckles were white and the fingernails bit into his palms.

He smiled through his tears. "No, my darling, it's not too late. Not for us."

"Keir. I..." Unconsciously, her head began to weave from side to side. "I'm sorry, so sorry," she whispered.

He turned toward her then and folded her within his arms. He held her as though he'd never let her go, but still he did not say what she so desperately craved to hear, that he loved her and wanted to marry her, that he wanted to make a home for her and Ann.

After a moment, she lifted her eyes, searching for his, unable to hold in any longer what was in her heart, her soul. "I...I love you," she said.

He stared down at her, his beautiful eyes a darker and more intense green than she had ever seen them before. Then he kissed her with passion, hunger and need.

"Oh, Danielle, Danielle," he whispered against her lips, "there are thousands of things I want to hear, to ask, about Ann—us, but right now all I want to do is make love to you, to show you how much I love you, how much I've missed you, how my life these past weeks has been hell without you."

"Me, too," she echoed softly. "But Jusie! Where is Jusie? We...can't...I mean..."

He leaned over and kissed the tip of her pert nose, drinking in the fresh fragrance of her skin, her hair. "Don't worry about Jusie. She's gone to visit friends. For the night. She wanted to make sure we had plenty of time alone." He grinned. "We had quite a conversation."

"You're crazy, you know," she said breathlessly.

"Crazy about you." He bent down and scooped her up in his arms. She seemed weightless, and he felt as if he could lift the earth.

In her bedroom they took their time undressing each other, stopping to kiss and touch, finally lying down on the bed together.

He circled her nipples with his tongue, bathing them in the dew of his mouth, causing her to suck in her breath with exquisite pain. Her hand fell lightly on the back of his head to keep him there.

"Oh, Keir, I can't believe you're here, touching me like this," she whispered, opening under him, drawing him down to her.

"I love you so much." He traced a finger down her thigh.

"And I love you. Oh!" She quivered as his fingers dipped into her. "Keir!"

She placed her hands between them, guiding him forward. But she no longer needed to direct him. He was there, parting her, entering, his hands caressing her breasts as he knelt between her thighs and immersed himself fully into her, then stopped, resting there. She raised her arms and brought him up to her breasts, anxious to please, to love him.

His hips shifted, beginning a counterpoint, playing a melody that was perfectly timed to his slow-thrusting theme. He held her, filled her more completely, more perfectly than ever before.

"You're perfect," he whispered.

She closed her eyes as he moved inside her, stirring something deep, something profound, something so wonderful that a soft dying cry came from his mouth. She shuddered and clung to him moaning softly, her eyes still tightly shut as she rose, then fell, gasping. A minute later, as the last of the spasms were passing, she felt his climax.

"I'm so happy," she said, a long time later.

"All I want," he said as he caressed her arm, "is for you to be happy."

He held her warmly in the crook of his arm. After a moment of contented silence, he confessed softly, "You know, you've never been off my mind. I kept finding you in every revolving door."

"I've never been without you," she answered, turning toward him with her heart in her eyes.

Thus began a play in separate acts with intermissions of kissing, talking and touching.

He told her about Natalie, how she was a substitute for her, that she was a wonderful person but he had never loved her. She spoke of the loneliness she had endured after they parted. He wanted to know the details of Ann's birth, and she told him.

After they had emptied their souls, they lay close together, arms wrapped tightly around one another. They fell into a deep sleep.

DANIELLE LOVINGLY glanced at a happy Ann, who straddled Keir's knee, egg mixed with grape jelly staining her cherub face. Then she raised her eyes, and they collided with Keir's brilliant green ones.

"Your daughter's a little pig, no doubt about it," Keir said, running his big hand through Ann's curls affectionately.

Danielle merely stood there, her heart swelled with love and pride at the picture father and daughter created together. With Jusie nowhere in sight, it was obvious that Keir had opted to bathe and feed Ann while she slept.

"Hungry?" he drawled, helping a squirming Ann down from his lap. "Sit down, and I'll prepare you a McBride special."

Danielle laughed, scooping her daughter up in her lap and giving her a squeeze. "Give Mommy a kiss then go get your coloring book and colors and show Dad...Keir...how well you can color."

"When are we going to tell her?" Keir asked a moment later as they watched their happily occupied daughter in the corner of the den.

"I'm...ready when you are."

He dipped his head and gave her a searing kiss. Pulling back, he whispered, "Let's get married. Today. This morning. Doesn't that sound like heaven?"

"Like heaven," she echoed into his mouth. Now, she thought, now he would tell her what she longed to hear, that he would give up his dangerous job, find work here in Texas, never leave her and Ann alone again.

"But we won't be able to leave right away. There's so much we have to take care of before we can go back to D.C."

The sudden businesslike tone of his voice sent a cold chill of foreboding through her. She raised her head to look at him. "Leave?"

"Of course." He rushed on. "We'll stay here until we can find a suitable buyer for the store, and Jusie—well, if she wants to go with us, I..."

Pushing him away, she lunged to her feet. "What?" Then before he could answer her she went on, shaking her head in bewilderment. "Leave? But why? I...I thought...I mean," she stammered, suddenly feeling as though she were foundering alone in the middle of the ocean in a life raft that had sprung a leak.

"Danielle, honey, what's wrong?" he asked, taking in her pale features. "I don't understand."

"Well, apparently neither do I," she whispered. "It's...it's just that I thought now that you wouldn't be working for the government any longer, we wouldn't have to leave." Her voice had dwindled almost to nothing.

The silence that fell over the room was formidable.

"I'm sorry if I gave you that impression," he said coldly, "but I have no plans to give up my work."

The silence stretched endlessly.

"I...I haven't changed, Keir," she said, unchecked tears beginning to trickle down her hollow cheeks. "I still want a real home, white picket fence and all for me...for Ann. And a husband who will always be there, not one who's constantly chasing danger."

"Correct me if I'm wrong, but this conversation sounds awfully familiar to me." Keir's tone showed evidence of the strain on his control.

"I won't deny that," she snapped at him. "But my God, Keir, after what we've just been through, what do you expect?" A shudder tore through her body. "I...I thought we'd be a real family." She choked back a sob. "If you're gone all the time, that's not being a family," she wailed.

He wanted to touch her so badly he could taste it, but something held him back. Something he couldn't name. Suddenly she seemed untouchable. His heart skipped a fearful beat.

"In the first place I won't be gone all the time," he reasoned. "And in the second place nothing is going to happen to me. You've got to believe that." His tone was pleading now. "Anyway, I have responsibilities, obligations to people other than myself. They depend on me. Right now, they're waiting on me to head an undercover operation that, if successful, could keep the Russians from walking off with any more of our technological secrets. I can't just back away from that."

"No. I guess you can't," she said bitterly.

"I love you and want to marry you. Isn't that enough?"

"How can you say that," she cried. "I love you, but I can't...I won't live with the shadow of fear. Not anymore."

He felt sick on the inside, sick that he was losing her. *Oh, God, not again,* he cried silently.

"Danielle," he reasoned patiently. "I know you've been through a living hell, but that's all over now. Put it behind you. We have a wonderful future in front of us. Don't throw it away. Let go of the fear, once and for all. Lean on me—trust me."

She answered him with silence, turning her back.

"All right, Danielle, you win. I won't fight you anymore. If living in a vacuum will make you happy, then so be it."

The door slammed shut behind him, shattering her heart into tiny pieces. She crumpled to the floor, too numb to cry.

*

SINCE HE HAD walked away without a backward glance over three weeks ago, she had tried to exorcise him from both her heart and mind, but thoughts of their parting and his bitter words continued to torment her soul. Fate had sent him to her, and she had sent him away. Dammit, if she didn't know better, she would say she was pining away.

Suddenly it dawned upon her that a home, family, roots were meaningless without Keir. He was her roots. Without him life had no meaning. To be completely fulfilled she needed Keir. Even though she dearly loved Ann, she could not replace Keir in her life. Nor could she deprive Keir from being a father to her child. She knew that now.

She realized, too, that it no longer mattered what he did for a living. He could be a government agent for the rest of his life if that would make him happy. It was no longer important. But accepting him, and loving him for what he was, was the important thing. She had made a grave error in trying to change him.

Jumping up, a brilliant smile changing her features, she cried jubilantly, "Washington, D.C., here I come!"

DANIELLE WAS nervous, but somehow she reached the door and pushed the bell.

Nothing.

Please, oh, please, be home, she cried silently.

The door opened, but it wasn't Keir who stood on the threshold, but a strange woman with a coat and purse draped over her arm.

"May I help you?" the woman asked formally.

Danielle circled her lips with her tongue. "Yes...uh...is Keir...Mr. McBride here?"

The woman—housekeeper more than likely, Danielle thought—raised her hand to push back a stray silver curl. "No, he isn't, not at the moment."

"When...when do you expect him back?"

"Not sure, ma'am."

"Would it be all right if I came in and waited for him? You see, I'm from out of town and I came especially to see him."

The woman looked both skeptical and uneasy. "I don't know, ma'am, I'm just leaving and I don't..."

"Oh, please," Danielle rushed on, a desperate note in her voice. "I'm a...friend. The name's Danielle Davis, and I've traveled a long way. I must see him."

The woman's kindly, wrinkled face was showing signs of weakening. She opened the door wider. "Mr. McBride has mentioned you." She smiled, taking in Danielle's pale, drawn features, then looked at her watch. "I have to go now. Have to pick up my grandbaby at the nursery. There's a bar in the den if you want something to drink and there's a cozy fire in the fireplace. Make yourself comfortable."

Danielle forced herself to smile. "Thank you."

Danielle, familiar with her surroundings, made her way into the den. She went to stand by the fire. But she didn't tarry there long. Jumpy as a cat on a hot tin roof, she began pacing the floor. *Fool! Life doesn't give third chances,* she thought.

She had to leave, to get out of there before he came home.

But her legs refused to cooperate. They were threatening to buckle beneath her.

Then just as she took a tentative step forward, she heard the front door open and close. She stood helpless, unable to move, unable to speak.

"Danielle!"

He stepped closer as though he, too, had seen a ghost.

"Are you real?" he whispered. "I was planning to leave tonight for Texas to tell you…" He paused on a ragged note. "To tell you that I can't live without you, no matter what."

Her mind was reeling. Had she really held this haggard-looking man in her arms? She had tried to negotiate with the person in charge of the universe to get Keir back. And now she was hearing the words she had longed to hear. She was afraid her heart would burst with happiness.

Keir put his arms around her, tightly, as though he would never let her go, and she was content to hold him and hear his heart beating. No other emotion could equal her love.

"Love me," she whispered, meeting his eyes, touching the gaunt shadows in his face as if to prove to herself that he wasn't a mirage.

He closed his eyes, his mouth shaking. "Oh, God, Danielle, darling, I love you so much and want you so much. For a while there I didn't trust my ability to stay sane."

"Oh, Keir," she said, "I felt the same way. Nothing seemed to matter if I couldn't have you."

His hold tightened. "My darling, my love," he said deeply.

Danielle sought the words to tell him what was weighing heavily on her heart. "I…I want you to know that it no longer matters to me what you do for a living," she said. "I'll support you one hundred percent, even if you're gone five days out of seven."

"Oh, my darling, you're priceless," he said, worshiping her with his eyes. "And you don't know how much your saying that means to me. But I have a confession to make. I had just come back from Cassidy's office, having told him I wanted a desk job, effective immediately."

Danielle gasped, causing him to pause with a sweet smile.

"I'm through trotting the globe, as you so aptly put it. Can you ever forgive me for being such a headstrong and selfish bastard, demanding you give up everything, but not willing to make any sacrifices myself? Life wasn't worth living without you."

"We're so lucky," she whispered, "to have been given a third chance."

"Marry me."

"Whatever you say."

Suddenly his face clouded again. "Would you mind very much living in D.C. part of the year, since my office is here? Maybe you could open up a bookstore here. I know how much your work means to you."

"We'll see, my love," she said. "But right now all I want is to be with you, no matter where it is."

Before he could say another word, Danielle locked her arms around his neck and kissed him, her lips filled with love and promise.

"Home, my darling, is where the heart is," he pledged softly, "and my heart is yours forever."

MARRIAGE, DIAMOND STYLE

Mary Lynn Baxter

The early-morning air was cool and fresh. It stung Matt's face as he looked toward the sky and took a deep breath. The dog at his heels stared with adoration at his tall, lean master.

He returned the animal's stare with a smile. The large black mutt had wandered up to Matt's front porch one day and hadn't budged since. Matt reckoned someone had dumped him on the highway and kept on going.

"Well, Sam, the weather's finally decided to cooperate." Matt felt Sam's warm, slobbery tongue on the back of his hand. "None too soon, wouldn't you say? Much more rain— and the loggers here will soon be history. Only bad weather's just a small part of my problems. Right?"

When the dog didn't respond, Matt sighed. If his luck *didn't* change, he was in jeopardy of losing his logging business—a venture he'd put his heart and soul into, not to mention every penny he had.

Matt threaded his hands through sandy-blond hair that the summer sun had turned almost white. Ordinarily Matt would have been in the woods, set up and waiting for dawn in order to cut the first tree. But today he'd let his crew off so he could get in working order what little equipment he had left. As he made his way to the edge of the woods, to the shop where he kept the logging machinery, Sam whined.

"Yeah, I know, life's a bitch."

Only that hadn't always been the case. Until this latest round of rotten luck, life had been on an even keel. At age thirty-five, and for the first time ever, Matt was where he wanted to be, doing what he wanted to do.

A runaway at the age of sixteen, he couldn't think of a time when he wasn't fending for himself. His mother had handed him over to a church home shortly after he was born. Years of enduring foster homes had followed. The day he'd turned eighteen, he'd gone to work for an oil company for low pay.

But it hadn't been long before he'd proved his worth. His reward had been a job in the oil fields in the Middle East.

Matt had liked what he did, especially the money, but he'd longed for roots, a place to call his own. So after years of desert heat, he returned to East Texas for good. He bought a house on several acres of land and went into the logging business. Though the hours in the woods were long, grueling and sometimes dangerous, he couldn't think of another place he'd rather be.

He was beginning to enjoy the fruits of his hard labor—then the first unexpected setback came. An accident in the woods claimed the life of one of his employees, a young man who was married and had a small child.

Matt's troubles hadn't ended there. Shortly afterward, his equipment woes had begun.

"Hey, boss, wait up."

Matt stopped in his tracks as his right-hand man, Elmer Cayhill, worked hard to catch up with him. He was a bear of a man and could outwork any twenty-year-old. Matt could hear his labored breathing.

"If you don't get rid of that gut, my friend—"

"I know," Elmer cut in, finally reaching Matt's side. "You're gonna be picking me up in the woods and carting me to the morgue. But if I can't have my beer, then I'll take the morgue."

Matt winced. "You're hopeless."

Elmer grinned. "So I'm told."

They walked in silence, the dog between them.

"You didn't stop by to discuss your health," Matt said at last.

"No, I didn't. I'm afraid we've lost another one." Elmer wiped his forehead, leaving a streak of grease across his face. "The big skidder."

A groan split Matt's lips. "Stolen?"

"No. Fire."

"Dammit, Elmer, what's going on?" Matt asked bitterly. "First a skidder caught on fire. Next, one was vandalized.

Then a loader was stolen, and now another skidder has caught on fire.''

"At this rate, you can't keep on going long, can you?''

Matt's laugh was hollow. "That's an understatement.'' Matt looked into the distance for answers.

"Well, I guess you'd best call the sheriff for the sake of your insurance.''

Matt's spine stiffened. "Speaking of insurance, I've got to call them, too.''

"Now that's the real kicker,'' Elmer drawled. "Think they'll cancel you?''

"No, at least not right now. But it won't stop them from sending a 'dress for success' down here to snoop around.''

Matt's shoulders sagged. He turned and trudged wearily toward the house.

BRITTANY had worked hard to make a place for herself in Walter Fleming's financial empire. Being the only child of the widowed insurance magnate was not easy. She wanted to please her daddy, ached for his love instead of the material things he had always given her.

She'd been in the third grade and had worked extra hard to make a perfect straight-A report card. She'd ridden home with her best friend, Sally. Sally had also made a perfect card, and when her mother saw it, she'd grabbed Sally, hugged and kissed her.

Brittany had watched from a distance and wished she had a mother like Sally's. But her mother had died when she was five.

When Walter arrived home later that day, she raced into his office flapping her report in the air. "Daddy, Daddy!'' she cried, her red curls bouncing. "I got straight A's.'' Her eyes shone as she waited, aching for him to hug her and kiss her just like Sally's mom had done to her child.

He did neither. Instead, he patted her on the head and said, "Wonderful. Tell Benson to drive you into town and let you buy anything you want.''

Her heart had throbbed until she'd thought it would burst through her small chest.

Why do you do this to yourself? For God's sake, she was twenty-five years old. It was past time she grew up.

Brittany dabbed her eyes with a tissue, then turned her attention to her work. Why, this Matthew Diamond was a menace, she thought. If the company had many more clients like him, they'd be out of business in no time. Something had to be done about him, and the sooner the better. Pushing away from her desk, Brittany stood, her back rigid, as if prepared for battle.

She heard a sharp, brief tap on her door.

"Come in," she said, and watched as Wade Bryant strode through the door.

"Perfect timing," she remarked as he plopped down in the chair in front of her desk. "I was just on my way to see you."

"Oh."

She heard the wary surprise in his voice. It was no secret that she and Wade didn't work well together. He resented her for who she was and didn't try to hide it. Unfortunately, Walter had complete confidence in him.

"I've been looking through that logger's file," Brittany said, bridging the lengthy silence.

Wade flicked a tiny piece of lint off his suit trousers, then looked at her directly. "Good. We'll discuss it at the meeting I've called at seven in the morning."

"I hope I won't be here."

Wade raised an eyebrow. "Just where will you be?"

"In Lufkin. Or rather, the outskirts, I should say."

"I don't think so." Wade stood abruptly. "It's not your case. I've decided to let Hamilton handle it, though I'm sure he'll be interested in hearing your assessment."

Brittany stood, as well. Her green eyes flashed. "Hamilton already has more cases than he can handle. I want this one."

"No way," Wade said flatly, and leaned over, planting both hands in the middle of the file.

Brittany swallowed the sharp retort that came to mind. If she lost her temper, she would play into Wade's hands. He tested her relentlessly, alert to something, anything, that would make her look bad in Walter's eyes.

"I'm perfectly capable of handling this case, Wade."

"I don't think so." His voice turned cold. "Diamond is obviously playing the company for a fool, and I want to get him."

"Me, too. I want this case, and if I have to, I'll go over your head."

Wade's upper lip developed an odd tic. "All right," he snapped. "But you damn well better come back with the ammunition to cancel Diamond."

He stared at her for a long moment. Then he pivoted on the heels of his polished shoes and walked toward the door.

He reached for the knob, only to have the door suddenly open. Walter Fleming stood on the threshold.

Wade inclined his head and strode past him.

Fleming turned to Brittany. "What was that about?"

"The Diamond case. Are you familiar with it?"

"Vaguely. Wade said he'd turn it over to Hamilton."

"I told him I wanted it."

Walter stared at her for an intense minute, as if he saw her for the first time. "That's my girl, a chip off the old block. Go to it."

When she walked out of the office a short time later, briefcase in hand, she couldn't seem to stop smiling.

BRITTANY BLINKED against the harsh sunlight. Even though the calendar said May, the weather felt more like summer than spring. Beads of perspiration gathered under the arms of her silk blouse.

Matt Diamond's part-brick, part-frame house wasn't bad. A bit on the small side, but neat and trim just the same. But it wasn't his house she had to worry about; it was his equipment.

It was so quiet and silent she began to doubt anyone was home. She saw the work shed nestled among a cluster of spindly oaks.

The truck's raised hood was the first thing she saw there.

"Mr. Diamond?"

The man that stepped out from behind the truck was nothing like she would have envisioned, not in a million years.

"Yeah?"

"I'm...I'm Brittany Fleming from the insurance agency."

He slammed down the hood of the truck and stepped into full view. "And Daddy's little girl, to boot—right?"

His hair, wet with sweat, should have looked shaggy because it was too long. But it didn't. She had the most ludicrous urge to reach out and wipe one greasy mark off his chest...

"It makes no difference who I am," she managed in a frigid tone. "But since you asked, I am the boss's daughter."

"Okay, so where's the check?"

She stood there subject to the same scrutiny she had given him. His deep-set blue eyes were like hot knives, dissecting her.

Brittany cleared her throat. "You know very well I have to investigate the legitimacy of your claims. I may as well tell you up front, the company is taking a dim view of your claims."

If the blatant sexual appreciation had been there a moment ago, there was no sign of it now.

"I need to see the damaged equipment, ask questions."

"Not today, lady. It's too late. I'm bone tired and I'm calling it a day."

Twin flags of color stained her cheeks. "Are you always this rude and uncooperative?"

He flushed. "I'll be in the woods till noon tomorrow."

"I'll see you after lunch, then." With that she turned and made her way to her car. She had the door open and was about to get in when she saw him lean against the hood.

"What is it now?"

"Your rear tire is low."

Brittany's eyes followed his. "Terrific."

"Want me to change it?"

"No, thank you," she said waspishly. "I'll take care of it when I get back to...civilization."

MATT WAS in a lousy mood. The last thing he needed was a high-and-mighty female who thought she was better than most folks, nosing around and questioning his actions and his integrity.

He'd seen the contempt in her eyes, and that was what made him the maddest. But he'd also seen the way she'd looked at him, as if she could eat him with a spoon. He hadn't been mistaken; for a moment, something had sizzled between them.

There had been a lot of women in and out of his life, but only one had ever gotten past the shield around his heart. He'd met Wendy Sheffield three days after he'd arrived in Saudi Arabia, in a grocery store, of all places. She'd been a teacher in an American school. In her quiet, sweet, unassuming way, she had managed to crack that shield, and he had thought at last he'd found a woman who understood him. He had wanted to share his life with her.

Only she'd gotten killed in an automobile accident six months after he'd asked her to marry him.

He was more careful now.

What he needed was to put that Fleming woman out of his mind, get cleaned up and eat something. He guessed Annie's Padlock Cafe would get his business again.

A few minutes later, Matt turned onto the farm road that would eventually take him to the highway. He saw her then. Actually, he saw her snazzy automobile first. The tire was as flat as flat could be.

Her arrogant statement, "I'll take care of it when I get back to...civilization," still echoed in the piney woods.

He threw back his head and laughed as he pulled his Ford Ranger pickup behind her car and got out.

"Well, well...what have we here?"

His mocking tone was more than she could take. "Don't you dare say it!"

"Say what?" He grinned and leaned against her car. "Say that I told you so?"

She lifted her chin slightly. "Go ahead, have your fun. But the last laugh will be on me. You'll see."

He crossed his arms over his chest and stared at her. "Oh,

how do you figure that? Seems to me I can fix your flat or let you sit here and fume.''

Brittany looked alarmed. ''You wouldn't. It'll…it'll soon be dark,'' she added on a plaintive note.

''Well? Say the magic word.''

''And just what is that?''

A display of innocence widened his eyes. ''If you don't know, then I guess I'll be on my way.'' He waved a hand.

''Don't you dare walk away from me!''

He kept on walking.

''All right!''

He slowly turned and waited.

Brittany balled her fingers into fists. ''*Please* would you change my tire?''

''Why, ma'am,'' he said mockingly, ''I thought you'd never ask.''

SHE FOUND HIM in the workshop the next day, standing over a huge chain saw. He wore faded jeans and an equally faded blue T-shirt chopped off at the waist, which made him look like the quintessential bad boy, the kind mothers see in their nightmares and girls see in their dreams.

She was no girl. Yet she was stricken with the same malady.

Matt lifted his head and stared at her. A muscle ticked in his jaw. ''I thought for sure you'd be in Tyler by now.'' His rock-hard gaze bored into her as if he searched for something. ''Since you're here, let's get down to business. If you know your business, that is.''

''Correct me if I'm wrong, but it's your business that's in trouble.'' She knew she was being childish and argumentative. Something about this man brought out the worst in her.

Matt's anger and impatience were obvious, but when he spoke, his words were calm and without malice. ''Look, let's call a truce, okay? All I want is my money.''

''Well, unless you cooperate, you won't get your money, Mr. Diamond. And whether you like it or not, you're stuck with the company. And me.''

He started walking. Brittany matched him stride for stride.

He was coiled tight, dangerous. Maybe that was where the challenge lay. She enjoyed flirting with danger, always had and always would.

"I need your employees' names, social security numbers and driver's licenses," she said.

"Do you mind if I ask why?"

Brittany searched for the sarcasm that was hidden in that question, but she couldn't quite pin it down.

"The company needs to run a criminal check on them."

"What about me?" He smirked. "Do they need one on me, too?"

"Yes." She flushed in spite of her efforts not to do so.

"Oh, that's rich. Surely you don't think—"

Brittany shook her head, stopping him. "The company's not picking on you."

"What about you, Ms. Fleming? Are *you* picking on me?"

"No," she said, with an exasperated lift of her shoulders, an action that pulled the material of her silk blouse tightly across her breasts. Matt's eyes fell to that exact spot.

Sparks exploded inside her as she saw the confusion in his eyes. Obviously he was disturbed as much as she was. What was happening here?

He ripped his gaze away, and the world suddenly righted itself.

Brittany forced a calmness into her voice. "What I'm doing is standard operating procedure."

"Right now, I'm only working Elmer Cayhill. And Billy Frost sometimes. My run of bad luck forced me to let the others go." His expression hardened.

Brittany consulted her notebook, then looked up. "Our records show you with seven pieces of heavy equipment. Out of the seven you've filed claims on four."

"They are legit claims, Ms. Fleming."

She prayed for patience. "You're not the only logger we insure, and to date no one has filed this many claims this close together."

"I don't like what you're insinuating."

Brittany's coral-glazed lips tightened. "I'm not insinuating anything. I'm merely gathering the facts."

He snorted. "Yeah."

A short, hostile silence followed. Brittany broke it first. "I need to see the skidder that caught fire and the loader that was vandalized."

"Follow me."

Silence accompanied them to the first heavy piece of equipment.

"Where did the fire start?"

"In the engine room."

"What about the fire extinguisher? Why wasn't it used to put the fire out?"

"Because the skidder caught on fire during the night, that's why."

She wrote down his explanation. "Let's see the loader that was vandalized."

"It's over there." Matt motioned with his hand, then waited for her to go ahead of him.

She'd taken a few steps when she turned to say something to him, only to nearly bump into his chest. His eyes found and lingered a fraction of a second on her lips.

Her face burning, she stepped away and murmured, "Sorry."

"No harm done," Matt said, in such an odd voice that it drew her eyes to his.

Brittany licked her dry lips. "Tell me about the loader."

"There's not a lot to tell. It was parked in the woods. The next morning the damn thing had been worked over. Tires were flat, and as you can see, they beat the hell out of the instrument panel."

"Anything else?" Brittany asked, her pen busy.

"Yeah. The SOBs put sand in the fuel system."

"Kids?"

Exasperation changed his expression. "Don't know. It could've been. But it could also have been other loggers. This can be a cutthroat business. Hunters—they're notorious for trying to run loggers off property where they hunt."

Brittany frowned.

"Not a pretty picture, is it?"

"No, it's not."

They were silent for a moment. The warm afternoon sun beat down on them. Brittany placed the back of her hand against her lips to keep from yawning.

He saw the gesture and smiled.

She stared at him, aghast.

"What's wrong?" he asked sharply.

Brittany held his gaze. "It's nothing, actually. It's just that you smiled, really smiled."

He blinked.

"For a second there, you were almost human."

He turned away, as if the sudden warmth in her eyes was too disturbing. "I'll bear that in mind."

"About the truck," Brittany said, realizing how close she had come to making a fool of herself. Who cared if he ever smiled or not? "I need to know—"

"It'll have to wait," he said abruptly, looking beyond her shoulder. "Company."

Brittany swung around. A young man who looked to be in his early twenties was beside the work shed. He had longish brown hair and sullen features.

"Who's he?" Brittany asked, frowning.

"Billy Frost, one of my hands."

"Somehow I can't see him working for you." She hesitated. "He seems a little... Oh, forget it. I don't know what I meant."

"You're right. Under ordinary circumstances, he wouldn't work for me, but since the accident—" Matt broke off suddenly and clamped his jaws together.

"What accident?"

"Never mind," he said tersely.

Brittany bit back a retort and asked instead, "Shall I leave you two alone?"

"I'm sure he's come to borrow money. My hands depend on me to work them, and when I can't, they're in deep trouble."

"I see."

"I doubt that," Matt responded flatly. "I'd be willing to bet you've never wanted for anything in your life."

Brittany opened her mouth to retaliate when he waved a hand and said, "Save it."

He turned his back on her and started toward the Frost boy.

"I'll leave, but I'll be back tomorrow," Brittany said.

He paused slightly, then kept on walking.

*

BRITTANY CURLED tighter in a ball on the rickety motel bed and moaned. She raised her head just enough to read the time on the travel clock. Four o'clock.

"Oh, lord," she whispered.

Cramps. Of all things to have happen. She'd felt great earlier. In fact, she'd jumped out of bed and gone to the high school track and run three miles. The cramping had started shortly afterward. Her day had gone from tolerable to terrible.

She'd tried to call Matt, but he hadn't answered. She had swallowed a couple of over-the-counter painkillers and gone to bed. She'd probably made his day by *not* showing up.

How had things gotten so out of hand? When had things gotten so personal? What was it about him? she kept asking herself. From the moment she'd seen Matt, she'd been aware of him on a different level—his dark face, his taut body, the heat that radiated from him...

Suddenly Brittany sat up and watched the room spin. That was preferable to thinking wayward thoughts about Matt Diamond.

What she needed to do was return to his place one more time so she could complete her report, make her judgment, then get out of this godforsaken place.

But not today. She couldn't face him today.

She sat up and realized she wasn't sick to her stomach. Courageously, she stood. Maybe if she brushed her teeth and showered, she might feel like eating something. She suspected hunger was contributing to her light-headedness.

When she finished showering, the second round of medicine had taken effect. She felt that she could face the world, especially after she put some food into her stomach. She knew where she was going, too.

Annie's Padlock. She'd noticed the place, a rambling wooden building surrounded by dozens of cars every time she passed it.

She walked outside and saw that the sun had set. She paused and looked up. The sky was streaked with colors. That was a good omen, she told herself. And so was Annie's Padlock. It was definitely the antidote she needed to revive her spirits.

MATT PULLED INTO the parking lot of Annie's Padlock. As he got out of the truck and walked into the cafe, he adjusted his eyes to the dimness. Still, he saw her. Right off.

His stride broke abruptly. Suddenly everything else around him became of secondary importance. He didn't notice that business was slow or that the counter was occupied by three men who were watching every move that Brittany made.

Her eyes had a faraway, dazed expression in them. Underneath were dark shadows that reminded him of faint bruises.

Those slight imperfections enhanced her refined features. She wore a pair of jeans—tight-fitting, he bet. Her red hair was loose and windblown. But it wasn't her hair that held his attention; it was her breasts, which were boldly outlined by the fit of her shirt.

He couldn't take his eyes off her. Sexually, she stirred him more, made him more aware of her than any woman he'd ever known.

He was livid because she was here—when she'd stood him up.

He cursed silently, then stepped up to her table.

"Surprise, surprise." Matt's gaze drilled her.

Brittany stiffened and opened her mouth. Before she could say anything, Matt spoke in a low, terse voice. "I waited all afternoon for you to show up."

A small crease appeared between her eyebrows. "I know, and I'm sorry." Her voice was husky. "I wasn't feeling good."

Matt snorted.

Her eyes glazed over. "Look, I fell asleep and when I woke up, it was too late. I tried to call...."

"Knowing that I wouldn't be in the house?" He heard the tremble of rage in his voice, but he couldn't control it.

She stared at him openmouthed, and her eyes were building up to a blaze.

"Hey, fellow."

At the sound of the unfamiliar voice, both Brittany and Matt swung around.

A man dressed in a dark brown business suit stood next to Matt.

"Is this fellow bothering you, little lady?"

Brittany opened her mouth to reply. Matt interrupted. "Butt out, mister."

The man hiccuped. "Oh, no. You butt out. I had my eye on her a long time before you came in, my friend."

"I'm not your friend," Matt said, steel in his voice.

"Matt..." Brittany rose, her face clouded with anxiety. "Matt...don't. Let it go."

"That's right, honey. You tell him. What do you say you and me split and—"

He never knew what hit him.

Matt doubled his fist and delivered an uppercut square in the middle of the man's chin. The man crashed into the table behind him. Dishes and glassware flew like tiny missiles around the room.

The entire room went graveyard quiet. Then everyone began talking at once.

"Oh, my God," Brittany whispered, raising horrified, accusing eyes to Matt. "How...how could you?" There was the smallest break in her voice, and her lower lip quivered.

Not out of fear, Matt told himself, but out of rage. He had embarrassed her. His backwoods antics had embarrassed the high-and-mighty Brittany Fleming.

Brittany grabbed her purse, whirled and walked past him.

He would have charged after her, but a waitress placed a hand on his arm. Her eyes shone. "That was real nice, honey, real nice. I wish I had someone to do that for me."

Matt shook off her hand, his eyes on the door. "Ask Harry to haul this piece of garbage out for me, will you?"

He strode out the door.

"Brittany," he called softly.

"Stay away from me!" she cried, twisting to face him. "Haven't you already done enough damage? Go away, damn you." She turned to get into the car.

Without thinking, Matt grabbed her arm.

Her gaze dipped to his hand, which surrounded her arm, then up to meet his fixed look. "Do you solve everything by using he-man tactics?"

It wasn't so much what she said that sent his temper over the edge, but the way she said it, with that contemptuous lilt in her voice. He hauled her against his chest. Their eyes met and held. The air between them vibrated with a raw tension.

"Matt...please."

She felt it, too. He heard it in her voice.

His anger deserted him. But not the heat. He wanted her. God, he wanted her.

"Matt..." Brittany's cry was a breathless whisper.

A warning bell went off in his brain. What the hell was he doing? He let her go suddenly.

If her car hadn't been behind her, she would have lost her balance. He dared not touch her, not even to steady her.

He turned, poised to walk away. She grabbed his arm. The muscles bunched under her light touch.

"Matt..."

"No...don't. Don't say another word." He took several steps.

"Where are you going?"

He stopped, swung around, his features contorted. "Going? Where am I going?"

She flinched under his cutting words.

"I'm going inside—alone."

"BILLY?"

Matt was almost to the workshop when he saw a figure move behind the skidder.

"Yeah, it's me," Billy said, moving into the open.

"What the hell do you think you're doing?"

Billy pawed the dirt with the toe of his boot. "Waitin' on you. Hopin' you'd have work for me."

Matt didn't like him hanging around his place. But then, considering the trouble he'd had, he didn't like *anyone* hanging around.

"How long you been here?" he asked.

Billy looked away from Matt's intense scrutiny. "Not long," he mumbled.

"It just so happens I can use you today."

His sulky features cleared. "Oh, really?"

"Yeah. You ready to go?"

Billy scratched his head vigorously. He eyed Matt carefully. "Ready when you are."

Matt turned his back on the kid and wondered what there was about Billy Frost that raised his hackles.

THEY BOTH heard the car. But it was Elmer who looked up. "You've got company, boss. I'm thinking it's that insurance dame."

Matt looked up, then swore. It had been a long, hot day in the woods, and the last thing he needed was Brittany prancing her tight little butt around here as if she owned the place.

"You wanna call it a day?" Elmer asked.

"What I want is for you to wipe that chicken-eating grin off your face."

Elmer's grin merely widened. "Anything you say, boss. See you in the morning." Elmer picked up his lunch pail and crossed to his pickup. "By the way, you know how I feel about that Frost kid—don't trust that little weasel—but I'll have to admit he sure as hell came in handy today."

"I know. And I was glad I could work him. Still, I feel guilty—"

"Don't. You can't help this run of bad luck."

"Thanks," Matt said, and watched broodingly as Elmer cranked his pickup and drove off.

He switched his attention to Brittany. She had gotten out of the car and was walking toward him. She looked wonderful, he thought.

Matt removed his dusty hat and slapped it against his leg. "You should've told me you were coming." His eyes were smoky, intent on her face. "So what are you doing here?"

"I've finished my report." She forced her expression not to show the turmoil his presence created within her. "Do you mind if I come in?" The words slipped out in a controlled rush.

Their eyes met. There was an element of raw emotion in the air.

"Suit yourself," Matt murmured. He motioned for her to precede him up onto the porch.

Brittany paused just inside the door, her eyes scanning the room. "Nice."

The room had highly polished wood flooring. A sofa and matching chair hugged a large area rug at one end. An entertainment center and fireplace dominated the remaining walls.

Brittany turned toward him. "It suits you."

He smirked. "I'm glad the lady approves."

"I wasn't being insulting."

He gave a tired sigh. "I know."

They stared at each other for a long moment. Finally Matt said, "So let's have it," as if responding to the look in her eyes.

"All...right."

"So when am I going to get my money?"

"You're not."

He took a menacing step closer to her. "Explain that."

"I think you're sabotaging your own equipment, and I intend to prove it."

His smile was lethal, a deadly weapon. And it stopped her cold. "You're crazy as hell!"

He stepped closer, until he was so close he towered over her. Her eyes widened, but she held her ground.

"Look, I don't like this any more than you do, but the facts are just that—facts. And I can't ignore them."

"You can't ignore them!" His lips twisted around the words. "I've paid my insurance premiums when I couldn't pay anything else." His eyes turned into icy chips. "You don't know the first thing about logging. You're just a spoiled brat who's window dressing for Daddy—"

Her hand acted with a mind of its own. She struck him hard across his cheekbone.

"How dare you talk to me like that!"

If she had said something else, he would never have acted. But it was the way she said it, as if she couldn't stand for him to put his dirty hands on her. Impossible, especially since every time she came near him, he'd ached to do exactly that.

He grasped her wrist and jerked her against him. Her breasts collided with his chest, and her legs slapped his thighs. He didn't care that he was hurting her.

"Let me go," she cried, struggling against him.

Her moist lips opened, partly from pain, partly from anger. Matt lowered his head and ground his hard lips into her soft ones.

She stopped struggling. He nudged her lips apart and touched her tongue. It was as if time had stopped; they seemed suspended in space.

Matt let her go. Silence, like a vacuum, fell around them. He didn't move, fully expecting to feel the sting of her hand across his face again.

Instead, a tiny sound erupted from deep within her throat. With trembling fingers she circled his neck and firmly drew his head down to hers.

Their lips met this time with such fierce suddenness that his legs felt like rubber bands. He tore his mouth from hers, then massaged it across her cheek.

"Please...don't." His breathing came in short, gusty spurts. "Don't play with me like this. You make me crazy. You have from the first day we met." He seared her skin again, then sank his hot, moist mouth into hers.

Brittany felt as if she were dangling off the edge of a cliff.

She clung to him, rising and falling with the rhythm of his kisses.

His budding hardness situated itself between her legs, generating an all-consuming heat. Brittany stroked his back and felt his taut muscles bunch. She wanted more and pressed harder against him.

He moaned, shifted to cup her buttocks and lifted her to her toes.

She tried to run her hands over his chest, but his shirt was in the way. She clawed at it, freed it from his jeans. Only it wasn't enough to feel his flesh; she wanted to taste it, too. She brought her lips to his chest. She sought out and found one pebble-hard nipple.

His voice was pleading as his tongue slid between her lips. "I want…you…"

With the same impatience Brittany had shown him, he tore her blouse open. One jerk of the front snap and the bra was open, then off.

His head dipped, and his lips closed around the tip of one breast. But his eyes sought hers. There was fear there as surely as there was hunger.

His hunger won. Within seconds, she was naked and pressed against him urgently. His clothes joined hers. He reached for her.

His calloused hands slid down her back and surrounded the cheeks of her bare buttocks. He lifted her off her feet and said roughly, "Lock your legs around me."

She did, and he backed her against the wall. Her thighs were liquid fire, enabling him to enter her swiftly, completely, hotly. His thrusts were forceful and deep, and she wanted this sweet pain never to end.

At some point he groaned, then strained against her even more, giving her all of him in one final thrust. Their moans came simultaneously. When it was over, his lips sought her pulse at the base of her throat.

Somehow, sometime, they had made it to his bedroom. They were locked in another embrace.

With an unsteady hand, he pushed her damp hair out of her

face and began to move gently, creating a friction that again set her on fire. He was tender, giving, and, at the very end, she couldn't be certain, but she thought she felt a tear drop.

HALF AWAKE, Brittany stared at the strange ceiling and groped for her bearings. Where was she? And why was she so stiff, so sore?

When she spied the Stetson hanging on the back of a rocker, her heart plummeted as if in a crashing elevator.

She climbed out of bed and, dragging the sheet with her, tiptoed to the kitchen. The note in the middle of the kitchen table was propped against the salt and pepper shakers.

"Make yourself at home. I'll see you later, and we'll take up where we left off. Matt."

Her face turned bright red, then deathly white. Not only was she mortified at what she had allowed to happen—but she was more mortified that he would assume she'd do it again.

Five minutes later, she was out the door and out of Matt Diamond's life. Forever.

*

"WAY TO GO." Her boss had eased a hip down on one corner of her desk. "It looks like you've nailed Diamond."

"We'll see." Brittany shuddered. Anything and everything about Matt affected her like that. "The equipment was hauled to the nearest repair shop so it could be analyzed. While we wait, I'm going to get started on the Hanover case."

"Well, if those shade-tree mechanics are like the ones in most small towns and run true to form, it'll be a couple more weeks until we get their report. Their tardiness plays into our hands, actually." Wade smiled a cocky smile. "He's on our timetable now. We got him. You know yourself, it takes at least thirty to sixty days to wrap up a case like this. Maybe longer, if we want to drag it out."

"In the meantime, what if he goes under?"

Wade pinned her with an odd glance. "He'll just go under. But that's not our problem. Right?"

Brittany smiled tightly. "Right."

Wade made his way to the door. He paused and turned. "I'll have to tell you, I didn't think you had it in you. Going for Diamond's jugular and winning."

"I wouldn't celebrate just yet, Wade. The case isn't closed. We have to *prove* Diamond's at fault."

"We will," he said airily, then closed the door behind him.

Brittany fought the urge to pick up the blotter on her desk and hurl it after him.

Had she really gone to bed with Matt? Had their bodies become one? Had he been inside her so perfectly that she forgot everything except him and what he was doing to her? Even after three weeks, thoughts of that night in his arms still had the power to send her stomach to her knees.

Her only consolation was that she wouldn't have to face Matt again. He'd made no effort to seek her out. She was sure he was as glad to be rid of her as she was him. More so.

She pressed a hand to her forehead and phoned her home phone for messages.

Two were from friends asking her to parties. The last one was from the doctor's office.

"Brittany, this is Joyce at Dr. Daniel's office. He'll see you tomorrow at the time you asked for."

Brittany looked around the office. Any other time, she might have felt the sense of pride and peace she always felt when she surveyed her domain.

The message from the doctor's office had destroyed any sense of well-being. It reminded her that she had missed her period. The first week she hadn't been upset, attributing the lateness to nerves. But after the second week, she'd been forced to rethink that reasoning.

Oh, Brittany, she thought, you stupid fool!

"ARE YOU SURE you don't need anything?" Matt asked into the phone.

"Just your company," Maria Frost said sweetly.

Guilt stabbed Matt. He knew he should visit Maria and her son more often. If it hadn't been for him, she would still have a loving husband to take care of her.

As if she could read his mind, Maria said softly, "When are you going to stop blaming yourself for Tim's death?"

"Never," Matt said flatly.

"It was an accident. You have got to come to grips with that."

Despite her brave words, Matt heard the tremor in her voice, and he damned himself for calling her in the first place. The last thing he needed was more guilt.

"You should be worrying about yourself."

"I am," he responded with dark humor.

"Haven't heard anything, huh?"

"I won't until those SOBs get good and ready."

"Surely that woman insurance adjuster saw how desperately you needed a settlement."

"Look, Maria, I gotta go now. I'll be by to see you and Skipper soon, okay?"

"All…right," she said, as if taken aback by his abruptness.

Matt placed the receiver in its cradle. He stared at it for a long minute, but he wasn't seeing it. Brittany's face swam before his eyes.

"Damn," he muttered, jumping up as if he'd been shot out of a cannon. He had to forget her; that was all there was to it. Their coming together was one of those crazy one-night stands, pure and simple. Her disappearing act had shown him that.

But even now, he couldn't block out the little sounds she'd made when she reached a climax….

MATT'S JAW slackened, and he blinked several times. "Well, well, well. So you decided to come back to Hicksville after all."

Brittany's heart flipped at the sight of him. "Do you…mind if I come in?"

"Why would I?" he said, shifting his weight so that she could pass him.

He closed the door and followed her into the living room. The silence was oppressive.

She knew he was stunned; she'd seen it in his face when he'd opened the door.

She couldn't stop staring at him. Her eyes swept over his hair, his tanned, shirtless chest, the faded, ragged cutoffs that molded his thighs. My, but he looked good....

He seemed to have read her thoughts—his pupils shrank to pinpoints, and his breathing turned harsh. "Why did you come back?"

Brittany couldn't answer. Her pulse throbbed in her ears.

He watched her, his eyelids at half-mast. "I'm waiting."

His tone was even, as though he was unaffected. She knew better. She heard the scraping sound underneath, like two pieces of sandpaper rubbing against each other. Sweat glistened on his forehead.

"I...we need to talk," she said.

His brows formed a scowl, making him appear more threatening than ever. "What you did was wrong, you know," he said unexpectedly, "running out without saying anything."

His face had a curiously vulnerable look to it. She turned away, numb and slightly sick. "I know."

"Then why did you?"

Reluctantly she faced him again. "I...I was afraid."

"Of me?"

Her breath came out a tight whisper. "No, of myself."

The seconds ticked away.

"Brittany..." His voice sounded hoarse suddenly, as though he had a terrible cold. He took a step toward her.

She backed away. "No...don't...please."

As if he remembered the last time she had said similar words to him, his eyes sparked, and tension stiffened his jaw. He seemed in danger of exploding.

"Matt...I..."

"What's going on, Brittany?"

She hugged slick hands to her sides. "I have something to tell you." There was a long pause. "I'm pregnant, Matt."

Shock stripped his face of expression. He was staring at her as if she wasn't there. Time slowed to a crawl. Each second extended itself a hundred-fold.

"I..." His lips snapped together as if it was impossible to say a word.

"I thought you had a right to know," she whispered, trembling inside.

A silence stretched.

"Are you sure you're pregnant?"

"Yes."

"There's no possible room for error?"

"Do you want to see the doctor's report?"

"No."

Another silence.

"Look, this conversation is going nowhere, so I'll be going...."

He reached out and his hand circled her forearm. "I don't think so. You're not going anywhere until this is settled."

She pulled away and eased toward the door. She had to get out of there before she made a complete fool of herself.

"As far as I'm concerned, it is settled."

"Like hell! If you *are* pregnant, no child of mine is going to be born a bastard."

"So what do you suggest, then?"

Her quietly spoken words fell into the silence like a chunk of lead.

"I suggest we get married, that's what."

Her heart jerked. "Do you...do you know what you're saying?"

"Yes. Will you marry me?"

Paralysis invaded Brittany's body. She couldn't move. She couldn't speak. Brittany realized that in her heart of hearts, she'd wanted him to say that. Matt was a stranger to her. Nevertheless, she loved him. She'd known that the minute he'd opened the door today.

"Brittany..." Matt's voice cracked.

She swallowed the tightness in her throat. "What?"

"Come here."

With a cry, she ran into his arms. He held her close to his heart.

Finally she pulled back and stared at him. "What now?"

"Set a date," he said thickly before kissing her on the mouth, a hot, searing kiss.

He felt dizzy, alarmingly light-headed and out of control.

*

SOMETIMES, she had to pinch herself to make sure this was real, that she and Matt had actually been married two months. What was more mystifying was that they were happy, which was not to say there hadn't been disagreements—there had.

At first, there was the awkwardness of two people living together who hadn't been privy to each other's bad habits and idiosyncrasies. Both had volatile personalities, and both were independent. Consequently, they had to learn to give and take. Brittany also knew Matt was frustrated because his insurance case was still under investigation and he hadn't gotten his money.

The most serious disagreement had come a week after they'd married. Matt had rented a friend's skidder and loader. The mill in Lufkin was buying all the pulpwood he could deliver. But that day Matt had come in from the woods early to shower and shave before they left for a barbecue at a fellow logger's house.

They had been dressing when she turned to Matt and asked, "Are you happy with your work?"

Matt stared at her with an incredulous expression on his face. "What kind of question is that?"

"We've never really talked about our future."

"What does that have to do with my work?"

"I think that would be obvious."

"Not to me," he said flatly.

"You wouldn't consider doing something else, then, something less dangerous?"

"Like what?" His tone told her he was not happy in the least with the conversation.

"Oh, I don't know." Her eyes pleaded. "It's just that we have a child to think about now...."

His eyes dulled. "You don't like living here. That's what this is all about, isn't it?"

"I never said that," she retorted.

"No, you didn't have to."

Tears welled in her eyes, and she held out a hand to him. "Matt...please...don't be mad at me."

His eyes were tortured. "Oh, God, Brittany, why I let you twist me in knots I'll never know."

He groaned and reached for her. They never made it to the barbecue.

That one incident had taught them both how thin-skinned they were and how much work was ahead of them.

All in all, though, the change in Matt had been quite remarkable. He was no longer the tense, angry loner he'd been when she'd met him. He seemed to genuinely enjoy being married.

If there was a murky cloud on the horizon, it was her daddy. Only after the marriage had Brittany driven to Tyler and told Walter.

"Have you lost your mind?" he'd yelled, his face growing redder by the second. "He's nothing but a damn redneck!"

"Daddy—"

"Don't you daddy me! What are you trying to do? Make me the laughingstock of my own company?"

"That's...a horrible thing to say." Waves of disgust crashed through her. "I'm pregnant, Daddy."

Walter turned pale, then said coldly, "Something you'll live to regret, I assure you."

Brittany reached out a hand. "Daddy, please...try to be glad. You've always wanted a grandchild."

"But not Matthew Diamond's. By God, have you forgotten that he's under suspicion for sabotaging his own equipment?"

"Matt says he's innocent, and I believe him."

"Well, I can see he sold you a bill of goods." Walter's

expression remained grim. "So I take it you're going to live in the woods."

"Right."

"Have you thought about the child growing up in that environment?" Walter shook his head. "I just hope you know what you're doing."

"I do." Brittany's voice almost faltered, but didn't. Not for one second would she let him know that she'd had the same reservations.

"What about your work?"

"Nothing's changed. I'll just use Lufkin as my base."

"I don't like it. I don't like it one damn bit."

"I'm happy, Daddy. Everything's going to be all right, you'll see." She leaned over and kissed his cool cheek. Would she ever please him? More to the point, would she ever stop trying? She doubted it, and that was what scared her the most.

BRITTANY didn't know what woke her. Was it the burning in her chest? Or was it the niggling pain in her lower stomach?

Why hadn't she listened to Matt and eaten only one piece of pizza instead of two? But they had been celebrating her fourth month of pregnancy and the movement of the baby for the first time.

She sat on the side of the bed. The pain kept on coming. Finally she got up and padded into the bathroom.

A few minutes later, she started crying.

She heard his feet hit the floor. Within seconds he stood inside the bathroom door.

"Oh, God, Matt," she sobbed.

He knelt in front of her and took her cold, clammy hands in his. "What's wrong, baby?" Panic weakened his voice.

"Help me, please." She clutched her stomach and bent over. "Oh, God. I'm bleeding, Matt, I'm bleeding."

"I'M SORRY Mrs. Diamond, but you lost the baby."

Those words. Those piercing, hurtful words. It had been six weeks since the doctor had come into the emergency room at the hospital and told her about the baby. And now the words struck her again as if someone had put a fist into her stomach.

She had carried the tiny life inside her only a short time, but she had wanted this baby so much.

The loss of the baby had hit Matt hard, as well. Yet they seemed unable to comfort each other. After he'd come in from the woods, long periods of silence would follow. He almost never smiled. They were more like strangers than ever before, except in bed. They couldn't communicate with words, but they had no trouble with their bodies. Their lovemaking was more intense, as if it bordered on desperation.

Work became her panacea for heartache. She pushed herself harder, begging for as many claim settlements as Wade would give her. She traveled to Tyler at least once a week, sometimes twice. But never far from her thoughts was the baby she had lost.

Today was no exception. She had driven until the tears made it impossible to see. Now, after getting out of the car and walking through a wooded area, she eased down at the foot of a tree and waited for the pain to subside.

It never did.

"MARIA, thanks for the coffee and cake." Brittany smiled.

Maria's face glowed. "I baked the cake for Matt as I always do—when I know he's coming."

Maria Frost was a good mother. While Matt had taken care of several chores for Maria, Brittany had played with the baby. Later Matt had joined the two of them on the floor. She'd been astounded at his patience with the child.

Now, as the two women stood beside the truck, waiting for Matt, Brittany held out her hand. "I hope you'll come see me soon."

Maria looked beyond Brittany's shoulder suddenly and waved. Brittany twisted her neck. Heading toward them was a young man who looked to be in his late teens or early twenties. He was one of Matt's loggers. She'd seen him while investigating the case.

"That's Billy, Tim's brother."

"Hi, sis," Billy said, lumbering up to his sister-in-law's side.

"Billy, this is Matt's wife, Brittany."

"Mrs. Diamond."

"Hello, Billy," she said politely, thinking how his eyes shifted in his thin face, and he never quite looked at her.

Suddenly an arm came around her neck. Brittany peered into her husband's face. He stared at her. "I see you've met Billy."

"Uh-huh."

"Matt, thanks again for all you've done this afternoon," Maria put in quietly.

"Ah, it's nothing. Only I don't know how much longer you can put off getting the house re-shingled."

Maria's face fell. "Oh, Matt, I can't afford—"

"Don't say that. Don't even think it. As long as I'm here, you can afford anything you need."

Billy laughed a humorless laugh. "He hasn't got work for me these last few months. But you heard the man, sis. Anything you want."

"Be quiet, Billy," she said tersely.

He shrugged and turned away.

Goodbyes were said, and Brittany and Matt headed down the drive in his pickup.

"Tim and I were the best of friends. He was several years older than Maria, and he thought the sun rose and set on her."

"Maria seemed devoted to him, too."

"She worshiped him. Billy worshiped him, too." He suddenly pounded the wheel with his right hand. "If only Tim had listened to me that day when I warned him about the skidder."

She laid one hand on his arm, offering what comfort she could. Then Brittany shifted her head to one side. "He hates you, you know."

Matt cut his eyes toward her. "Who?"

"Billy."

"What makes you say that?"

"I saw the way he looked at you. Hate definitely shone from his eyes."

"I guess he has reason to," Matt said bleakly.

"You know better than that." Her tone was sharp. "It was an accident. Maria certainly doesn't hold you responsible. Why should his brother?"

"It's just that he was so close to Tim, relied on him for everything."

Brittany shivered. "I don't trust him."

Matt searched her face before turning back to the road.

THIS AFTERNOON was the second time she had gone to the Livewell Fitness Club in Lufkin and worked out. She was making strides to get her life back on track. She had hoped that work, combined with physical exertion, would help fill the void inside her.

She glanced at her watch and saw that it was late. Matt would be home soon. She reached for her gym bag and stepped out of the car. She was just starting toward the house when she saw a movement out of the corner of her eye.

Someone was in Matt's workshop. A frown marred her brow, but she pushed aside the flutter of fear and marched toward the shop. She had her hand on the knob when the door suddenly opened.

Billy Frost froze in his tracks.

"What are you doing here, Billy?" Brittany demanded, her tone direct and sharp.

"I was looking for a tool to fix a faucet leak for Maria," he said quickly. Too quickly.

Brittany pursed her lips. "Did it ever occur to you to ask permission to borrow something?"

"No one was home." His stance bordered on belligerent.

"Then you should've left." Brittany crossed her arms and leaned against a wall. "You know what I think, Billy?"

"No."

"I think you're lying."

His face flushed a deep, ugly red. "I don't care what you think," he shot back.

He darted past her and out the door. She ran after him, but he was on his bicycle and pedaling as if the very devil were after him.

"You little boneheaded jerk," Brittany muttered, thrusting her hands deep into her hair.

"Hey!"

She spun and watched as Matt climbed out of his truck. "Was that Billy I saw tearing off through the woods?" A frown added to the tiredness of his face.

"One and the same," Brittany responded tightly. "I came home from the gym and caught him in the shop. Said he was after a tool so he could fix a leak for Maria."

Matt grunted. "That'll be the day."

"That's what I thought." Her insides clenched. "I think it's Billy who's behind your equipment troubles."

He laughed. "Billy? No way. He's worthless as hell. He doesn't have enough sense to get in out of a good hard rain, much less steal and damage equipment."

*

"BRITTANY THINKS Billy's behind our equipment problems."

Elmer's mouth fell open. "Billy? He don't look like he has enough smarts to do anything like that."

"I feel the same way."

Elmer had opened his mouth to say more when the crunch of automobile tires interrupted them.

Matt spun, thinking it was Brittany. She was due back from Longview, where she'd been working on a case.

When he saw the Lincoln Continental, he breathed an expletive.

"I take it your visitor's someone you don't want to see."

"If my gut instinct is right, which it usually is, that's my father-in-law."

Elmer followed Matt's gaze, then whistled through his half-rotten teeth. "One of those, huh?"

He said "those" as though it were a contagious disease.

"I wouldn't know. I've never met the man."

Elmer's jaw flapped open.

"My wife's never seen fit to introduce us."

BRITTANY'S BREATH hitched in her lungs when she saw her daddy's car in the drive. The day had been a long and tiring one.

How long had Walter been there? she wondered, killing the engine and getting out of the car. She had a hand on the front doorknob when she looked up and saw them walking out of the workshop.

As they approached her, Brittany tried not to wince.

"When did you get here, Daddy?"

"Oh, 'bout an hour ago, I'd say. Matt was kind enough to show me around the place. In fact, we've had quite a nice visit."

Brittany clamped her teeth together so that her mouth wouldn't flop open.

"I decided it was past time I met my son-in-law."

Brittany shook her head to clear it. "Well, I'm glad you did, only—"

"Stop spluttering, child, and invite me in. I'm dying of thirst."

Ten minutes later they were in the living room, sipping coffee.

Walter emptied his cup and looked directly at Matt. "If you've got another minute, I have something I'd like to talk over with you."

His tone was casual, Brittany thought, too casual.

Matt, who stood by the fireplace, straightened slightly, but said nothing.

Walter kept his eyes fixed on Matt. "How would you like to move to Tyler, go to work for my company?"

Breath escaped from Matt's lungs like air from a punctured tire. But he still didn't say a word. He merely looked at Brittany.

The room filled with a suffocating tension.

Walter stood and looked at Brittany. "The doctor's told me I need to take it easy."

"Oh, Daddy," Brittany wailed. "Why haven't—"

Walter held up his hand and stopped her flow of words. "I'm not going to the cemetery, but I do plan to slow down. Why don't the two of you talk over my offer. I need to go, anyway."

"But Daddy…" Brittany spluttered.

He leaned over and once again pecked her on the cheek. "I'll see myself out."

When they were alone, Matt turned to her and asked, "Was this your idea? Did you put him up to asking me?"

Brittany let the angry questions hang in the air, then said, "Would it be so terrible?"

Matt's face swelled with rage. "I think it stinks."

Brittany felt a new heaviness inside her. "Won't you even think about it?"

"No," he said, baring his teeth. "You can be at your daddy's beck and call if you want to, but not me. I'm *not* going to work for your daddy." Matt's nostrils flared. "Not now. Not ever!"

He turned and stormed out the door.

MATT BARELY talked to her. He shut her out completely, and there was no way to reach him. He continued to blame her, thinking she'd gone behind his back to Walter.

If she had learned one thing about her husband, it was that he was proud. So proud that he took Walter's offer as an insult.

She set the alarm and got up so she could talk to him before he left for the woods. She walked into the living room and found Matt sitting on the side of the couch where he'd slept the night before.

His head was bent, and his face was in his hands. She stepped toward him, and he looked up.

"What do you want?" he asked, his voice remote.

She winced at the stab of pain that took her breath. "I…think we should talk."

"I told you, we have nothing to talk about." His eyebrows were drawn together, his face pinched.

The bottom of her stomach fell away. "I didn't know Daddy was going to make you an offer."

"Maybe not. But you were damn well for it, weren't you?"

Brittany tried to swallow, but her mouth was too dry. "I worry about you—"

"Bull," he spat, lunging to his feet. "You worry about yourself, about being away from Daddy and all your other highfalutin friends."

He didn't give her the chance to reply. He left, and stayed gone from daylight till dark. He was so tired when he came in that he barely managed to eat a few bites.

Her eyes searched his face and glimpsed a flash of longing in his eyes. Then, before she could say anything, the phone rang.

Brittany groaned, but it never occurred to her not to answer it. Rushing across the room, she lifted the receiver.

She listened, then said in a strident voice, "Tomorrow?" She listened again, then frowned. "I'm sorry. I forgot."

Matt used the counter for a prop and watched her, his expression wary.

Shortly, Brittany placed the receiver on the hook and muttered, "Damn."

"Walter?" Matt's tone was brisk.

"Yes," she said, her face troubled.

"Is something wrong?"

"No. There's nothing wrong. It's just..."

"Spit it out, Brittany. I'm a big boy—I can take it."

Ignoring the edge in his voice, she said, "Daddy's having a political fund-raising dinner—"

Matt pushed away from the cabinet. "So? What's that got to do with you?"

Brittany took a steadying breath. "I promised him a long time ago that I'd act as hostess."

"I take it you're going home, then."

"Yes."

"Are you coming back?"

Silence, sudden and total, descended over the room.

The fact that he even asked her cut to the core. Since they had stayed together after she lost the baby, she had felt they had a chance to have a real marriage. And somewhere along the way, she had convinced herself that he had to love her.

But the time had come to hear him say the words, to tell her that he loved her. Now.

"Can you give me a good reason I should?" Brittany's voice trembled. *Say it, Matt! Say you love me and that you don't want to live without me.*

The seconds turned into a minute. He stared at her as if he'd never seen her before. She felt cold. And brittle. If she moved she feared she would break into a million pieces.

His hands dropped to his side. "No, there's no reason for you to come back."

As if he'd struck her, she recoiled. Oh, God, was this the end? Was her marriage over?

*

"SON OF A BITCH!"

Matt's mumbled curse echoed off the walls of the workshop. Someone had walked in and helped themselves to tools, and the building had been trashed.

Matt felt sure the culprit was Billy Frost. The last time Billy had approached him was three days ago. Billy had asked for money. Again.

Matt had turned Billy down flat. No more money, he'd said. Billy had gotten furious.

"You owe me!" he'd shouted, his face red. "You owe me for what you did to my brother."

"I don't owe *you* a damn thing," Matt had responded, his lips stretched into a thin, tight line. "The only reason I keep you around is because of Tim. But there's a limit to my patience."

Billy had looked as if he wanted to say something, but wisely hadn't. Mumbling to himself, he'd sulked off.

Now, as Matt took a thorough mental inventory of his tools, he reminded himself that Brittany had seen Billy's true colors from the beginning. He paused in his thoughts and recoiled as if he'd been kicked in the solar plexus.

Brittany had left four weeks ago today.

The palms of his hands were suddenly slick with sweat, and the pain in his soul was almost unbearable.

He thought he'd been doing her a favor by sending her away. Brittany had never belonged in his world. She was like an exotic hothouse plant that had been uprooted and replanted in the wild.

But maybe he had been too hasty. Maybe she was made of stronger stuff than he'd given her credit for.

Had *he* been the weak one? The coward, afraid to share himself, his emotions with someone else? No, dammit! He wasn't a coward. He wanted a home and family. But only if he could have Brittany.

So prove it, a voice taunted. Get up and go tell her you love her and that you're not worth a damn without her. Even if you have to beg, tell her.

Regardless of the outcome, he couldn't live with himself if he didn't try.

His mind buzzed. He had to cut another load for the mill at dawn. The minute he got through, he'd head for Tyler. And Brittany.

Suddenly he no longer felt a zillion years old.

SHE'D BEEN HOME for four weeks. But she hadn't fooled anyone, especially not her friends, not her co-workers and not her daddy. Broken hearts were hard to disguise.

Brittany had been home two days before she'd mustered the courage to tell her daddy about the breakup of her marriage. The dreaded words, "I told you so," kept her mum.

"Did my job offer have anything to do with your leaving?" he asked.

She answered his question with a question. "Why did you make that offer, Daddy?"

"I did it for you," Walter said stiffly.

"No, you didn't," she countered, peering at him with pain-filled eyes. "You did it for you. You still can't bear the thought of your daughter being married to a redneck logger."

Walter straightened.

"You had no intention of letting Matt have a responsible job." It was a statement, not a question.

She saw Walter's face tighten as she hit a nerve. He didn't say anything. He didn't have to. His silence had spoken louder than words ever could have. And had cracked her heart a little wider....

Now Brittany sat in her robe and watched through the French doors as the rain pounded the deck outside.

She wondered if it was raining at Matt's place. In a wretched whisper, she sobbed his name. She missed him with every fiber of her being. Nothing made sense without him. So why had she let him push her out of his life?

Brittany sat up suddenly, as though she'd been slapped. Why, indeed? What she should've done was call his bluff, make him look her square in the eye and tell her he didn't love her.

Brittany stood quickly, too quickly. Her head swam. Damn, she needed to eat something.

There wasn't time. She didn't have a second to lose...or she just might lose her nerve.

She dashed into her bedroom and slipped into a pair of jeans and a shirt. With keys in hand, she dashed to the front door, only to hear the bell chime. She jerked open the door.

"Daddy!" Her shocked tone conveyed her surprise. "What is it?"

He rubbed his forehead. "It's Matt. He's been hurt."

"Oh, no!"

"A loader overturned and pinned him underneath."

She fell into a chair, clutched at her stomach and waited for it to stop lurching.

"But he's going to live—the doctors are certain."

"Thank God," she wheezed. "But how did you know? I mean—"

"A man named Elmer Cayhill called the office, and when

they refused to give him your home phone number, he told the secretary about Matt.'' Walter paused. ''I thought I should be the one to tell you.''

''I have to go to him,'' she whispered.

Walter stepped in front of her. ''I think you should leave well enough alone.''

''What...what are you saying?'' Tears flooded her eyes. ''He's my husband.''

''Soon to be ex.''

Brittany flinched.

''For God's sake, Brittany. Let it go. Let him go. He's not good enough for you.''

''How would you know what's good for me?'' she cried.

He seemed taken aback at the venom in her voice. ''I'm your father, that's how.''

''Oh, please, spare me.''

His face turned red. ''Don't you dare talk to me like that. I forbid you to—''

''You forbid me? That's a joke. You can't forbid me to do anything, Daddy. Not anymore, that is.'' Tears ran down her face. ''I love you, and lord knows I've tried to please you all my life because I thought that by being perfect you would love me back. I still want your love, but it's no longer the most important thing to me. Matt's is.''

Later, while her car dispensed of the highway miles, she realized there had been tears on her daddy's face.

SHE ENTERED Matt's room and tiptoed to the side of the bed. Except for a scratch on one side of his face and a bruise on the other, Matt looked like his old self.

But Matt could be paralyzed, the doctor had told her. Forever. She placed a hand to her mouth to keep from crying. Oh, God, no.

Brittany lifted her head suddenly. Could she stand it? Could she stand by him? If not, now was the time to leave.

The decision was clear. But then, it always had been.

''I love you, my darling,'' she whispered. ''And I won't let you down.''

For the next two days Brittany remained by his side, though she was certain he never knew it. When he started to moan and his eyes glazed with pain, the nurses gave him a shot.

But the long hours with only short doses of sleep were wearing on Brittany. After Maria and Elmer had practically pushed her out of Matt's room, she had gone to the nearest motel and straight to bed.

Now, as she stood in front of his door again, she felt her knees knock together. It had been three days since his surgery, and she expected Matt to be awake. She had no idea how he would react to her presence.

"What are you doing here?" he asked when she pushed open the heavy door. "If you've come just because I got hurt, then—"

"I came because I love you."

They stared at each other.

"I love you, Matt," she whispered again. "And even if you are paralyzed—"

"Paralyzed?"

Brittany could only nod.

"Have you seen the doctor this morning?" Matt asked.

"No...no I haven't," she said around the huge lump in her throat.

"I'm not paralyzed, Brittany."

She laughed and cried at the same time, murmuring, "Thank God. Oh, thank God."

Only, Matt wasn't laughing. He was staring at her with a strange expression on his face. "Are you saying you thought I was paralyzed?"

"Dr. Kent...said there was a chance you could be."

"And knowing that, you were willing to stay?"

Her gaze never wavered. "I never could have *not* stayed."

"Brittany—I love you, and I was coming to tell you that the day of the accident, to beg you to forgive me."

"Oh, Matt," she cried, rushing toward him.

The nurse found them locked in each other's arms.

*

"Is THAT a new robe?"

Brittany flashed her husband a demure look. "Mmm, you noticed." She purposely ran her hand over the turquoise silk as if stroking it.

His eyes darkened. "Oh, I noticed, all right. I notice everything about you."

They were in the bedroom at Matt's house, *their* house. Three months had passed since Matt's accident.

His recovery had been slow, but without complications. Through it all, Brittany had stayed by his side. They took long walks, they swam in the creek, they read books together. But most of all they loved and they laughed.

The only real excitement was Billy Frost's arrest. He had been caught in the act of stealing another logger's equipment. Once he was arrested, he admitted to stealing Matt's as well.

Brittany had never been happier. She felt his eyes on her as she brushed her hair.

"I love you," he said, his eyes filled with passion. "But you look better without the robe, you know."

His voice and leering look brought a smile to Brittany's lips. She untied the robe and stood before him, completely naked. She heard Matt's sharp intake of breath.

"Do you notice anything different about me?"

"Only that you're the loveliest creature I've ever seen," he said in a strangled voice.

"Is that all?"

He pulled her down beside him on the bed. Words were forgotten as his mouth closed over hers.

The wanting was sharp inside her, the pleasure edged by a need that knew no boundaries. Matt sensed her mood and matched it.

Although she hadn't expected anything more than a special closeness, she climaxed in a rush of flawless pleasure. When it happened a second time, moments before he spilled inside her, she cried out with delight, a delight that blended with his.

"ARE YOU AWAKE?"

Matt's raspy voice interrupted Brittany's slow descent into sleep. She snuggled against his chest, and his hold tightened.

"By the way, your daddy called today."

"Oh. What did he want?"

"You, of course."

Her fingertips massaged the nape of his neck. "I wish we could all—"

"I invited him to dinner tomorrow night."

Brittany's hand stilled. "You did?"

"Yep, and he accepted, too." Matt tweaked her on the nose. "I kinda felt sorry for him. He sounded—oh, I don't know—sort of blue."

"He is blue. He knows he screwed up trying to keep me away from you, and he's trying to make up. He never calls now that he doesn't tell me he loves me."

"'Bout time he realized how special you are."

"Matt, are you sure you haven't noticed something different about me?" Her voice sank lower.

He pulled back slightly. "Is something wrong?"

She smiled. "No, nothing's wrong. I'm pregnant."

Silence stretched through the room.

Brittany looked into the depths of his eyes. Something there stole her breath.

"Oh, Brittany, love." Matt leaned over and placed his lips against her stomach.

Flutters of pleasure darted through her.

Matt lifted his head. "How far along are you?"

"Four months. I was pregnant before the accident, only I didn't know it."

"Does your daddy know?"

"No. I thought we'd tell him together. Later."

"Why later?"

"Because...I'm scared..." Her voice cracked. "I'm so afraid after—"

"Shh," he said. "Don't say it. Don't think it. Everything is going to be all right, you'll see."

She placed her palms against his cheeks and searched his eyes. "I love you."

"Don't ever leave me again," he pleaded. "Stay with me as long as I live."

"As long as we both shall live," Brittany promised.

In September 2001,
save $1.00 off the purchase of any

DREAMSCAPES

title.

Silhouette®

DREAMSCAPES

WHISPERS   OF LOVE

$1.00 OFF!

any Dreamscapes series title.

Visit Silhouette at www.eHarlequin.com
T5V4CDSUSR
© 2001 Harlequin Enterprises Ltd.

Silhouette®
Where love comes alive™

In September 2001,
save **$1.00 off** the purchase of any

DREAMSCAPES

title.

Silhouette®

DREAMSCAPES

WHISPERS   OF LOVE

$1.00 OFF!

any Dreamscapes series titles.

Coupon valid until December 31, 2001.
Valid at retail outlets in Canada only.
Limit one coupon per purchase.

52603323

Visit Silhouette at www.eHarlequin.com
T5V4CDSCANR
© 2001 Harlequin Enterprises Ltd.

Silhouette®
Where love comes alive™

BREATHTAKING, ROMANTIC SUSPENSE

THAT'S

HARLEQUIN®

INTRIGUE®

Save $2.00 off the purchase of any 3

INTRIGUE®

series titles.

$2.00 OFF!

any three Harlequin Intrigue series titles.

RETAILER: Harlequin Enterprises Ltd. will pay the face value of this coupon plus 8¢ if submitted by customer for this product only. Any other use constitutes fraud. Coupon is nonassignable. Void if taxed, prohibited or restricted by law. Consumer must pay any government taxes. For reimbursement submit coupons and proof of sales to: Harlequin Enterprises Ltd., P.O. Box 880478, El Paso, TX 88588-0478, U.S.A. Cash value 1/100¢. Valid in the U.S. only.

Coupon valid until December 31, 2001.
Valid at retail outlets in the U.S. only.
Limit one coupon per purchase.

107450

5 65373 00051 9   (8100) 0 10745

HARLEQUIN®
Makes any time special ®

BREATHTAKING, ROMANTIC SUSPENSE

THAT'S

HARLEQUIN®

INTRIGUE®

Save $2.00 off the purchase of any 3

INTRIGUE®

series titles.

$2.00 OFF!

any three Harlequin Intrigue series titles.

RETAILER: Harlequin Enterprises Ltd. will pay the face value of this coupon plus 10.25¢ if submitted by customer for this product only. Any other use constitutes fraud. Coupon is nonassignable. Void if taxed, prohibited or restricted by law. Consumer must pay any government taxes. Nielson Clearing House customers submit coupons and proof of sales to: Harlequin Enterprises Ltd., 661 Millidge Avenue, P.O. Box 639, Saint John, N.B. E2L 4A5. Non NCH retailer—for reimbursement submit coupons and proof of sales directly to: Harlequin Enterprises Ltd., Retail Marketing Department, 225 Duncan Mill Rd., Don Mills, Ontario M3B 3K9, Canada. Valid in Canada only.

Coupon valid until December 31, 2001.
Valid at retail outlets in Canada only.
Limit one coupon per purchase.

52603150

HARLEQUIN®
Makes any time special ®

Save $2.00 off the purchase of any 2

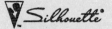

I N T I M A T E   M O M E N T S™

series titles.

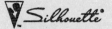

I N T I M A T E   M O M E N T S™

Romance, adventure—excitement!

$2.00 OFF!

any two Silhouette Intimate Moments series titles.

RETAILER: Harlequin Enterprises Ltd. will pay the face value of this coupon plus 8¢ if submitted by customer for this product only. Any other use constitutes fraud. Coupon is nonassignable. Void if taxed, prohibited or restricted by law. Consumer must pay any government taxes. For reimbursement submit coupons and proof of sales to: Harlequin Enterprises Ltd., P.O. Box 880478, El Paso, TX 88588-0478, U.S.A. Cash value 1/100¢. Valid in the U.S. only.

Coupon valid until December 31, 2001.
Valid at retail outlets in the U.S. only.
Limit one coupon per purchase.

107468

5 65373 00051 9   (8100) 0 10746

Silhouette®
Where love comes alive™

Save $2.00 off the purchase of any 2

 **Silhouette**

INTIMATE MOMENTS™

series titles.

 **Silhouette**

INTIMATE MOMENTS™

Romance, adventure—excitement!

$2.00 OFF!

any two Silhouette Intimate Moments series titles.

RETAILER: Harlequin Enterprises Ltd. will pay the face value of this coupon plus 10.25¢ if submitted by customer for this product only. Any other use constitutes fraud. Coupon is nonassignable. Void if taxed, prohibited or restricted by law. Consumer must pay any government taxes. Nielson Clearing House customers submit coupons and proof of sales to: Harlequin Enterprises Ltd., 661 Millidge Avenue, P.O. Box 639, Saint John, N.B. E2L 4A5. Non NCH retailer—for reimbursement submit coupons and proof of sales directly to: Harlequin Enterprises Ltd., Retail Marketing Department, 225 Duncan Mill Rd., Don Mills, Ontario M3B 3K9, Canada. Valid in Canada only.

Coupon valid until December 31, 2001.
Valid at retail outlets in Canada only.
Limit one coupon per purchase.

```
52602984
```

Silhouette
™ *Where love comes alive*™